SMITTEN

Vivienne Savage

Copyright © PAYNE & TAYLOR 2016

Payne
&
Taylor
Publishing

All rights reserved.
ISBN-10: 0-9903817-7-3
ISBN-13: 978-0-9903817-7-8
www.viviennesavage.com
Editor: Shay VanZwoll

Table of Contents

Chapter 1

With a thin, white cotton shawl wrapped around her shoulders, Ēostre stood on the balcony overlooking a verdant California valley. The cool morning breeze kissed her skin and swept the smell of meadow flowers to her.

A few years ago, the state had suffered one of the worst droughts in history — but due to dragon magic, the land had entered a period of renewal. Storm dragons like Ēostre made rain fall from the heavens and wash away desiccated flora, replenishing depleted bodies of water. Earth dragons had emerged to rake their claws through the soil until dust bowls bloomed with new life, grass, vibrant flowers, and trees. And the humans, ever ignorant of magic, praised everything but the actual source of their good fortune.

In Ēostre's opinion, it was a travesty the mortals weren't allowed to appreciate the truth: the creature once feared as their greatest enemy had become their only ally. If they came forward to the humans, they could do more for the ailing planet to make the world a better place for all.

"Penny for your thoughts," a gentle voice said from behind Ēostre.

Chloe stepped through the open door with a silver tray, two mugs atop it beside a small, clay teapot. She lowered her load to the circular table and claimed a seat.

"My thoughts are weighed by old concerns and nothing more," Ēostre said. "Did Saul send you?"

"What? No," Chloe said a little too quickly. For all of the time she spent among supernatural beings, the dragon-blooded woman had gained nothing of their secretive personality. She remained an open book, perpetually airing her thoughts to the rest of the immortals in her company. "I came on my own."

Ēostre pressed her lips together, her mouth forming a thin line. Since moving in with her son and daughter-in-law, she'd been besieged by numerous attempts to entertain her.

"He worries," Chloe admitted, confirming Ēostre's suspicions.

"Of course he does. Such is Saul's nature. He worries I'll retreat from the world and return to my hibernation at the top of a long-forgotten mountain peak." She chuckled a dry, humorless sound and joined Chloe at the table. "Perhaps it is time for me to leave for a while—"

"No!" Chloe blurted out.

"You desire my continued presence in your home?" Ēostre asked. She raised one fine, silver brow.

"Why shouldn't I?" Chloe asked.

"Most female dragons experience a sense of territorial possessiveness when it comes to their homes and hoards. From what I have studied in recent years since my return among the awakened, I had come to believe such was true of human females regarding their mothers-in-law as well. Do you not feel threatened by me?"

The bright-eyed young woman stared wordlessly. Without another word, she tilted the teapot and poured dark, spiced liquid into the cups. Beside them, honey, cream, and sugar filled tiny bowls decorated with delicate, painted blossoms.

"Perhaps you are more dragon than I previously believed," Ēostre murmured softly. Chloe's features had taken on a stoic expression. "It has never been my intention to make you feel uncomfortable within your own home. I will leave at once and move into the apartment I rented in Sacramento—"

"Ēostre, no," Chloe interrupted her with a gentle, firm voice. "I know you're the 'Monster-in-Law' and according to all forms of entertainment, we're not supposed to like each other, but that's not the case here. Astrid loves you. Hell, Saul frets every day that you're going to leave again for another century. Most of all, Ēostre, I *like* having you here. You're family, and you've never done anything to make me feel unwelcome or unloved. Please stay."

A rare surge of emotion clutched Ēostre's throat until she blinked to stave off her unshed tears. "You are my son's beloved. I would never do anything, unwarranted, to jeopardize that."

The best part about reawakening had been discovering her family had grown. Chloe and Saul helped her to navigate the new, modern world and Astrid filled her days with childish delight. They'd surrounded her with their love and banished the void left by Fafnir. Ēostre felt less alone. Less out of place and time.

The next best thing was rekindling a friendship with Maximilian, her deceased mate's closest friend and ally. He was an incredible man, and she'd been honored when he asked if she had the time and the will to help him undertake a career in politics. It was unprecedented. No dragon ever became involved so openly in mortal government, not since the council dragged their world into secrecy.

Chloe reached across the table and took Ēostre's hand without ending the eye contact between them. "What's bothering you? Saul told me you only hide away like this when you have a lot on your mind. Is it about Maximilian's presidential campaign?"

"No. That does not worry me. Although it won't be necessary, we could buy the election if we wanted and force the other two candidates to bow out. In three months, I predict he shall win on his own." She squeezed her daughter's fingers before drawing her hands back to her lap.

"What's the problem then?"

"The final meeting is to occur between all leading members of the supernatural world. Dragons, witches, and other magical beings will send representatives to decide on the matter of reversing our vows of secrecy. This is a vote we cannot buy, and its outcome changes everything. *Everything* we have done has been leading up to this one moment."

"Right. Because he's already known as the governor of California, and this'll only put him in the public light even more. So if he runs as a human man, he'll have eight years of time in the spotlight before he has to make a disappearance, fake his death, or eventually fall into obscurity, right?"

"Correct. The humans will expect him to age and become gray as the years go by. He was not a young man by their standards when he entered the governor's office, but if we come forward to the world, we will only do so after he has become the president. On the record, Maximilian is fifty-five."

"He doesn't look fifty-five," Chloe mused. "And you don't look forty-nine. Hell, I don't look forty-five and neither does Saul. You know, he told me it's been centuries since you two could pass for mother and child in public."

"We could once, long ago" Ēostre confirmed. "It's strange to play as his older sibling. Of course, with magic, I could alter my appearance but…"

"You're vain," Chloe said bluntly, much to Ēostre's embarrassment.

"Yes," she admitted. "As our kind often are."

While Ēostre wanted to openly claim her only child, she also craved the sense of belonging she once had as a highly sought-after advisor among the humans. Back when her kind first retreated into secrecy, a few ancients even older than Ēostre had convened, voted, and determined it was to the benefit of all supernatural creatures to work their magic from the shadows. There, they could accomplish more without the risk of courting appearances from dragonslayers and witch hunters. When the other supernatural creatures agreed, there was no turning back.

She wondered if they had truly believed humans would be any match for them. Only the cockiest wyrms, like her dearest, beloved Fafnir, ever succumbed to slayers. If they'd wanted, dragonkind could have banded together and crushed human resistance long before they'd created weapons of war.

Chloe stirred milk and honey into her tea while Ēostre did the same. They shared a companionable silence, sipping caramel vanilla chai while the sun rose in the distance. It became a radiant ball above the horizon and sent out streams of magenta and orange over the azure sky.

"How do you feel about the dragons coming out to the world, Chloe?" Ēostre finally asked.

"About which part? How do I feel about no longer having to hide what I am, or about the danger related to some human taking offense to what we are?"

"All of it."

Chloe tapped her nail against her lower lip, a thoughtful look on her face. "I feel like it's a good change. We're all stressed. Technology is moving forward and we'll have to move with it if dragons and the supernatural are to thrive. How can we enjoy our lives from the shadows, always afraid of what someone will see or find out? We have to become a part of normal, everyday life until we are the *new* normal."

"You have spent time with Maximilian," Ēostre guessed. Chloe had seemingly echoed many of the fire dragon's points on the subject of ending the secrecy.

"No. I've believed this for a while. Honest. Astrid may still be a child to you, but without dragon blood in her veins, she'd be old enough to marry and have a family of her own in a few years," Chloe said.

"Not so soon, I would hope," Ēostre replied with a chuckle.

"Well, no." Chloe laughed. "But what I meant was, if people could accept us as we are, she could spend more time with human children of her physical age. She could go to school and socialize with peers rather than be home taught. She's lonely here. No matter how much Saul and I play with her, or how often we arrange playdates between her and Javier, she wants friends."

Ēostre turned her thoughts to her grandchild. Despite Astrid's seventeen years of age and advanced intellect, she physically resembled a child no older than twelve.

"We considered enrolling Astrid into online college courses next semester. She's ready, and she's anxious to learn," Chloe continued. "Eventually, she and Javier won't be the only half-dragon children, either."

"You and Marceline have opened the metaphorical floodgates," Ēostre agreed, her tone dry but humor-filled. "In a world open to our kind, she would be free to pursue such interests."

"Exactly," Chloe said. "So, Grandma, you have a big job to do."

Chapter 2

Maximilian Emberthorn sat within a luxurious office in downtown Sacramento. With the sun streaming through the window to his rear, he sipped coffee and stared at the computer screen before him. Business was booming, stock prices were up, and California's citizens loved him.

And none of it brought him true happiness. None of his vast accomplishments, the wealth attained through his company, or the power gained as governor of California filled the gaping hole left by his deceased daughter Brigid.

"Sir, you have a phone call on line two," his personal assistant informed him through the intercom. After a pause, she added, "It's Loki Agnarhorn. Should I tell him you're busy?"

"No, that's not necessary, Hilary. Thanks. I'll take the call." Max plucked the phone from the cradle and placed it between his ear and shoulder. "Hello, Loki."

"Good evening, Maximilian, my friend. How does the day fare for you?" Loki's majestic voice, carrying a deep Scandinavian accent, rumbled and boomed through the phone line. Maximilian imagined the dusty old wyrm chatting in his dragon form, punching numbers on the dial pad with the tip of a claw.

As much as some dragons abhorred humans, they held a proportionate fascination with the rise of technology. They loved gadgets and gizmos of all kind, and of course, so did Maximilian, otherwise he wouldn't have founded his own electronics company.

"What do you want?" Max asked warily.

"Is that any way to address a family friend?"

"When that friend calls only to ask favors? Yes. Let's cut to the chase. What would you like me to do for you?"

"My lead software developer and I have created an absolutely fantastic new application intended for the android mobile phone. I'd like to license it exclusively to your company, of course."

"Of course," Max said dryly. "And what does this fantastic new application do for the user?" He twisted to his computer again and scanned the endless flood of Twitter messages on the screen.

"Organization," Loki said. He went on to describe, in great detail, a program allowing a mobile phone user to safely store everything from grocery lists to bank account numbers and passwords at the push of a button.

"And it takes dictation." Maximilian rubbed his chin. "That's impressive. I'll have Hilary deliver a prototype of the XTC Jewel tomorrow. Load it with the app and have the device returned to me. I'll place it up for consideration."

"Consideration?" Loki repeated. "My creations require consideration?"

"What sort of businessman do you take me to be, Loki? Did you honestly believe I would trust you again after the fiasco with the GPS mapping application ten years ago?"

"That was no fault of mine. How was I to know the code had been stolen? This is one hundred percent legitimate, a creation of my own design."

"And I will scrutinize it closely before making my decision."

Dead silence hung on the line between them, an awkward lull Maximilian irritably endured.

"I see. Is this what your own flesh and blood must endure, cousin?"

Max raked his fingers through his hair. "This has nothing to do with blood, and everything to do with proper business protocol."

"Yet you bring up my past mistakes, rubbing my nose in them as you would a dog who has piddled on the new carpet. A human being killed your only cub, and you have not only forgiven this human, but befriended the very family protecting her, while refusing to forgive transgressions — much more minor — from your own family. Is blood not thicker than water, as the humans say? I do not understand you, Maximilian." The grave, grating voice on the other end of the phone paused. "Nor do I understand why we must call you by this preposterous human name. Why do you not use your given name?"

"I haven't used that name since I first began to live as a human at the turn of the nineteenth century," Maximilian replied gruffly. "Perhaps old age has addled your mind, but I have always been a friend to the Drakenstone family."

"To Fafnir," the other dragon snorted.

"And to his widow, Loki."

"And to his widow," the other dragon agreed reluctantly. "But how has this human inherited such loyalty, when she has done little more than serve as a milk-machine for a halfling spawn? Murdered Brigid—"

Maximilian couldn't take another second. The mention of his child's name incensed him and rage swept over his body with a rush of molten heat. The hand resting on the edge of his desk clenched down, splintered the wood, and the surface buckled. "Enough! Chloe Drakenstone did no such thing," Max spoke heatedly into the phone. "Say another word of it and I will scrape the ashen scales from your worthless, charred carcass."

Loki silenced.

"For years, I have bided your disrespect, your meddling, and your prattling commentary with humor for the sake of your mother, but I will accept it no longer. My Brigid made her own choice and our egotism cost her life. Nothing more. You will not pass judgment."

"Belenos—"

"Your gutless attempts to sow dissent and weave treachery have failed. Meddle in my affairs again and I will finish the skinning Thor began a century ago. Then I will reduce what remains of you to *slag*."

"My apologies. I had only meant—"

"Whatever you intended is meaningless," Maximilian cut him off brusquely. "As for your product, I'm positive it's shit as usual. I wouldn't even load your software onto my competitor's cell phones."

Max ended the call and leaned back in the seat, breathing deeply.

"Sir?"

"I'm fine, Vincent." Max waved off the suit-clad security agent in his doorway. The man's amber eyes focused on the splintered desk and he didn't move.

"If there's a threat to your control, I need to be aware."

Werewolves are too damn perceptive. And stubborn, Max thought. "Only an annoying family member. It's nothing, I promise."

Vincent flashed a toothy grin then pulled the door shut. It opened a second time, less than a minute later.

"Max?" His secretary peeked around the edge of the barely-cracked door, concern on her face.

"Nothing to worry about, Hilary," he assured her, too. For her benefit, he managed a small smile.

"Are you sure? Should I evacuate under the guise of another fire drill?"

"No, that won't be necessary. I'm in control."

He dragged in a slower, deeper breath to demonstrate his decreasing temper. "I am quite fine, Hilary. See?"

"You certainly are," she said around a nervous chuckle. "Peace incarnate. Lunch arrived fifteen minutes ago while you were on the phone. Would you like yours?"

"Yes please."

Hilary stepped away from the door and returned with a to-go box from a local burger place. Maximilian might have the appearance of a stuffy Hollywood socialite, but he didn't eat like one. He promptly opened the box and scooped up the messy triple-decker burger. The sweet scent of barbecue sauce and smoky bacon rose from the greasy meal.

Hilary laughed as he stuffed his face.

"What?" he asked around a mouthful. "I'm starved."

"Your face," she teased. "You looked so gleeful. So, do they take care of you like this at the state capitol building?"

Max grimaced. "No. It's awful. If I ask for a simple, five-dollar burger, they look at me like I'm a crazy man," he grumbled. "I fear for what happens once I'm the president. There's probably some special chef creating masterpieces of tiny filet mignon cubes and caviar. And because I haven't entrusted all of my staff with the truth, a few of them have tried to turn me into a vegan." He grimaced.

"You're lucky to be a dragon. If you were a normal guy, I'd wonder how you find the time to do all of this," Hilary said, chuckling.

Max dug into his fries and glanced at the window, thoughtful. "I haven't paid a visit to this office in weeks, Hilary, and you know that. I've left most of the day-to-day activity of running the company to the senior vice presidents."

"True. We miss you, too. I suppose we'll see even less of you once you're president. You won't have time to run this at all."

"I won't," he answered sadly. "But never fear, no one will dare fire or demote you in my absence upon threat of flames and death. I sent out a memo."

"I know. And because I won't find a job better than this, you'll see me here in eight years when you're back. Besides, I know you need me here to keep an eye on things. I don't trust the board any more than you do."

Once Maximilian caught up on the personal business matters most important to him, he departed the office with his security team, wondering if it would be the final visit for some time.

If he lost the election, he'd return to a content life at the state capitol, complete the remainder of his second term as governor, and settle for a quiet life in the technology sector until it became time to leave the public eye.

But if he won... oh, the possibilities! No dragon would ever be forced to abandon another life they enjoyed.

He took the long, scenic drive home with the radio blasting rock and roll — it was the best time in the history of mortal music, in his opinion, but Ēostre disagreed.

Ēostre. He smiled as he punched in the gate code and slid the black Cadillac into the drive. The thought of his close friend warmed his blood. Would she be settling down for a family dinner with Saul, Chloe, and Astrid? Or had she given her family the slip in favor of campaign management?

"Must you always take the long route?" Vincent parked his motorcycle behind the car.

"I must. If I win this election, you know as well as I do my driving days are over."

The wolf smirked and disappeared around the back of the house. Max had long given up on inviting the man inside. All four agents assigned to him belonged to the same pack and all were equally introverted but dedicated to their duties.

Max took the white steps of the governor's mansion at a brisk pace and let himself into the quiet home. The estate was too large for a bachelor, but he'd always held some small hope of finding a mate to share it with. He'd even prayed to the Ancestors on one brief, pathetic occasion of loneliness, wishing to find his other half, then laughed bitterly when he came to his senses.

How could the Ancestors introduce him to his ideal mate when she'd been there before him all along? In Ēostre, he saw everything he wanted, everything he could ever need. Wisdom, strength, and beauty were all wrapped within one elegant dragoness.

Unfortunately, Ēostre had already found and lost her beloved. He had watched the death of Fafnir reduce her to a shade of her former, radiant self. And she also had no interest in Max beyond friendship and putting him into the White House.

Max tossed his jacket onto a coat hook, loosened his tie, and beelined to the informal parlor. The daily post waited for him on the coffee table beside a mug of fragrant, light roast coffee. His live-in maid saw to his day-to-day needs, and he paid her handsomely for putting up with his crap. Not that she complained about having his coffee and mail ready for him each day.

"Lynette?" he called.

"Just cleaning up my mess in the kitchen!"

She appeared around the corner and stepped into the open entranceway, a big grin on her face. "Unless you have any other needs, Max, I'm leaving for the night. My boyfriend scored us tickets to a late concert in Los Angeles tonight."

Max glanced at the time. They'd be stuck in rush hour traffic no doubt. "You should have left an hour ago. The cars will be bumper-to-bumper now."

"Oh it's fine," the thin, young woman said. Lynette was a failed ballerina, tiny in frame, but lacking the grace to transform a childhood hobby into a career. Like her older sister, Hilary, she knew about Max's true nature and appreciated the generous salary he paid in exchange for secrecy and loyalty.

"In the future, call me if you need to leave. I can fend for myself."

"You may know how to operate a coffee maker, but you'll never make it as good as I do," she teased.

Max grunted. "I don't know what you do, but it's liquid gold in a cup when you make it."

Lynette beamed. "I know. Those are the secrets you learn when you've worked as a barista for a while."

"You should let me in on them." He sipped the scalding hot brew without blowing on it. "Tell that boy he had better drive safely with you in the car."

She rolled her eyes. "Of course, Dad."

Her words washed over him with the same effect as a bucket of ice water. He sat rigid and still in his seat, gripping his coffee mug in one hand. Hairline fractures spread beneath his thumb. Lynette couldn't possibly understand what she'd said wrong or why it deeply affected him. Almost seven years had passed since he'd picked the girl out of a mile-high application pile, and in seven years, she'd become a daughter to him.

But she'd never called him "Dad" even to tease. After a struggle to find his voice, he said, "Enjoy your concert."

"Thanks! Dinner is in the oven. You *can* take it out in an hour when the timer rings and handle it from there, right?"

Max scoffed. "I've been feeding and caring for myself for centuries, thank you."

"Sometimes I wonder," Lynette retorted. She ducked through the double doors of the front hallway and sprinted outside, shutting the door behind her with an excited slam.

Max's fragile smile wavered. Lynette was a good girl. The girl his Brigid should have been.

Instantly, the sweet coffee became sour in his mouth. He set the oversized mug aside and slouched back on the couch with his fingers interlaced behind his head. The mail went ignored, and instead, he fell prey to memories of his daughter. Her ghost haunted his thoughts at every turn, an ever-present reminder of his greatest failure.

Where did I go wrong with her? Was I too lenient? Too tolerant of her spiteful tendencies?

Hours later, after consuming every last crumb of the roast left in the oven, Maximilian retired to the upper level, showered, and settled into his personal office where Facebook distracted him for an hour, the time divided between inane chat in messages and idly liking photographs flashing over his wall.

It was all an absolute waste of time. He procrastinated until well after midnight, pouring a few cups of cold coffee from the pitcher Lynette left in the fridge. Eventually, he took the entire thing back to the office. She made it strong and sweet with flavor shots and cream, perfect for adding a pair of ice cubes.

Lynette's coffee-making skills had been the final test before he'd hired her back then. She was fresh out of high school, a young barista at Starbucks leaving two parents behind in Nevada for the first time. When her mother and older sister drove with her for the interview, he'd become enchanted by their close family. When her mother had the audacity to quiz the governor of California about his intentions, he'd offered both girls a job. One to look after the other, he'd said, after promising he had no romantic interests.

"I've gotten nothing done," Max realized at 3 A.M. Where had his night gone? He rubbed his face a few times and glanced at the open doorway. The shadowed hall beyond it led to his bedroom.

Because he dreaded sleep and his recurring dreams, he dawdled for a while longer and eventually settled into reading the current legislation on the table.

"Such a ridiculous waste of taxpayers' money," he muttered. "We already have a law concerning pets in outdoor restaurant seating. Whose absolute nonsense idea was this?" He searched the wording, found a minute difference, signed it, and slouched back. He didn't give a damn if restaurants allowed dog owners to sit outside with Fido while sipping their expensive lattes.

He considered purchasing a dog, perhaps even visiting a shelter, and had finally convinced himself to rescue a large parrot when his phone suddenly rang. Accustomed to receiving phone calls from his fellow dragons at all hours of the night, he plucked it from the cradle and answered without checking the ID.

"Hello?"

"What are your plans for this weekend?" Ēostre asked.

Max leaned back and stared at the heap of paperwork strewn over the desk. "The California legislature has been busy. They expect me to read these things called bills, and once finished, I am to sign my name to them. Can you believe it?"

Ēostre's exasperation amused him. "Smart ass. I am quite aware of your duties. My surprise is that you plan to work over the weekend."

"What can I say? I enjoy my reputation as a workaholic."

When Ēostre chuckled, the warm sound created flutters in Max's belly. Even her laughter sounded magical. "I have a better idea, Maximilian. Would you accompany me tomorrow for a difficult and most harrowing adventure?"

"Adventure to where?"

"A car dealership. I find myself in need of a personal vehicle." She paused, and the words rolled from her tongue like syrup. "I want a car like yours."

"Like mine?"

"Exactly like yours."

"Then take this heap of trash and be away with it."

"You don't mean that."

"You're right, I don't," he admitted. "Will Saul or Leiv not go with you?"

"I didn't ask. While Leiv is well educated on the matter of automobiles, and my son is quite generous with his time, both have prior obligations this weekend. So? Will you come?"

Maximilian gazed at his never-ending pile of work. There was only one answer. "Of course."

Chapter 3

Ēostre arrived at noon, courtesy of her own magical portal. After ending her call with Max, she stepped through a shining ring of lavender and silver, twinkling with stardust shimmers.

The governor met her in the entrance hall, still sipping his morning coffee. "I would like to state at the moment how amusing I find it that a woman with the power of teleportation finds it necessary to purchase an automobile."

"I very well can't vanish and appear on a whim among the mortals, Maximilian," she reminded him. "At least, not until you have become the president."

The portal collapsed behind the dragoness as she stepped up to him. Barefoot, Ēostre stood nearly six feet tall, and her four-inch Louis Vuitton pumps brought her to Max's height.

"That makes it no less entertaining, whether your vehicle shall be for appearances only or to provide you transportation. Besides, do you even know *how* to drive?"

"Saul, Leiv, and Chloe have all given me lessons." She sniffed daintily. "I have a driver's license." She glanced around. "Where's your bodyguard?"

"They never come inside, but he'll shadow us throughout the day. I think the poor kid had a heart attack when I told him I planned to accompany you to test-drive cars."

"He'll get over it."

Once outside and alongside the sleek Cadillac Maximilian drove for his day-to-day business, Ēostre walked her fingers over the pristine finish. "Black has never suited you, Maximilian, but this is a handsome automobile. Take me to purchase one like this."

Max opened the passenger door for her. Something about the kind gesture, one he'd done several times in the past, made her fingertips tingle and a shiver race down her spine.

"There are many things you must know before we reach the car dealership," Maximilian warned once behind the wheel. "Money may be no object, but the point is to never allow the salesman to know your pockets are bottomless."

Ēostre twisted away from the window and raised a brow at her friend. Max wore his casual best, dressed in a white designer shirt and dark slacks. If he were a mortal man, she'd call him crazy for wearing a light leather jacket in the absurd Californian heat, but it looked good on him.

So did the dark stubble on his cheeks. Their hair grew slowly, and as the days passed, he stopped shaving for work. No matter how much she fussed at him about maintaining appearances, she couldn't convince Max to pick up a razor past the middle of the month.

"Our faces are quite well-known, yours even more than mine. You're the most popular governor to lead this state since the Terminator. They'll know we have money."

"They will know *I* have money. You are Ēostre Feuersturm, and as far as they know, merely my campaign manager."

She fixed him with a dubious look.

"If you'd chosen Drakenstone as your legal name, this would be an entirely different situation." Maximilian hesitated. "May I ask why you chose to abandon your familial name?"

"I had wanted to avoid unnecessary association with Saul until we decided how to handle the obvious similarity in our ages. My son appears to be thirty years old, and I scarcely look a day over forty. In human terms," Ēostre said.

"Yes, in human terms. I'd never given it much thought until I ran for governor." Maximilian rubbed his chin and gazed away from the road ahead of them, his amber eyes flicking to the signs in passing. "How old do I appear?"

Ēostre pursed her lips. "Forty-five at the most, but I'd call it a stretch to be honest. Your smiles always make your crow's feet and laugh lines more apparent. When you *do* smile," she added.

Max chuckled. "The public loves a man with a genuine smile. I haven't forgotten your advice, Ēostre. I'm working on it."

"You are. I've seen the improvement, Max. You've gone from a melancholic, taciturn grump to a man the people can safely trust," she praised him. "And I'm trusting you right now with part of my nest egg. Saul could only liquidate so much of my wealth into usable currency." Ēostre sighed.

"If you took advice as well as you gave it, you'd have a sizable bank account by now," Maximilian reminded her.

Ēostre bit the inside of her cheek to refrain from firing off a snide retort. Max could banter with the best, but she'd rather spend their drive in pleasant conversation than playful jabs. Instead, he idly gave her tips about how to handle the salesman, and once they arrived, he offered his arm and led her to the dealership's door.

Sunlight filtered in through large floor-to-ceiling windows, illuminating the polished floor and several pristine Cadillacs. A carpeted area to the side boasted leather couches and a coffee machine with a variety of single-serving pods to choose from. A tray of cookies, freshly baked by the smell, nearly lured Ēostre over until Max caught her attention with a whisper against her ear.

"Remember my warning, sweetheart. No matter what he says, the price isn't carved in stone. The dealer will expect you to haggle."

"And haggle I shall," she replied. Her voice was light-hearted, but the brush of his stubble past her skin covered her arms with goosebumps.

A lone salesman sipped coffee at a nearby desk, but he beelined over to them after one glance at their fine attire. The man himself stood several inches shorter than Ēostre, and even without her heels he would have only reached her shoulder level. He drank her in, like a fish thirsting for water, his eyes lingering over her svelte curves before they returned to her face.

"Welcome to Cline Wilson Cadillac, I'm Sammy. What can I do for you today?"

"Ēostre," she introduced herself. "A pleasure to meet you, Sammy. We came to look at the CTS models."

"I'm Max," the fire dragon beside her said while shaking the man's hand.

The salesman watched Max closely, a silly smile frozen on his face and recognition in his eyes. "Oh, wow. It's you."

"Ah. I've been recognized," Max said.

"A pleasure to have you in our dealership, Governor. So, you said you were both interested in a new CTS. Looking to upgrade your own model?"

"*I* am purchasing the car," Ēostre corrected the salesman. "My *friend* has merely accompanied me to help."

"It's her first time," Maximilian explained. "I merely tagged along for moral support."

Sammy blinked. "Ah. Well then, are you set on the CTS or would you like to see some of our other models?"

"The CTS, please. I'm familiar with Max's vehicle and would like one of my own."

"Excellent. Let me show you what we have on the sales floor and we'll go from there."

The entire time Sammy walked her through the floor models, Ēostre was keenly aware of Max's presence behind her. Each time he leaned in close to murmur advice in her ear an electric tingle zipped up and down her spine.

"The white, while perfect for you, will show every speck of dirt and dust," Max pointed out. "I suggest the blue, otherwise it will become green and yellow once spring arrives."

"Perhaps I'd prefer the red, to be bold and daring," Ēostre spoke out of impulse.

Max blinked, startled, but he covered it with one of his dashing smiles — the genuine sort that made her toes curl.

"I think red would suit you nicely, Ēostre."

No better than it suits your hide, she thought. She flushed with satisfaction and turned to face Sammy as the man returned with keys in hand. Once he presented them to her for the test drive, Ēostre was set loose on the streets of Sacramento.

"How do you feel about the way it handles?" Max asked from the rear seat. Sammy rode on the passenger side, occasionally offering directions for Ēostre to follow their test drive route.

"It handles far better than that ostentatious brick my s— that Saul drives each day." The wheel slid like glass beneath her hands, and the motor's methodic, gentle purr became almost peaceful whenever Sammy quieted. "I love it."

So she bought it, beaming quite proudly while penning her name across the check. Spending vast sums of money had never felt so good. Max offered his arm again as they descended the dealership steps and walked to his car, empty-handed aside from a folder of receipts, warranties, and paperwork. Ēostre had been disappointed to discover that because of all of her luxury add-ons, they would have to order the car and it would require time to arrive.

"How does it feel to be the owner of a new car?"

"I'm hardly an owner without the vehicle," she bantered back.

"Nonsense. You'll have yours in less than a week, shiny and new with a bow on it."

Ēostre chuckled. Somehow, Max always brightened up any situation. It was part of what made him such a good politician.

"Let me buy you lunch, for being a good sport through the whole tedious affair," she offered. "Honestly, I was certain Sammy was going to request your autograph."

"Yes, well, about that…" Max rubbed his nape, his expression sheepish. "He did, when you stepped out to the ladies room. I even took a selfie with him that's sure to show up on Facebook within the next fifteen minutes, if it isn't already there."

A small snicker escaped. "Good press is good press, at least. You made an impression, and I didn't empty my accounts. A successful afternoon."

"I should have known you'd be all right when it came to the haggling. You're shrewd in whatever business deals you engage in." Max pulled into a parking lot. Ēostre eyed the two large horse statues flanking the entrance, recognition brightening her eyes. The Chinese restaurant had become a favored place to eat out and cemented her love for orange chicken and fried rice. She couldn't help herself. In the weeks following her awakening, there had even been a period of time when her family had threatened an intervention if she didn't vary her diet.

"No shop talk," Max warned as they were seated in a cozy booth. "How's the family?"

"Saul and Chloe are well. Astrid is a remarkable child, and eager to see her uncle again. Things you already know."

"Perhaps I may know these things, but it never hurts to ask. It's been too long since I've been to the manor for a visit."

"Then you should remedy the situation, no?" She glanced over the menu for something new to try. "Maybe we can plan an outing before your active schedule becomes even busier. A few breaks will be good for you."

"I'd like that."

His acceptance sent a bright rush of pleasure over her skin, so intense she worried the warmth added a flush in her cheeks. She cleared her throat and glanced away to sip from her glass. Max, stubborn as any red dragon could be, was relentless when it came to his work. Convincing him to take breaks during their early campaign trail had been as easy as pulling teeth from a drake.

"Do you remember when the idea of fine dining was a roasted elk or buffalo?" Max asked. "How things have changed."

"And men now pay for a night out on the town, instead of hunting it with their own bare hands."

"You find that peculiar?" Maximilian leaned forward and whispered, "I find it more unusual that women pay for the night out on the town."

"The women of this time are quite able to fend for themselves. No more damsels in distress awaiting a hero to rescue them."

"I must confess to missing some aspects of those days, my friend. You will never know the joy of spiriting away a beautiful princess, and the reward of devouring the hapless dimwit who comes to her rescue."

"So you assume."

"And how many princesses have *you* abducted?" The dragon raised both of his brows and grinned at her, brimming with the charisma that won his voters over. Ēostre cursed internally, hating that it worked on her, too.

"Oh, a handful I suppose."

All the more intrigued, Maximilian chuckled and called her bluff. "And what did you do with your stolen princesses? I am eager to know. Please do tell. Perhaps I'll learn something from you."

"Whereas you and others did it for the fun, or the free meal that followed, I offered a few of them advice. Those who took it went on to be better leaders."

The dragon's big, gloating grin dimmed, but a peaceful smile remained in its place. "Ah, Ēostre the Selfless. Always the serious one. You and Fafnir were true opposites in every way. Do you do nothing for your own enjoyment? I may be a workaholic but even I know how to take time away to enjoy a selfish moment of peace for myself."

"We all view fun in different ways," she defended. *Still, perhaps he has a point. All I've done since I awakened is work. Babysit and work. When do I take time for myself?*

"When we first initiated this partnership, you told me you were up for any challenge. I have one task more for you."

The mystery behind his unnamed proposition intrigued her. "Oh? What might that be?"

"You are to do one selfish deed only for yourself. An act to expressly benefit you and no one else. We shall even place a wager upon it."

"Does the purchase of a car not count?"

Max waved his hand and shook his head. "You admitted that was for looks. I'm speaking of doing something wholly for yourself, Ēostre. It must be to please you and you alone, with no external motivation."

I would be pleased to take him home to my bed, she thought to herself in a sudden bout of self-honesty.

"Well?"

This is absurd. These thoughts have nothing to do with Max and everything to do with the amount of time since I've had a lover. That's it, she convinced herself. Returning to clear and rational thought became more difficult when Max reached across the table to take her hand between his both of his warm, strong hands. He didn't have the baby smooth fingers of most human males, or even most politicians. His fingers were rough. Strong.

"Or do you fear gambling with your firekin?"

Ēostre shook her head.

"Do you find my request unreasonable?"

"No, I was thinking. How much time am I allotted to find such a truly thoughtless act of narcissism?"

As Max leaned back in his seat, his eyes lit with a mischievous sparkle. Light spilled through an adjacent window, casting copper and golden glints of color against his hair. "Until election three months hence. I doubt you should need so long a time, but you've surprised me before."

"And the wager? What prize does the winner claim?"

"One piece of treasure from the other's hoard. A single piece which may be anything the winner desires."

"Then this shall be like stealing sweets from a wee cub. I'll have taken my choice from among your most precious jewels within the week," she boasted.

"We'll see."

Chapter 4

While Ēostre didn't win her bet during the week, she did accomplish another impossible feat within the time. With the permission of the elder council, she organized a final summit to take place in a neutral zone chosen by the so-called "inferior" creatures.

Sometimes, Ēostre loathed her fellow dragons.

What a preposterous bunch of nearsighted buzzards, she thought. As the hosts of the caucus, she and the rest of her winged kin occupied seats at the high table at the forefront of the room.

It was the grandest conclave ever formed between supernatural creatures, with no expense spared. They assembled in Chicago, and in the heart of the Windy City, Ēostre had found an elegant, oversized conference room at an upscale hotel for their use. Members of every shifter tribe and nation arrived from all corners of the world.

And now, both sides were presenting their final arguments for or against coming out to the world.

"This is a fool's errand, Maximilian. Do you believe the humans will look upon us with smiles and kindness? We speak of weak-willed pissants who will go to war over verbal slights," Loki said. "What do you think they will do once they discover we aren't fictitious constructs of their own imagination?"

Ēostre whipped her head to the left to make eye contact with the smirking dragon three seats down. Loki made her skin crawl. He and her older sibling were often at odds, but what she wouldn't give to see him under Thor's huge claws now.

"As if we, with fire in our veins, do not fall prey to the same fits of temper," Max said. "I have learned to curb my urges, and humans may be taught as well. They are children who merely require more of our guidance. Our nurturing. In time, they will gain wisdom."

"Or they will declare war against us and seek to eliminate our kind," a bronze-skinned ancient rumbled, breaking his silence for the first time since their hour-long meeting began. Tlaloc didn't speak often, but when he did break his silence, it was to voice his disapproval of anything human.

"They will not. There has never been a better time to present our existence to the mortals," Maximilian said. "Whether they like it or not, we are part of this world. We shaped civilization and gave them the tools to enjoy it as freethinking human beings. There is not one dragon or older supernatural creature among us able to claim they do not prefer the times of the golden age when kingdoms rose and flourished under our aid. As proud creatures, as their benefactors through the centuries, we should no longer hide. We must offer our guidance in the open."

"Offer or force them to take it, Maximilian?" Watatsumi asked. His fingers ran through the immaculate, sleek strands of a chest-length black beard after phrasing the gentle question. "Will they listen once they know the truth?"

Maximilian opened his mouth to speak, only for Ēostre's brother to speak up in his stead. "It is doubtful, but we cannot allow potential negative consequences to distract us from what is most important. The humans must understand this world belongs to one and all. It is not a limitless resource to be squandered," Thor rumbled. The mighty storm dragon glanced to his left, seeking agreement. Ēostre smiled at him and nodded her head in appreciation.

"I must admit that when Ēostre first spoke of this mad scheme to me, I had my own reservations, but I can see the wisdom in this decision and how it will help to protect the world for our own future generations. For us. I have watched forests dwindle and waste away, depleted by human greed." Druantia, another elder dragoness, smiled at Ēostre from her seat at the high table. Their friendship had lasted centuries, and Ēostre had never appreciated the earth dragoness more. With her russet skin and dark eyes, Druantia resembled a member of one of America's native tribes.

"I agree," Teotihuacan said calmly. "If we do not take this planet now, one will not exist in the future. Centuries from now, we will be the ones living in this stinking cesspool the humans have created. We must act and strike while the iron is hot and allow them to discover they are not alone."

"While the iron is hot?" A black-haired dragoness slapped her hand against the table. Her voice raised to a shrill tone. "It will certainly become hot once the mortals have turned to chemical warfare to be rid of us. What shall be done after they unleash nuclear winter?"

Ēostre rolled her eyes. "They will not destroy their own planet to remove supernatural beings from the world, Mahuika. We are too many, and we are also forgetting our esteemed guests."

She gestured with a hand toward the seated representatives from the other paranormal communities. A few shapeshifters belonging to the more timid animal species nervously avoided eye contact, fidgeting in their seats.

The leaders of the more-cagey, predatory breeds disguised their feelings behind stoic masks. Among them, a few witches watched with keen, studious eyes, too smart to be shaken by the presence of a few dragons.

Or too dumb. Ēostre could never tell when it came to human mages.

"Ēostre is correct. Many of us hold positions of power around the world. Furthermore, we have an ace in the hole if such becomes necessary," Agnes said. The old woman steepled her fingers and smiled cruelly. If any of her kind resembled the hags of legend, it was Agnes, with her crooked spine and enlarged nose. Deep creases lined her face, and whenever the witch spoke, Ēostre expected pieces of it to crumble to dust.

"And what ace is this?" Max asked, his voice brimming with skepticism.

"The werewolves are prepared to deploy. They'll turn the most socially powerful humans and bring them into our world whether they want it or not."

Max cut his eyes toward the section of wolves from around the world. Most of them appeared to be in agreement. "Many of you could die in the attempt. I would not recommend it. If this route of action is taken, we will never earn their trust and peace will never exist between the sides of mortal and supernatural. I must ask you to reconsider this plan."

Ēostre shivered. "Turning humans should always be a last resort. We want to minimize casualties on all sides. There's no need for a loss of werewolf *or* human lives."

"We're prepared for that. It's nothing our packs haven't done before to keep our people safe, and we'll do it again for the community as a whole," a young werewolf alpha said. Jason, a leader from the wolves of the northern states, rolled his shoulders as nonchalantly as a man discussing the weather.

Another pack leader named Argus twisted in his seat to stare harshly. "We did not discuss this."

"But the wolf cub is right!" The cry came from a massive, broad-shouldered bear shifter among a section of equally brawny men and women. Bear shifters tended to run a narrow range of sizes and shapes, resembling Olympic athletes and sports players. "We have the strength to crush them and implement the changes we want! Even the werewolves understand the law of survival. Today, the bear clans vote for change. The time for hiding like cowards is over."

"Thank you for that very rousing speech, Brutus," Ēostre said, using her gentlest tone. "What do the witches say, Pythia?"

"Our covens remain undecided," Pythia answered. The older woman's face was set in a frown. She was well respected among many of the southern good witches of the United States, and she'd become a leader of her own coven in the recent years. "*Some* of us remember the Salem Witch Trials." She and Agnes exchanged cool stares.

Ah, so that's it, Ēostre thought. *So dark and light have taken opposing sides in every way. Should I take this as an omen that the dark opposes secrecy and the light favors it?*

"It won't happen again," Agnes said. "Those times are in the past."

Pythia shook her head. "I haven't forgotten any of my past lives. I can recall every mistake humanity has made since the massacre of the first natives on American soil. This will be another, and it will be our fault once they realize witchcraft is real. They'll burn all of us."

"Humans can openly declare to be Satanists now and no one is burning them at the stake. I think those days are behind us," Ian pointed out. Argus chuckled from his seat beside the eagle shifter. "Key members of the government know we all exist, they've been using our services for years in their wars and to protect this beautiful country. They won't sacrifice that for the ignorant masses. They need us too much and I've been working my ass off to make sure they'll always see us as allies."

Ēostre smiled, thrilled to have both men on her side. Ian MacArthur, Argus, and her son Saul had a good working relationship. When he'd first introduced her to them, she'd had her doubts, but the shifters had power in their communities. Ian had even promised to place political support behind Maximilian. She took a moment to admire him from her higher table in the conference hall.

Ian was one of those shifters who had taken a human mate, and he knew better than most that mortals were willing to accept the supernatural as equals. He flashed her a big smile, the shifter's younger features at odds with his pale, almost white hair.

"Then, if all have said their peace, it is time to cast your votes. You will find a tablet in the arm compartment of your chair. Please select either yes, no, or recuse. Your votes will remain anonymous."

Ēostre punched in her vote and watched Maximilian do the same. He'd sat beside her at the beginning of the meeting — startling her, since he usually joined the old doddering fire wyrms who never missed a chance to reminisce about the beloved days of King Arthur. Razing villages. Stealing princesses. Devouring knights… things better left behind them.

She wondered how much of their sordid past would emerge, and whether human rights activists would scream for reparations as they searched their family trees for proof of ancestors who were consumed by dragons. The idea made her chuckle as she returned the tablet to its compartment. Maximilian nudged her leg with his thigh, wanting in on the joke.

"Nothing," she mouthed to him. His inquisitive, bright amber eyes lingered on her face. She shook her head.

Twenty minutes passed before the last tablet lowered. Some had made their decisions quickly. Others had taken their time, clearly filled with inner turmoil over the decision.

"Have all finished?"

Heads nodded and expressions remained tense.

Maximilian remained on the edge of his seat beside her as she tapped a finger on the computer console. A projection shined from a spot on the ceiling to the far wall in front of them, displaying the results for all to see.

Yes! The vast number of positive responses left her speechless. The stunned flame dragon at her left stared at the projection screen, then a grin slowly overtook his handsome face.

"It's done." Excitement trembled in her voice as Ēostre announced the results, "We have received overwhelming support for worldwide exposure. Within a year of Maximilian entering the Presidential office, the supernatural world will emerge to take our rightful place among humans as equals."

"Hell yeah!" a young shifter called out.

Despite the scowling faces peppered among the group of ancient wyrms, Ēostre turned to the man beside her and hugged him tight. "We did it, Max."

Chapter 5

In the subdued lighting of an extravagant hotel suite, a trio of dragons with scowling faces convened to discuss the aftermath of the most historic vote in draconic history.

Mahuika's dark eyes raked over the men standing by the door. Both were handsome brutes, the one on the left more refined than the brawny ancient beside him. She'd chosen them for being the most outspoken during the debates, for their reactions after the poll, and the very nature of their fierce reputations.

"I am glad you both chose to join me this evening," she greeted them in the Draconic tongue.

The larger dragon, Tlaloc, wore his features in an impassive mask. "I find my curiosity stimulated. What could you possibly have to discuss with me?" Tendrils of his hair fell in an ebony river around his powerful shoulders, framing a darkly tanned face that could have been carved from stone.

"I am also intrigued," Loki said.

"On this day, I witnessed your disgust, your disappointment, and your fury. That is why you are called to meet with me in secrecy. Something must be done about Maximilian and Ēostre's foolish behavior, and it must be done soon before they have the chance to ruin everything we have worked to achieve. But I must ask, *why* did you allow this to happen?" Mahuika asked.

"Why did I allow it to happen? What could I have done to stop it?" Tlaloc demanded. The man rose to his full, awe-inspiring height, a giant among them with an impressive, terrifying aura. His bronze skin was flawless with the exception of a long, white scar slashing across his lip and chin from the days of war.

Mahuika fell back a step, immediately contrite. "Apologies. I merely meant to ask why you had not sought the counsel and aid of your fellow great wyrms. Together, their presence may have intimidated the weak-willed and skewed the vote in our favor. But please, come with me. Let us be seated first."

She led them deeper into the deluxe suite until the men were treated to a view of downtown Chicago, and their choice in seating arrangement on a plush sofa and nearby armchair. Her fingers glided over the leather of the adjacent seat and patted the cushion. Loki, accepting the invitation, sat to her left while Tlaloc sat opposite them in the high-backed chair.

"Had this been a vote among dragonkind alone, common sense would have prevailed. But it was not. Involving the lesser races in this debate was a wise strategic maneuver," Loki said.

"It has long surpassed a debate," Mahuika said hotly. "What they have decided this day shall destroy everything."

Loki stroked his stubbled chin. "Only if he becomes president. We have not lost yet, my friends." His gray-green eyes flicked to Mahuika's idle servant. A short distance away, the girl knelt in the corner on a single pillow, hands resting on her lap and face downturned to avoid eye contact. Her tiny, thin white slip barely covered her thighs. "But does your slave find us unworthy of performing her duties?"

Mahuika snapped her fingers at the female deer shifter. "Wine, girl. Be quick about it. We have thirsty guests."

"My apologies, Mistress." The doe flew from her chair to pour wine for three. She served in silence, hopelessly unable to conceal her flushed face and embarrassment. Raising her chin, Mahuika watched her pet's trembling hands with smug satisfaction.

As glasses exchanged hands, Mahuika twisted to face Tlaloc. "I have seen the results of your great wisdom in the past, Tlaloc. You and Loki are known as two of our greatest schemers, and I refuse to believe you will sit idly by as Ēostre brings ruin to us all. Is there nothing we can do?"

"There is nothing," Tlaloc said in a contemptuous voice, "short of killing him before he ascends to their human throne. I know little of this time period, but what I have learned from my son and his mother tells me we should annihilate every sniveling human from this planet. We should fly as we once did in the past."

"No, my friend. You do not understand the might of their weapons. They have missiles," Mahuika hastily said.

"And what is a missile to me, the great Tlaloc? I will open the earth itself and swallow their cities into the abyss." The black dragon made a fist and growled. "We will wipe the earth clean of them."

Loki shook his head. "She is right. You don't understand the power of the weapons these mortals hold. The strength of a missile is incomprehensible until you have witnessed the resulting devastation. Far worse than any magical tempest or dragon's fire. They could destroy entire nations within seconds and leave only scorched earth in their wake."

"We'll have to show him, Loki."

They presented Tlaloc with a brightly lit pad, angling the screen for him to have a full view. Loki swiped his fingers across the device and pulled up several images for the older dragon to observe.

"This is the aftermath of Hiroshima," Loki said. "The weapon was deployed in the 40s, while most of us hibernated in our lairs. The destructive power is far beyond anything I can do with my breath weapon. They even, unknowingly, killed an ancient slumbering in her lair. I fear this being used against me."

"As should we all," Mahuika said.

"I…" Tlaloc's stunned features told Mahuika everything she needed to know.

Loki pressed a button on the pad. "Now *this* is the power of modern-day technology."

Tlaloc didn't utter a word as the video footage rolled, displaying a war-torn village in the Middle East. Homes smoldered in the aftermath of a drone strike.

"A few decades ago, we on the grand council decided to become involved, discreetly, in the manufacturing of these items. They contain fail safes, programmed back doors able to render them completely dysfunctional," Loki said. "But it won't take long for them to realize they can't use these against us."

"Mark my words, should Ēostre's half-baked plans come to fruition, everything will change," Mahuika hissed. "These demanding humans would see us living by their laws and traditions."

Loki chuckled dryly. "Your slave girl will be freed. As I understand, slavery has been abolished across the world in all civilized countries. They won't stand for it."

"As will yours, Trickster. There is much for all of us to lose."

"Maximilian's arrogance will cost him. We will not weep and lament this decision. We will combat it in the only way we know how."

Tlaloc set his jaw and stared beyond the window. For the second time since their meeting began, emotion broke through the stony facade. "You are right about the changes to this world, but I am not fated for this task. It is a duty for the young dragons of this era."

"Tlaloc, you must—"

He shook his head again. "It has taken this to realize I am a creature stuck behind, far in the past. I do not understand the things you speak of. This technology. These flying disasters of the skies are unknown magic to me."

"But we need—"

Tlaloc cut her off a second time. "May the Ancestors guide you. As for me, I hope to awaken in a new and better age."

With sorrow in his eyes, the ancient rose from his seat and turned to the door. He reminded Mahuika of Teotihuacan in so many ways, from his proud stance to the powerful body beneath his cream-colored khakis and button-down shirt.

Teo must have loaned his father a change of clothes.

"Must you leave so soon?" Mahuika asked. Gliding her fingers over one shoulder strap, she slid the dress lower. The soft upper swell of her plump bosom, and little else, became exposed.

Loki watched her with ravenous eyes, his attention fastened to the hint of areola peeking from the top of her neckline. She'd taken him in without a struggle.

"I am mated, as you well know," Tlaloc said.

"And yet Xochiquetzal is not here." Her voice softened when the stoic man's expression transitioned to disapproval. She eased from the couch and approached, slowing her walk to a sensual stroll. "I saw her among the voters. Did she take the side of the heretics who would place us all in danger?"

Tlaloc remained silent, but his green eyes fixed on the exaggerated sway in her hips.

"She *has* sided with your son, hasn't she? It is a shame. Teotihuacan is such a fine dragon. I would have considered claiming him as a mate, but he has dishonored himself by choosing a lowly human. Why would he shame his parents in such a way?"

"It is his human pet who pollutes his view of the world. This is not what I taught him."

With one of the male dragons already under her sway, she pressed her palm against Tlaloc's abdomen, felt the muscles tense beneath her fingers, and slid her hand downward over the taut definition. With only his button-down shirt separating them, she imagined how easy it would be to part him from his clothes. Dragons were no stranger to hedonistic pleasures, and having the two handsome men at once was the perfect way to consummate a partnership.

She realized her mistake too late. Tlaloc's hand gripped like a vice around her arm, threatening to crush the bone. He leaned over until she was forced to bow backwards and yield to his remarkable strength.

"My apologies!" she cried out. "I meant no insult, Tlaloc." His hold cut off the blood flow to her hand, making her fingertips tingle and pulse mercilessly to the rhythm of her heartbeat.

"Try a trick like this again, Mahuika, and not only will I take your wings, I will then allow my *mate* to finish the job."

"I meant nothing by it!"

The agony was exquisite. While his human nails weren't as sharp as talons, he possessed the same magic in either form. Acid burned through her veins, and beneath his touch, the skin blistered. No matter how she pulled and twisted, Tlaloc had her anchored securely in place to receive the full brunt of his fury.

"I apologize!" she shrieked again until the older dragon released her. Another growl rumbled through his chest and he shoved her back, before stepping through the door without another word.

Loki waited until the door had shut behind the other ancient before he spoke up, "I could have warned you that would happen."

Mahuika shot him a dirty look, and for the sake of not risking her chances with another elder dragon, she kept her thoughts to herself.

Chapter 6

Ēostre paused in the shade of a palm and fanned herself with a handout from the primate house.

An unforgiving sun shone from above, and more than ever, the storm dragoness wished she and Fafnir had chosen a home with more temperate, enjoyable weather like Seattle, where peaceful rains and cloudy skies beckoned. But no, her mate wanted scorching heat and perpetual sun.

The tail end of September had brought in grueling ninety-degree days and cloudless skies. Ēostre would have given her weight in treasure for a break.

Astrid skipped ahead, calling behind her, "C'mon, you two! We're going to miss the feeding!"

Where does she find the energy to move in this abysmal heat? Ēostre wondered. As if sensing her grandmother's plight, the girl stopped to crouch beside the upraised walls surrounding the lion exhibit.

A lazy male lion basked in the summer warmth while a trio of his female companions patrolled nearby. One flopped beside their wild-maned mate, and another slumped in the shaded grass. The third keen-eyed lioness stared Astrid down, only to back away and retreat when Ēostre braved the sun again and stepped up beside her granddaughter.

"Intimidating the locals?" Maximilian teased from her other side.

"I didn't do anything but walk over for a look," Ēostre protested.

"Perhaps your frown terrified her."

"I am not frowning."

Andrew, the agent shadowing them for the day, chuckled quietly from a respectable distance away, proving wolves had extraordinary hearing.

"Grandma doesn't like the heat," Astrid offered to the conversation. She turned her small face up to Maximilian and beamed. "Uncle Max, does that make you like my mom and dad?"

"And like you," he replied. "Although your grandmother is one with the storms, you and I have fire in our souls. I would say you seem to have inherited more of your grandfather's spirit."

While they talked, Ēostre discreetly gestured to the open air. She turned her face to the blindingly bright sky and closed her eyes. Seconds later, fluffy and thick cloud cover rolled in from the east.

Max turned to raise a quizzical brow at her. "Ēostre."

"It was necessary!" she protested.

As a young couple walked by, the woman fanned herself and uttered, "Thank God. It's like we're finally getting a break from this crap."

Ēostre glanced at her friend.

"There's no need to be smug about it," he mumbled.

"Would you like me to take a picture of you with your wife and daughter, sir?" A cheerful, smiling employee with a camera around her neck beamed at them. "The lions are in the perfect spot for it today."

Ēostre searched the area for another couple, and failing to locate any other family near them, she stared at the employee. "Excuse me?"

"Why yes, we would," Maximilian said after the initial awkward pause. He slipped his arm around Ēostre's waist and tugged her in close, and before she could protest, Astrid bounced over in front of them. The little girl hammed it up for the camera, but her playful antics failed to distract Ēostre from how natural it felt with Max's arm circling her waist. His warmth enveloped her at once with the scent of cedar and woodsy cognac. She discreetly turned her head, breathed in his cologne, and half-melted against him. He made it easy.

"Smile!"

Ēostre attempted to put on a dignified smile, but a single glance at Astrid ruined it. The young girl had twisted to throw her arms around both adults. The resulting photograph was wildly inappropriate and absolutely adorable.

I'm smiling like a loon, Ēostre thought as the woman revealed the digital preview.

"Here's your number, sir. If you take this to the ticket kiosk at the end of your visit, you can purchase your photographs."

"Appreciated," Max replied. He pocketed the scrap of paper as the woman walked away.

"Why didn't you say anything?" she asked under her breath.

He shrugged. "Did you want to tell her you're Astrid's grandmother?"

Ēostre considered it. "No, but—"

"Allowing her to assume otherwise causes no harm and saves us the effort of making explanations. Your identification may say forty-eight, but your face says thirty, my friend." He took her hand in his and squeezed her fingers. "I took my cue from Astrid when she failed to correct her."

"Uncle Max is right. Mom told me to never call you grandmother in public if a human can hear us. Besides, who cares what they think?" The girl beamed at them, revealing plenty of her mother's personality. "C'mon, the gorillas and zebras are this way!" Astrid bounced on her toes, pigtails swaying.

They wandered down the winding pathways while Astrid bolted from exhibit to exhibit along the way. She pointed out every creature, big and small, her enthusiasm contagious.

"Look, zebras. Are they just like horses, Uncle Max? Can people ride them?"

"Far from it. They're meaner and grumpier, of course, you would be too if you were taken from your home and shoved into a much smaller place to live."

"The lions don't seem to mind."

"They do. I assure you, these creatures, much like the male lion we saw, would appreciate a grander and more spacious territory to roam."

Astrid's nose scrunched up. "I wish I could give them a bigger place to live. They want to run."

They continued past the zebra enclosure at a sedate pace, pausing to pick up frozen lemonades from a snack stand.

"You know, I make annual donations to this zoo," Maximilian murmured as they traveled a path through the section dedicated to African wildlife.

"Oh?" Ēostre's eyes cut toward him. Max walked beside her with his hands clasped behind his back, a mischievous smile on his bearded face.

"I'm quite friendly with the director. Friendly enough to acquire certain privileges for a special someone," he ventured. "Astrid, how would you like to meet the animals up close without glass between you?"

"Absolutely not," Ēostre said.

"Let her live a little. She has dragon's blood in her veins. She's meant to explore and undertake great adventures, is she not?"

"Please, Grandma, please!"

"All right. Fine. Far be it that I should be the one to be prudent and use my common sense. This stays between the three of us without a word to your mother and father."

Grinning, the dragon shifter stepped aside and removed his cell phone to make a call. Moments after its completion, a big door marked with "Staff Only" in bold white text opened.

He hadn't been joking about his connections.

"Come." Maximilian nodded toward the door, and without further word, he slipped Ēostre's hand into his right, took Astrid's in his left, then guided the girls toward the zookeeper waiting at the door.

The park employee was a bright-eyed woman in her mid-thirties. She wore khakis paired with a green polo shirt, the park's logo stitched over the breast. The name tag with her smiling photo introduced her as Maggie.

"Hi!" she greeted them with enthusiasm. "My boss called and said there's a group of animal lovers who would love to meet our friends back here. Would that be you?" she asked Astrid specifically.

"Yes, yes!"

"Great. I'm Maggie. And who are you?"

"I'm Astrid, and this is my Uncle Max and Aunt Ēostre!" Astrid always did a fantastic job of acting her apparent, physical age, but this time her enthusiasm wasn't a show.

"It's a pleasure to meet you, Maggie. Thanks for this," Max said.

"Yes, thank you," Ēostre agreed.

"No problem. Come on. If you follow me, we'll get to do some really fun stuff."

"Do you have any babies I can look at?"

"Here, let me show you the jaguar cub. He's docile enough for you to pet if you promise to be gentle with him."

"Oh, I will, I promise," Astrid vowed. She trailed after the veterinary technician with a big grin on her face and a bounce in her step.

Ēostre and Max trailed behind and witnessed a fun-filled hour of joy for Astrid. Around three, they peeled her away to allow the vet tech to return to her duties.

"I want to be a zookeeper when I finally grow up. Uncle Max, can I?"

Ēostre opened her mouth to speak, but Max beat her to the punch.

"My sweet, you may be whatever you wish to be when you grow up. That's the magic of being an adult, and no one else may decide for you." Then his warm, amber eyes drifted to Ēostre. "But it never hurts to listen to the advice of loved ones and family."

"Well, I've decided I want to work at the zoo," she insisted with conviction.

As far as Ēostre knew, Saul had already planned on pulling Astrid into the family business. She grinned. Her son was in for a rude awakening, his little girl already developing her own mind and personality apart from his own.

Astrid led the way around the park, revisiting her favorite exhibits, until Ēostre was sure her feet would never recover from the exertion. She received a reprieve when her granddaughter took a seat on a bench to eat a grilled turkey leg while watching the animals roam.

"Astrid has shown immense interest in the zebras," Maximilian commented.

"She loves animals of all kinds. For a while, Saul feared she would become the world's first dragon vegetarian."

"She wouldn't be the first, actually. Watatsumi's daughter survived on kelp until adolescence." He chuckled. "Couldn't bear to harm her ocean friends."

"We're beyond that worry with Astrid, thankfully."

Astrid devoured a meal impressive enough to challenge most grown men. Without taking a break, she sprinted away to the nearby playground equipment. "Thank you for joining us today, by the way. You've really—" Ēostre glanced to the right and encountered an empty seat.

The flame dragon had disappeared, beside her one moment, gone the next while Ēostre was watching the little girl play. No doubt gone to do more mischief with his money. *How much did he pay for Astrid to enjoy a private petting session among the wild animals?* Ēostre wondered.

She texted him and received the standard response: I'm handling business. BBS.

When he returned fifteen minutes later with a cocky grin on his face, Ēostre's dread intensified.

"What did you *do*, Maximilian?"

"I made the first investment in Astrid's future career. That's all."

"What did you do?" she repeated.

"I bought her some zebras."

"You bought a herd of zebras?" she shrieked. Several passing tourists glanced over, prompting her to lower her voice. "Max, what were you thinking?"

"I wouldn't call three a herd."

"Three zebras? Three zebras, Max? Did you not think to consult me or even ask the child's parents if it's acceptable? Sweet Ancestors, you're the future leader of this country. You can't walk about throwing money at everyone to have your way."

"If it truly makes a difference, the animals were to be transported to another zoo out of state in exchange for some komodo dragons, but the deal fell through. It caused an immense amount of grief; there's been cutbacks in this department, and one of the animals requires more care than what they can reasonably afford. So I offered to sponsor the animals for them."

Ēostre sighed in relief. "So they won't be going to Drakenstone Manor. Why didn't you say so?"

"Oh, no, they will." Max held up his hands in the face of her withering look, and quickly continued. "However, their main caretaker shall be visiting the manor five days a week to give Astrid lessons in their care."

"Saul and Chloe will *love* that. How soon should we expect their arrival?"

"Ah. Today. They appear to be very eager to be rid of them for some reason."

"What?! Doesn't that provoke even a little suspicion, Maximilian? Who prepares three zebras for transportation to unknown territory without so much as an investigation into the home? How do they know the grounds will be prepared for their arrival?"

"I phoned Leiv and told him about the surprise. He assures me Mahasti shall have everything ready." Then he grinned even wider. "Besides, I *am* the governor of the state and Saul Drakenstone the billionaire is quite well-known for his studio's phenomenal treatment of animals in their movies. As if we would besmirch our reputations." He scoffed.

"That is not the point."

While Ēostre considered the murder of the future U.S. President, Astrid wrapped her arms around his waist and squealed, hugging him. "Thank you, Uncle Max, thank you!" She'd overheard it all, making it impossible to force Max to undo his troublemaking.

The drive home was filled with exuberant chatter about her new friends. Astrid had picked out a book in the gift shop on their way out and regaled them with facts and trivia from the backseat.

"That is fascinating," Max said from the passenger seat. "Yes, sweetheart, tell us more. Your grandmother appears particularly interested in the mating habits of wild African boars."

Ēostre wanted to strangle him.

"Astrid, why don't you go get cleaned up and ready for dinner," Ēostre suggested as they parked in the driveway. "Say goodbye to your uncle."

"Aww. Can't he stay for dinner?"

"Sorry, my dear. I have a teleconference meeting in less than an hour that I can't put off."

The girl sulked, but she hugged him one last time before sprinting away to scrub up for dinner. Once she was gone, Ēostre opened a portal to Maximilian's home office. The shimmering gateway hung suspended between them, revealing his comfortably appointed accommodations on the other side, as if looking through a window.

"You're such an ass," she said to him.

"You wound me, Ēostre." He lifted a hand to his heart. "Now go enjoy your educational evening and don't forget our wager. Look at the happiness my gift has brought Astrid."

She grumbled and gestured toward the portal. "Go on or you'll be late. Be sure not to let that New York journalist bully you into a corner, and ease up some on the correspondent from Wyoming. You want to win their votes."

"I know, I know. Now go on upstairs and enjoy your evening with your family."

Max surprised her with a quick hug. Before she even had the chance to recover her wits and return the friendly gesture, Max had released her and stepped through the gateway.

Andrew stepped over from the car he'd borrowed for the day and eyed the opened portal with a grimace.

"C'mon, pup. It won't bite."

"So you always say," the wolf grumbled at Max. "Enjoy your evening, Ēostre. Sorry for the menagerie."

"Thank you, Andrew, and good night."

The gateway closed behind them with a soft pop moments before Chloe walked onto the porch.

"Ēostre? I thought I saw Maximilian standing on the drive."

"I sent him and his guard home. He wanted to say hello, but the drive from LA took longer than planned."

"Oh bummer, I'd hoped to hear what he thought of everything. So how does he feel about having a security detail?"

"He loathes it and undermines their attempts to protect him at every turn. But if he didn't have an official team on the books, he'd have pressure to allow the Secret Service to guard him. As it is, he can only put them off until after the election as it is, since he'll be required to have even more security once he becomes the President-elect."

They moved inside where cool air greeted them. On the brink of collapse, she sank into a chair at Chloe's dinette table and graciously accepted a glass of ice water. "I have never walked so far and so long in a human guise in all of my life. Not even when we visited Disneyland four years ago."

Chloe laughed and pushed over a tray of sweets. "She wasn't quite as, uh, energetic then."

"She has certainly grown into a fine young woman." Ēostre furrowed her brow. "Which leads to my news. There's something I must tell you, Chloe."

"What? Astrid wasn't naughty, was she? She streaked past me and to her room before I even had a chance to ask about the day."

"No, nothing like that. In fact, quite the opposite. However, you should know that—"

Astrid sprinted into the room. "Mom, Mom! Uncle Max bought me zebras! He bought me zebras, and they're here now!"

As quickly as she entered, Astrid was off again. She skidded out the door and down the hallway toward the foyer.

Chloe slowly turned around to face her mother-in-law, her blue eyes wide. "What?"

"Uh… about that."

"When were you planning to tell me that our daughter now owns a team of zebra?" she demanded.

"Now, before she interrupted."

Chloe scowled at her.

"Well, you *do* have the room," Ēostre pointed out. "When Fafnir and I chose these lands to raise Saul, we carved out our territory for many miles in each direction."

Chloe's mouth pressed into a thin line.

"I'm sorry, darling. I couldn't say no. He'd already written the check and Astrid eavesdropped on our conversation before I could decline them. How could I be the horrible grandmother who refuses after seeing her precious face light up with glee?"

A sigh escaped the other woman. "Since when did Max start going to the zoo with you and Astrid anyway?"

Ēostre paused. Why *had* she invited Maximilian along on her Saturday outing with Astrid? She could have taken him anywhere on any other day.

"Well?" Chloe persisted.

"I suppose I thought he'd enjoy an afternoon away from politics…" she hedged.

"At the zoo."

"Well, he is a friend."

"A friend who you've spent a lot of time with lately during and away from work," Chloe continued. "Are you two—"

"Chloe?" Saul called into the kitchen, interrupting the two women. "Why are men in my driveway with a trailer of zebras?"

Ēostre exhaled a sigh of relief. Her son's abrupt arrival drew the attention back to the issue at hand — three zebras needing a home among the livestock inhabiting the fertile plains of Saul's property.

"They're gifts for Astrid."

"Mother," the dragon said in an exasperated breath. "We discussed this once in the past. No expensive and extravagant gifts for Astrid. Certainly not a herd of animals. Who will care for them?"

"It's fine, Saul," Chloe said. "Leiv will think it's amazing, then thank us for giving him a new project to undertake with the girls."

Saul hesitated. "All right," he agreed. Chloe had firmly wrapped him around her pinky finger, and it was as if she could do no wrong in his eyes. He smiled warmly at both women, the irritation fading from his features immediately. "I shall return to speak with them."

Chloe pounced the moment her husband left.

"Are you and Max dating?"

"No!" Ēostre blurted out.

"I don't know too many single men who gleefully go along with an equally *single* woman and small child to the zoo."

"There is absolutely nothing between Maximilian and me. It was innocent fun and nothing more. I merely thought a good friend, who happens to be very lonely, would appreciate an outing in the sunshine away from his job."

"Ēostre, if there is nothing between you," Chloe said gently, "why defend it so thoroughly… unless, of course, you want something between you. In the month that's passed since the vote, I've seen you two grow closer and closer."

"I… well…" She tried to voice an eloquent denial, but nothing came to mind.

"I won't press anymore. You're used to being the one who gives everyone else advice — whether we want it or not," Chloe said with a brief pause and cheeky smile, "but everyone needs a hand sometimes. I know you dragons take years to do what we humans decide in days, but… Max is a good man. If you *do* like him, don't wait too long to ponder on it."

"Mom! Mom! Come look at the zebras!" Astrid called through the front door.

"That's my cue to leave you be. I guess dinner is delayed until we get these guys settled."

"You go on, dear. I'd like to shower and freshen up after that long day in the sun."

After Ēostre retreated to her bedroom for a shower, she couldn't help but wonder if her daughter-in-law was on to something.

Did she have feelings for Maximilian? More importantly, did she want to risk ruining the comfortable friendship between them to find out?

Chapter 7

Early October ushered in the perfect day for a rally beneath the open blue skies of Virginia. Max stood in front of a podium, addressing a boisterous crowd of future voters.

"During my drive to this conference, I passed at least two homeless veterans," Maximilian announced to the crowd. "It's unacceptable to treat our heroes this way. When I am elected as your president, I promise to bring the same reforms implemented in California to *every* state, helping our soldiers and sailors after they've served their time for our country. During my term as president, I swear no hero will ever go hungry or without a roof above their head. They are owed more than that."

Cheers erupted from the crowd, as he'd expected considering the military-heavy population. He knew exactly what to say to them, what to promise, and what topics to avoid. Even more importantly, he knew how to keep his word once they elected him to the presidential office.

A woman clothed in a red, white, and blue bikini top over tiny denim cutoffs waved a banner declaring her love for him while shouting similar comments. A short distance away from him on the platform, Ēostre made a disgusted noise in her throat and looked away. She wasn't impressed by some of his female voters. At all. But she also held her fellow women to a high standard.

They'd flown to Virginia for a last-ditch effort to win over the state. So far he was leading in the popularity polls by a hairsbreadth, making the race too close for his comfort. Max's adrenaline was still pumping by the time they reached his hotel suite.

The other guy was putting up a better fight than expected, and it didn't help that Loki was out to sabotage him by publicly supporting the other candidate, Thompson, and funneling money into his opponent's campaign.

It was enough for Max to feel tempted to contact Thor and put out a hit on him. A couple hundred thousand gold coins for one good thrashing. But Ēostre had sweet-talked him out of the idea and also made him promise he wouldn't personally deliver justice with his own claws.

"All right. I think I'll go freshen up and change. Dinner out?"

"Yes, of course. Excellent idea. We'll be sure to ride the public transportation as well. I read some comments online about how much the green community loves my willingness to take the bus."

Ēostre fixed him with a look. "I suppose fine dining is off the table?"

"You guessed it. Tell Vincent to prepare to earn his pay today."

"Then I shall return once I have dressed down."

Ēostre shut the door behind her and left for her own hotel room. In the time it took to wait for her return, Max showered, changed, and settled on the couch in the suite's main room to check his email. Half an hour passed before a knock jarred him out of his thoughts.

"It's about time," Max announced as he jerked open the door. "I thought I'd starve waiting for…" He trailed off, stunned by the sight in front of him. Another female dragoness stood framed by the open door, her hair messy coal black waves around golden-brown, bare shoulders. She wore a strapless, curve-hugging jumpsuit in a bold shade of red, and stilettos that brought her chest high. Mahuika was tiny for a dragoness. But her tits were as amazing as he remembered.

"Hello, Maximilian. Your hired muscle did not want to allow me to see you, but I managed to convince him otherwise."

"Would you like me to escort her away, sir?" Vincent asked. The werewolf in his impeccable, impossibly tailored suit waited on Max's command.

Max shook his head. A wolf could never force a dragoness to do anything she didn't want to do, but he had no doubt Vincent would try. They were purely hired for looks and to keep away the human or shifter rabble. Against his fellow dragons, they were useless. "No, that won't be necessary."

"Let me know if you change your mind, sir."

Without awaiting an invitation, Mahuika stepped forward into the suite. Maximilian shut the door behind her and suppressed the apprehension crawling down his spine. "Why are you here?"

"Did you not see me among the members of the crowd? I came to provide my support to you."

"You must have been far in the back or I'm certain I would have noticed."

"Well, I could hardly distract you when you had the crowd eating out of your talons."

"I suppose you must want something. What is it?"

"Is that any way to treat the mother of your cub?" She pouted.

Max scoffed and crossed back toward his desk. "Let's not use labels that hold no meaning, Mahuika. You may have birthed Brigid, but you were no mother. Now, the question still stands. What do you want?"

A tiny wrinkle appeared in Mahuika's brow and her mouth turned down at the corners. "To speak with you, Maxim. Only to speak. We were once very civil with one another and I hoped things could be that way again someday."

"I am being civil. Now, please tell me what's on your mind."

"Your speech was moving. So much so that I would like to offer you my support. Both to your campaign and our emergence into the public eye."

Mahuika had been as outspoken against his plans as some of the other elder dragons. Her words did nothing to assuage his skepticism.

"Now you are willing to support me?"

"Yes. I was wrong. I am not too proud to admit this to you now. Watching you and seeing the love these people have for this human persona, it has humbled me and made me realize the affection may remain once we are open with them."

"I see." His apprehension remained, but he was willing to hear her out.

"So, may we talk about my ideas?"

Max nodded toward the sofa. He poured two glasses of brandy from his private stash and joined her. The dragoness edged closer than necessary until their thighs touched and the sweet scent of cinnamon and clove reached him, laced with an underlying, pleasurable aroma.

"Now that you're guaranteed to win the presidency, have you considered the importance of a first lady?" Mahuika asked. She smoothed her hand over his shoulder in a soothing rhythm. "These Americans practically expect it."

"I wouldn't be the first unmarried president," Max replied in an even tone.

"Is this country not obsessed with the promise of maintaining family values? When the big secret comes into the open, your citizens will search for similarities between you and them. They will try to humanize you. See you as more than a beast who breathes fire." The words rolled from her tongue as she pressed to his side, completing the invasion of his personal space. "They will want to see you as a man."

"What do you imply I should do, Mahuika?"

"I can make your existence more palatable by becoming your wife and giving you a child. We will show them dragonkind is not so different."

Max's spine stiffened. Her arrival had doused his entire mood with cold water, but the promise of another baby inspired a yearning he hadn't felt in years.

No, he *had* felt it more recently. He'd felt it when Astrid threw her skinny arms around his neck and kissed his cheek. When she'd screamed with joy and squeezed him so tight, he'd thought of his Brigid and his thoughts were consumed by her for the rest of the day.

"You gave me the impression you didn't want a family when I once courted you."

Mahuika playfully walked her fingers down his chest until she reached his abdomen. Max's t-shirt rose with the next effortless stroke, exposing washboard definition. Old memories of having her beneath him awakened his cock with a throbbing pulse. He visualized her above him, rocking to the sensual rhythm of their lovemaking.

He'd lost count of the nights he'd had her beside him, bare and glistening in the light of a bubbling lava pit. She'd been the perfect lay, the woman who taught him to enjoy making love as a human.

"When I gave you Brigid, I was not yet ready to settle with a single male for the rest of my life. But I am ready this time. Don't you miss our cub? Can you claim a single day has passed without her in your thoughts? Give me the chance to bless you with another, and we will raise the little one together."

He missed Brigid so insanely it hurt, but Mahuika had never shown an ounce of interest in his daughter during her life. She'd been an incubator. Nothing more.

"You loathed the idea of revealing ourselves to the mortals. Be truthful with me this time. What inspired this change of heart? Why come to me *now* when you've had centuries to return?"

"I did hate it," she admitted. "But I've come to accept your ideas as truth. Is that so bad? You've always been a very, very persuasive dragon."

Max gently, but firmly, dislodged her from his side. "You've given me ideas to consider, but at a later time. I have a meeting."

"Mmm. All right," she replied, surprising him. "Try not to ponder it for too long." She stood on tiptoe and brushed her lips against his cheek. Her mouth lingered by his ear when she reached it, breath warm against his skin. "I have fond memories of our last matings and the long months until your seed took root."

"Mahuika…" He breathed her in, and finally the familiar scent made sense. Mahuika had chosen to meet him at the peak of her heat cycle, making her scent absolutely irresistible. It was the ideal time to impregnate her. The only time to guarantee she'd be gravid with his child within months.

Her lips closed around his ear lobe and her index finger traced between his shirt and the thin leather belt around his waist. "We could begin now, Maximilian. What were the chances of my fertility cycle arriving now when you need it most?"

One in a million. No, a billion. Those were impossible odds, the kind dragons attributed to fate and the Ancestors giving their blessings.

Raw lust consumed Max's thoughts and spread hotly through his loins in a white-hot pulse of arousal, pushing out all rational thought. His hardening cock pressed for freedom from his jeans, accompanied by the overwhelming desire to bend Mahuika over the desk to sate his need. He hadn't taken a lover since before Brigid's death, over fifteen years ago.

When Maximilian gazed down at the receptive female dragon in front of him, it wasn't tawny skin and dark hair he craved. His aroused mind crafted a vision of Scandinavian beauty: fair, freckled, and tall.

Ēostre. She would be over at any moment, fresh-faced and ready to celebrate their success. According to the emails he'd read and the blog posts online, the Virginia voters had loved every moment of his speech. She was who he wanted to see.

"No," he gritted out before parting their bodies again. "As I said before, we will speak of this another time. I have somewhere to be within the hour."

"Somewhere to be? I came to you at the height of my breeding season, and you have somewhere else to be?"

"I do," Max said replied before seizing her by the upper arm and striding to the door. He opened it wide. "Always nice catching up with you, Mahuika. Thanks for stopping by."

With fury in her brown eyes, she stalked past him and into the hallway. Her heels made muted thumps against the carpeted floor.

"Future visits with her are to be declined, Vincent. I doubt she'll make a scene if you're firm, but you're also not to place yourself in unnecessary danger to remove her. Thank you."

Some dragonesses didn't change, and he was a fool if he thought Mahuika had it in her to be anything more than a conniving harpy.

***

Mahuika rubbed her thumb over the enchanted jewel given to her by Loki and braced herself as a torrent of magic washed over her body. She was whisked promptly from one location to the next, arriving to the point of its creation.

The laid-back sorcerer lounged on a sofa with an open book while one of his servant girls delivered a foot massage. Another fed him from a bowl of plump grapes. A third, to her left, held a platter of seared beef cubes speared with toothpicks, creating an unoriginal, wholly predictable scene of male pampering. She rolled her eyes at the sight and stalked up to them.

"Did he accept?" Loki asked.

Mahuika snarled her response. The three servants, timid squirrel shapeshifters, squeaked and fled the room, tumbling fruit and bite-sized nuggets of savory meat in every direction. Loki sighed and waved away the mess with a hand gesture.

"Hm. That surprises me greatly. I expected the great Belenos of Gaul to eagerly accept your offer to bear him another child. He would have been under your thumb for certain then," Loki mused.

"But he isn't. Now what are we to do? Your entire plan hinged on Maximilian becoming the protective, doting father."

"And unwilling to risk an uncertain future for his cub." After a disgusted snort, Loki leaned back in his seat, and with one hand, patted his lap for Mahuika to join him. She slid into place without question. "I am not without an alternate plan, Mahuika. Did you believe me to be so simple I would not foresee this outcome as a possibility?"

Mahuika didn't answer. Loki's reputation preceded him, but centuries had passed since his last great plot. Without an ounce of hesitation, she lied through her teeth, "Of course not. You are Loki, the great god of schemes and trickery."

"There's a good girl." Loki's nose skimmed her throat. As he breathed in the potion perfuming her skin, his palm glided over her breast and squeezed. "Perhaps you should shower before I take what your dear friend took for granted."

Mahuika tilted her head back and gazed into his green eyes. A sly smile curved her lips. "Maybe that's what I want," she purred, her voice seductive and low.

"Or perhaps your pride has been wounded by Maximilian's denial," Loki surmised. A growl rumbled on the tail end of his words as he traced a fingertip down her form-fitting outfit. The dragon-shifter's claws appeared in an instant, slicing through the material without damaging the flesh beneath.

"It's because of that sniveling silver bitch. If she didn't have him wrapped around her talons, I could have had him today."

"Maybe, maybe not. We will never know. What I do know is that they have become closer since her awakening." He paused and tilted his head, inspiration brightening his green eyes until they flowed like emerald fire. "Talk to the crone. I've heard quite the juicy rumor regarding a certain collection she's amassed over the centuries. One treasure in particular should interest you deeply."

"What sort of treasure?"

Loki clicked his tongue at her. "Tsk. What fun is there if I tell you everything right away?"

"How would you know what Agnes has in her hovel she calls a home?"

"Your jealousy is showing, my dear. The witch owns half of the antique galleries in the country and has come across all manner of things, many of which I have bartered for."

"So you've laid eyes on this one object?"

"I watched her acquire it." A slow smile gradually transformed his face into the picture of mischief, resembling the Cheshire Cat. "And it rankles her to no end, knowing I witnessed one of her greatest crimes. Tell her Loki has called in her aid, and together, we will punish Belenos for his transgressions against us."

"But Loki, he hasn't done anything against her. The hag wants to come out in the open, remember? What will make her help us when she wants what he does?"

"Because," he answered while circling his thumb over one dusky nipple, "if our brethren were to discover what she possesses, she would suffer a fate worse than any mortal death. They would hunt her to the ends of the earth."

"You make it sound as if she has a dragon sleeping in her cellar."

"Not quite, but close enough."

***

"What do I wear?" Ēostre wondered out loud.

Since returning from her hibernation, she'd received frequent lessons from her new daughter about modern-day fashion. Chloe loved to dress her, and the only thing she loved more than dressing Ēostre with her choices of wardrobe was introducing the dragoness to favorite stores and watching her acquire a style of her own.

Ēostre had developed a true love for leggings and oversized shirts when the mood didn't call for a sophisticated wardrobe.

"Is it too warm for leggings? No, it's never too warm for leggings," she determined. She imagined the outfit she desired and pictured the dresser drawer in her mind's eye. The folded pile of quicksilver material appeared in a flash and landed upon her open palms.

After showering away the day's stress, she wiggled into the leggings and wore them with a mid-thigh-length white tunic. She even traded the day's earlier choice of fancy pumps for flat, roman-style sandals. With her hair worn loose around her shoulders, Ēostre admired her reflection with a smile.

"I look magnificent," she spoke to the air. Perfect for the cameras and paparazzi who would no doubt photograph them together. Before the dragoness could take a step toward the door with her purse, her tablet rang with an irritating notification to alert her to an incoming Facetime request. She checked it.

"Hello, Astrid my love, what may I do for you?" she asked the girl.

"I want to talk about boys," Astrid said bluntly, wearing a stern expression on her youthful face.

"Oh?"

"Yeah," she replied. "They freaking stink."

This should be a good one, Ēostre mused. She listened intently to the start of Astrid's next points, and it didn't take long before she was chuckling through the video call.

"So he isn't your friend anymore because he ate the turtles?" Ēostre asked to clarify.

"He's an ass, and I don't really want to visit anymore, but Mom and Dad said I have to."

"What other mean things does he do?"

Astrid sighed. "He pushed me over on the beach with his dragon form and rubbed wet sand all over my hair," she complained. "And then he wouldn't apologize when Aunt Marcy told him he had to do it. Aside from that, he never wants to visit here. He never comes away from his stupid island. I don't want to go see him tomorrow and they can't make me! He's a stupid baby, and playing with him isn't fun anymore when Mom visits Aunt Marcy and Uncle Teo."

With a grandmother's patience, Ēostre listened as Astrid listed the younger dragon half-breed's crimes against her. Javier had only turned seven recently, and was prone to childish behavior Astrid no longer found acceptable at her older age, even if he had an older child's mental acuity. "I see. I see. Do you want to know what I think, little one?"

"Yes!"

"The next time he is mean to you on the beach, I think you should punch him in his nose, sit on him, and rub his face in the sand. And then do you know what you should do?"

"What?" Astrid asked, hanging on to her every word.

"Call Mahasti and tell her to take you home, but *not* before you tell Javier everything you have said to me. You tell him he has hurt you, and that you refuse to come play with him again until he learns better manners. That when he feels able to apologize, he must come play with you at your home. This way you do not have to argue with your mother and father because you have talked to him about how he has wronged you."

"But he's only seven," Astrid said. Her brow knit again. "I can't punch a seven year old."

"But he is half-dragon, and thus stronger than any other seven year old. Chloe and Marcy have raised the both of you as humans, but what they do not realize is that they must also raise you as dragons. We do not deal in corporal punishment and spankings, but we do warn our little ones with nips when they cause harm. He doesn't realize his own strength and must learn the hard way to be gentle."

"Okay," Astrid said without a complaint. "I love you."

"I love you, too."

"Can I ask you something else?"

"Of course. You may ask me whatever you want."

65

"Um, this isn't for me. It's for a friend," Astrid began. "But you give the best advice and it's always better than what Daddy or Mom says to do."

Laughing all the while, Ēostre settled on the cozy loveseat in front of the suite's flat screen television. "What does your friend need to know?"

"If someone likes a person, but that person doesn't know it, how should someone tell them?"

The question caught Ēostre off guard. Had Astrid already developed a crush on Javier? Technically, she had reached the physical age in which most powerful dragon parents considered finding mates for their children, and Saul hadn't looked any older when Fafnir made arrangements with Maximilian. He and Brigid been intended since her birth.

No, of course not. The boy is too young, Ēostre determined. At seventeen, Astrid resembled most twelve-year-old girls, but Javier barely passed for five despite inheriting his father's massive height. *Maybe she's met someone at one of those homeschool support groups Chloe takes her to.*

"By being as honest as possible, sweetling. If you like someone, you must always tell them unless some greater reason exists for why you shouldn't."

"Like if they're already married or mated?"

"Exactly," she said. "Because it is never right to usurp another dragon's mate. Unless that mate is horrible and their cruelty has been witnessed by three people. Then in accordance with our laws, anyone may intervene to challenge. If they are soul bonded, one may never challenge at all."

Astrid became quiet for a moment, then she said, "Dragon laws are weird." Her small nose scrunched.

"Do you find such a law confusing?"

"Well, yes. Daddy doesn't hit my mom or anything but the other day, while we were watching a movie, she told me some husbands hit their wives because they're big babies who don't know any better. And she said the wives stay with them because no one sees what's happening and they're afraid to get help."

"That is true," Ēostre said sadly. "And it has been true since the dawn of time when humans first began to couple with one another. But when it happens among dragons, it's between mates who have not yet pledged their soul bond. No male or female would dare to harm the dragon they have vowed to love for eternity. It would be like wounding oneself. It takes immense amounts of love to create a dragon's soul brand, Astrid. Very much. It cannot be done by force and must be accepted by a willing heart."

"Oh."

"So you see, such instances are very rare for us. We dragon females may often be smaller than males, but our breath weapons are more powerful, our claws are sharper, and we are quicker."

"And smarter," Astrid said.

"And far smarter," Ēostre agreed, laughing at her grandchild. "And once we have found a male unworthy, we never stay."

"Why doesn't Uncle Max have a mate?"

Ēostre hesitated to answer. She thought of the man in the next room, kind, generous, and everything any dragoness could want. It wasn't for his lack of trying. Over the years, she'd watched countless females cast him aside for simple, often egotistical reasons. His horns weren't long enough. His feathers were too drab, and they wanted to birth a cub with feathers like shining embers. They hated his red hair or loathed his freckles, which had practically vanished as he aged. Even his hair had darkened to a subtle cinnamon shade she adored.

Her friend Belenos had matured like the finest wine.

"Because, my love, many of our fellow dragonesses are unworthy of him."

"Aren't you worthy?"

"I... I suppose I am," Ēostre answered honestly.

67

A heavy fist thumped against Ēostre's hotel room door. She twisted around to face it and swore under her breath. "I'd better go, Astrid. I promised to join Maximilian for dinner."

"Oh okay. Have fun!" Astrid ended the video chat without fuss.

Ēostre hurried to the door and yanked it open to find Max appropriately dressed down in jeans and a t-shirt. It was contradictory to the sophisticated businessman she knew but oddly fitting for the occasion. Not that it was the first time she'd seen him in jeans. Or a t-shirt, its sleeves taut around his biceps and stitches strained. There were photos circulating the web about Max, speculating whether or not he'd kept a certain former governor as a physical trainer.

"Max, I am so sorry."

"It's fine," he responded curtly, and then as if seeming to realize his tone of voice, he followed up with a gentler, "I thought something important must have delayed you."

"It was a video call from Astrid," she confessed. "But never mind that, what's wrong? You seem… irritable."

Maximilian made no effort to smile, and from that, she already knew something was wrong. So rather than grab her purse and head for the door, she took his hand and guided him to the couch.

"Let me order in, all right? General Tso's and shrimp lo mein for you?"

"Okay," he agreed easily.

Ēostre didn't pry, but Max's bad mood hung around him like a fog for the next two days. He curbed it when in front of the cameras, but whenever they were alone, he brooded in silence and failed to engage her in conversation. Knowing he would consult her when he was ready, Ēostre let him be.

***

The request for her advice came three days after their return to Sacramento. Max had been asked by a prominent technical college to speak at their winter graduation ceremony — whether he was elected or not in November — and Ēostre thought it would be easy to convince him to agree.

"I would be honored," he replied quietly.

"Your face tells me otherwise," Ēostre said. "Did something happen while we were in Virginia?"

Max's low and humorless chuckle worried her as much as the troubled expression on his face. "I find myself in need of your wise counsel. Which is no surprise, as I seem to seek it more often than usual as of late."

"That's what I'm here for, Max. I'm your advisor, so please, speak your mind and let me do my job."

After a tight nod, Max focused his hazel eyes on the city beyond his office windows. They were the most beautiful color — golden amber with tiny specks of blue that reminded her of the heart of a flame.

"Do I need a first lady, Ēostre?"

"A first lady?" The question startled her as much as his change of mood. Her fingers gripped the leather. "What brought this on?"

"Answer the damned question," Max snapped. "Give me your honest opinion. Is the presence of a first lady required in the White House? Does the American public expect me to have a wife and family?"

Ēostre struggled to regain her composure, put off by his surge of temper as much as she was unsettled by the question. She repeated herself, "What put such a foolish notion in your head?"

Maximilian's eyes flashed, fire behind the warm caramel color.

"Belenos… What's wrong?" Her voice softened as she left her chair and crossed the desk to meet him. She sat on the edge of it, facing him, and crossed her legs.

"Mahuika paid a visit after the Virginia speech," he said gruffly. "She seems to think a wife and child would humanize me to the public, and as such, has offered me both."

"I see," Ēostre murmured. "And does her offer tempt you?"

"Very much," he replied honestly. "I have never blamed Chloe for taking Brigid's life. If anyone is to bear the blame for those sad events, it should be me for turning a blind eye to my daughter's cruelty. I spoiled her from birth. I coddled her, Ēostre. I loved my child so dearly I gave her anything she asked until she grew wild, beyond my control. I coveted Saul for a son, and thought if only he would give up his human pet, we could become so much closer and fulfill Fafnir's wishes. I thought… I thought Saul would become a good influence to tame the ferocity she acquired from her mother." The fire dragon shook his head. "Instead, I have lost her."

"Bel—"

"If I had commanded her to release Saul from his obligation, she would be here beside me today."

"She wouldn't have listened to you, Belenos. Brigid never listened to you. You gave her every opportunity to make the right choices for herself. None of us can do anything more than teach our offspring right from wrong. We cannot force them to make the right choices."

"I should have tried harder," he whispered. "If only I'd done more to raise her differently from her mother."

Ēostre pressed her palm to Max's cheek and directed his head until their eyes met. "Tell me this — if Brigid inherited her willful personality from her mother, why consider breeding with Mahuika again?"

Max didn't answer.

"Do what your heart tells you." She stepped away and to the cabinet behind his desk, where he kept glasses and a decanter of fine cognac. After she poured him a glass, she recorked the bottle and returned it to the shelf.

"Would you judge me if I accepted her offer?"

"I…" She stopped to gather her thoughts and chose her words carefully. "I would ask myself if she is the example you would want at your side when you lead the country."

"Each move I make will be scrutinized and studied," he agreed, nodding. As he slouched back in the seat and raised the glass for a sip, the humor returned to his eyes. "You evaded my question though. That isn't what I asked."

"She wouldn't be my choice for a proper match," Ēostre admitted beneath his gaze. "I don't believe she'd be good for the office, either. Or your reputation."

"Still not what I asked."

Ēostre pressed her lips in a thin line. "As your campaign manager, yes, I would judge you for the poor decision."

"I'm not asking my campaign manager. It was a question for my closest friend."

"I think you could do better. More importantly, you *deserve* better."

"Then I will seek a better match," he told her, wearing another one of his crooked smiles. The kind that brightened his eyes and made him seem more approachable than any other volcanic dragon Ēostre had ever met in her two thousand years.

A palpable sense of relief rushed over her, and only then did Ēostre realize, it wasn't that she didn't want to see him with Mahuika — she didn't want to see Maximilian with *any* dragoness.

Because she wanted him for herself, and knew the day another female dragon chose him, it would also be the day she lost her closest friend. Losing Fafnir had been hard enough, but having Max stolen beyond her reach would be next to unforgivable.

If you like someone, you must always tell them. The words spoken to her grandchild came back to haunt her.

How could I possibly act on these feelings when he has never looked at me with anything more than the love for a friend? Ēostre wondered. Was her desire for Maximilian genuine and true attraction, or a lusty byproduct of a century-long period of abstinence while mourning?

Contact with unrelated dragon males over the years since her awakening had been brief, and those she did talk to were often already bound in mated relationships. Ēostre frowned.

"Is something wrong, Ēostre?"

She shook her head and put a pleasant smile on her face. "I was only thinking of how correct you are about my need to indulge in some selfish activities."

"Ah. At last, this moment has come. I am the master and you are the apprentice. Let me train you, my young Padawan, in the art of putting oneself first."

Ēostre rolled her eyes and shoved his shoulder. "Are you quoting mortal movies at me again?" At least it was a decent one. "I can come up with something on my own, thanks."

"Are you sure? Last chance to back out."

"I'm not backing out. In fact, I have a great idea."

Maximilian's dubious expression delivered a blow to her ego, but she chuckled anyway and leaned close enough to hug him.

"I know it's only noon, but I'm going home. Astrid wants to cook dinner and I promised I'd return on time to eat it fresh from the oven."

"I see she takes after her mother."

Ēostre chuckled. "Saul has improved since that casserole disaster, thank you very much. You should join us. I'm sure she'd be happy to provide for her Uncle Max as well."

"A tempting offer but one I must take a rain check on. I have a few pressing business matters to conclude."

"Perhaps next time," she said, pleased when he answered her with a smile.

Unlike her son, who usually summoned his genie to sweep him along the California interstate to his mountainside retreat, she enjoyed the long drive and used the time to clear her head and unwind to music. She was halfway between Sacramento and the manor when an incoming call jarred her from her thoughts.

"Did you forget something?" She forced a chipper tone after accepting the call through the automobile's speakerphone.

"I did," his rich voice spilled from the speakers. "I had intended to ask something else of you before our conversation veered to tenser subjects regarding Mahuika. An invitation arrived this morning to Senator Duhane's 55th birthday party next Friday. Care to join me?"

"You've only invited me to keep you out of trouble."

"Naturally. I'll be swarmed by single mortal women if I go alone."

"Ah, so I'm to be your guard."

"More like an oasis of sanity. So, will you attend with me, or shall I be forced to tread lightly on eggshells in fear of destroying your hard work on this campaign?"

"At this point, Maximilian, you would have to pour gasoline over a box of kittens and spit fire on them to ruin what we've done."

"I know. But one can never be too cautious."

Chapter 8

Ēostre stood within her daughter-in-law's favorite department store, staring flabbergasted at the piece of metallic silver fabric dangling from her hands. If one could call it fabric at all. It was more like a slingshot. Or a shiny rubber band. She turned it over and flipped it, but viewing it from another angle didn't make it magically expand.

Struck by impulse, she whirled to face the nearest customer beside her. "Excuse me, would this suit me? Is it too small?"

The other customer looked offended by the question, her youthful features contorting into an exaggerated, horrified mask. "Too small? Pffft, if I had your legs, I'd wear that thing everywhere just to have an excuse to show them off. I'd be pumping the gas in my bikini, girl."

"I'm not too old for it?"

The girl couldn't be older than thirty herself. Her brows raised a mile then she tossed her head back and laughed. "Are you shittin' me? Nah. I'm probably older than you are. Get the bikini and rock your stuff at the beach. The weatherman said we're going to have perfect weather for it this weekend."

"Awesome," Ēostre said, testing the word. It felt strange, alien, but somehow right at the same time. She could get used to modern-day slang, even if her stubborn son continued to struggle with the change in the times.

She swept a few more articles of clothing from the racks and checked out to hurry home and enact her master plan. Originally, she'd gone out to purchase the perfect cocktail dress for the senator's birthday bash, when an oversized sign alerted her to an end-of-season blowout on swimwear.

Ēostre was still on cloud nine when she reached Saul's driveway.

"Grandmother! Happy birthday!"

While it all seemed to happen in slow motion, Ēostre felt powerless to stop it. One moment, she was crossing the driveway with shopping bags in hand, and in the next, her grandchild was streaking across the pavement as a bolt of fiery lightning and aurorous feathers, too quick for the human eye to track. "Happy birthday!" she cried again.

"Astrid, no!"

The child didn't know her own strength or realize how quickly she'd grown into her dragon form. Two years ago, Astrid had been no larger than a shetland pony, but the creature who collided into Ēostre now outweighed a sedan.

"Oh no!" Chloe cried from the porch.

The collision sent Ēostre flying, and with no hope of coming out of it unscathed in her human body, she transformed in a blink. Pieces of Ēostre's favorite pantsuit flew like confetti, expensive shreds of cream linen and silk fluttering in the breeze.

If she'd braced herself against the impact in her dragon body, Astrid would have undoubtedly been hurt. Instead, Ēostre rolled with the momentum, all the while clutching the smaller cub against her chest.

"Ēostre! Astrid! Are you both okay?" Chloe screamed from the porch.

"I... I think so." She and her grandbaby had rolled into the grass for several yards where they landed against a fence bordering one of Leiv's pastures. "Your child hits like a hill giant."

As Saul and Chloe rushed across the grass to meet them, Ēostre lowered a sobbing dragon cub to the grass and frantically examined her for injuries.

"I'm sorry. I didn't mean to!"

"It is all right, sweetling. Where are you hurt? Where are you injured?"

"I hurt you. I didn't mean to hurt you," Astrid blubbered. "I'm sorry! I don't know how it happened, I was running and suddenly—" Her sobs intensified, shaking her entire body.

Ēostre didn't find a single broken feather after running each of her clawed digits over Astrid's body.

"Is she hurt?" Chloe cried.

"No. I must have protected her well," Ēostre said, voice laced with uncertainty.

"My daughter is strong," Saul said. He brimmed with pride as he set his hand atop Astrid's head and stroked the growing nubs curving back from her brow. Female dragons didn't develop their horns until they reached breeding age. "There is no need to cry, little one. Your grandmother is fine."

"But I hurt her. I didn't mean to hurt her, I didn't mean to."

Chloe gazed helplessly up at Ēostre. Her daughter, in her dragon's body, was taller than her by a foot and twice as broad.

"Shhh, my love. I know. Come. Let your mother and I clean your face. I am quite fine, see?"

Later, after Ēostre and Chloe had washed Astrid's face and given their reassurances again, they enjoyed a peaceful family dinner. It was Ēostre's 2244th birthday. Even though dragons only celebrated their bicentennials, Astrid always insisted on her father and grandmother acknowledging each year.

"Has she gone to bed?" Ēostre asked when Chloe returned downstairs.

"Oh yeah. She's knocked out. All of the drama must have exhausted her, I guess. Plus she was outside with the zebras most of the day before you came home. She's teaching them to trust her dragon form."

"Ah." Ēostre pursed her lips and gazed out the window into the fading twilight.

"What? You think it's a bad idea?"

"Oh, no, it was not the zebras on my mind. It was Astrid herself."

Concern wrinkled Chloe's brow. "She feels really bad about it all still. I'm sorry about your suit…"

Ēostre waved away her distressed apologies. "No true harm done. Only…"

"Only what?"

"She hit me dead on, Chloe. I… don't understand how she came out of it uninjured. I tried my best to protect her, but something is wrong."

"I know."

"No, Chloe. You do not understand. The way she came at me was…" Ēostre slowly inhaled and closed her eyes, reliving the experience through her memories. "She became as a bolt of lightning itself. It is enough to make me believe the legends of St. George. Like Saul, she is fire and lightning, I believe, and perhaps something more."

"But I'm human. I don't understand, Ēostre. A dragon and a human shouldn't produce a stronger half-dragon."

Ēostre shook her head. "While I do not understand it, I know what I saw and felt. Your child is very, very powerful, and if we do not begin to teach her to harness her powers safely, someone may be hurt next time."

Chloe loosed a long, slow breath. "Okay then. What can we do?"

Ēostre liked that about Chloe. The woman took everything in stride.

"I would like to ask Maximilian's help with honing her fire abilities."

"Saul can't teach her?"

"Who do you think taught Saul?" she asked, chuckling. "You must understand, Astrid may not grow as fast as a human, but as far as dragons are concerned, she is a prodigy and far ahead of our learning curve. I nursed Saul until he turned thirty-one."

Chloe wrinkled her nose, failing to suppress the horror emerging on her face. "Ēostre. That's ahh…"

"That is equivalent to a human toddler." Ēostre raised a hand about two feet from the floor, indicating a very, very tiny person. "I told you that for the sake of comparison."

"Oh. Okay." Chloe's face smoothed and the furrow in her brow disappeared. "Whoa. That kinda sucks. I hope he was at least a good one."

Ēostre laughed again and hugged her daughter-in-law. "Our children develop slowly, Chloe. Very slowly, but for us the years seem to pass as days. Saul was an amazing cub, with none of his father's temperament," she said. "My friends envied me, and we loved him dearly."

As Ēostre curled up on her corner of the sofa with the remote to the television, Chloe fiddled with the corner of a couch pillow. Time together as friends came naturally, a relief to both women when they began to explore everyday activities together with Astrid.

"Saul makes it very easy to love him," Chloe chuckled. "Ēostre, can I ask you a question?"

"Of course."

"How did Saul and Brigid wind up promised to one another? As far as I could tell, they didn't even like each other."

"They didn't," Ēostre replied. "It was a match made between Max and Fafnir. We had hoped to ally our families through a bond stronger than friendship."

"And it backfired."

Ēostre sighed as she thought back to the century before Fafnir's death. Saul had felt utterly betrayed when the two elder dragons proudly informed him of their decision, but he'd been a good sport about it, agreed, and said he would do his best to earn Brigid's love. Easier said than done when the self-absorbed female dragon snubbed him at every turn.

"Brigid was a… willful child. Headstrong. She saw the betrothal as an opportunity to toy with Saul. You see, at the time, Fafnir and Maximilian were certain her age factored into her refusal. They believed she would change if given time to travel the world as our young often do upon reaching adulthood so they waited eagerly to put their theory to the test. Before they could, Fafnir was killed by a traveling dragonslayer."

"You mean, like, a knight in armor and all that?"

"Yes, Chloe. This happened in the late 1800s… There were and still *are* humans who realize we exist, but their numbers are few and the stories, as well as the training, are passed through their families. From parent to child, they teach their methods to kill all of us without discriminating good dragon from bad."

"I didn't mean to make you rehash all of those memories, Ēostre. I'm sorry."

"No." With a sad smile on her face, Ēostre shook her head and turned her eyes to the nearby window. The starlit world beyond their living room reminded her of long nights in the grass beside her beloved with their cub tucked between them. How she missed those days. "My memories are precious, and sharing them with you brings me joy."

Saul stepped into the room, oblivious to the weight in their discussion. "Mother, would you mind giving us a moment? I need to speak with Chloe alone. We'll be right back."

Ēostre waved him off and rose from her seat. "I intended to retire to bed early this evening in any case. Don't trouble yourselves over me." With a pause by Saul to kiss his cheek, she bid them both a good night and ascended the stairs to the upper level.

Since Saul didn't trust his daughter with more than a window, afraid she'd sneak out for late night flying lessons, Ēostre slept in the only other second floor bedroom with a full-sized balcony. The second story view overlooked stretches of grass and beautiful California valley. It was difficult to believe it was the same territory she and Fafnir once claimed centuries ago. Still, it remained unchanged in many ways, remote and out of the way of humankind.

Not that she had anything against humans. Her third most favorite person in the world was a human. Chloe had been mortal once before Astrid's magical blood mixed with her own.

And then there was sweet Astrid, who was half-human, half-dragon, a perfect blend of both worlds with the advantages of both races and seemingly none of the flaws.

How could other dragons like Tlaloc not understand how amazing human beings could be once they saw past their differences, prejudices, and hatred for one another? For every wicked mortal, there were fifty who were better, but convincing her fellow drakes of such seemed an impossible feat.

"Grandma?" Astrid called from beyond the door. Her small fist knocked gently.

"Yes, my love? Come in."

Astrid cracked open the door and peaked inside. Typically, she turned in hours before the adults. "I noticed your lights were off. Are you going to bed early? May I sleep with you tonight?"

Ēostre eased into a sitting position and rolled her right shoulder. She winced when the muscle protested, but at least it was no longer tender and swollen. A little magic made everything better.

"Of course you may. Come." She patted the empty space beside her and pulled back the sheets. Astrid wasted no time in wiggling into bed beside her and snuggling close.

"Grandma?"

"Yes, sweet?"

"Was Grandpa like Uncle Max?"

"Very much like him in some ways," she told the child. "And they were the best of friends for as long as I knew them both."

"I wish I'd met him."

Ēostre squeezed the girl close and kissed her golden head. Me too, my sweet. Me too."

Once Astrid's peaceful face went slack and her chest moved in the tranquil rhythm of sleep, Ēostre took her mobile phone with her to the balcony. There, she lowered into one of the patio chairs and dialed Max.

"Happy birthday, Ēostre. Pleasant night with the family?"

"You remembered?"

He laughed. "I could never forget your birthday Ēostre, but you beat me to the call. Was the day enjoyable at least, or did you spend it working hard?"

"I purchased my dress for Duhane's party, spent time with the family, and then Astrid joined me in bed."

"Ah. I do not know whether to pity or envy you, then I remember Brigid's wild sleeping habits and sleepless mornings of her tossing and turning beside me."

"I will not sleep a wink for most of the night," she agreed, "but that isn't why I called you."

"Oh?" His chair creaked with movement, and soothing notes of jazz filtered into the line. She easily pictured the man comfortably seated behind his office desk, a snifter of brandy beside his keyboard, music playing in the background. Shirtless. Clothed in only a pair of boxers — if he was clothed in anything at all.

"I am ready to win our little wager, Maximilian. For my completely selfish act, I have decided I want you to take me to the beach. I want reservations at Catalina Island's best hotel."

Dead silence came from the other end of the line until she picked out his measured breaths and finally, seconds later, his laughter.

"How is that a truly selfish act? Did you know you are the only dragon I have ever known to sunburn?" he inquired.

"Because you'll be my Speedo-clad manservant," she crowed triumphantly.

Maximilian's stunned silence sent her into a fit of childish giggles. He finally ended it with a gently uttered, "I don't own a Speedo."

"Then you'll buy one. If you can throw away an undisclosed sum on zebras for Astrid, you'll buy a tiny swimsuit to wear beside me. Come prepared to apply sunblock."

"Ēostre."

"Clear your Saturday and Sunday. G'night," Ēostre said. She crawled into the bed and beneath the sheets, satisfied with the outcome. Max would live to regret his challenge, and she would be the victor.

"I hope he's prepared to lose one of his treasures," she mused to the quiet bedroom. "Because I intend to win."

***

Maximilian upheld his part of the bargain and agreed to humor Ēostre's idea for a spontaneous weekend getaway. After enduring a dull cocktail party honoring his acquaintance in the Senate, she deserved it.

They reached Catalina Island sometime after two and passed the time until check-in by lounging in the lobby with fancy tropical mixed drinks from the bar. Ēostre balanced her tablet over her lap, peeking up on occasion for a stealthy peek at Max.

Good. Her victim was none the wiser, absolutely ignorant to what she had in store for him.

"I can hear you cackling, Ēostre. What are you doing?"

"Oh, nothing," she assured him.

"I can't believe this is how you chose to spend your wager," Maximilian mumbled under his breath. "Of all the things to do."

"You told me it must be truly selfish, and trust me, I've only just begun to use this to my advantage." Smiling sweetly, Ēostre sent Maximilian to the front desk, where he paid the exorbitant fee for their two rooms overlooking the ocean.

If she'd been wise, she would have told him one for the pair of them was enough, but in hindsight, that seemed like too much at once.

This is so silly of me, Ēostre thought. *Where has all of my common sense gone?* Max's presence gave her flutters in her tummy, and whenever he was near, it was as if she had a head filled with sawdust. She smiled as she watched him converse with the hotel employee, receive their keys, booklets, and return.

Andrew lurked nearby and monitored the exchange. All of his squad members had accompanied them to the resort island, dressed down in casual wear so as not to draw attention to themselves or their charge. They were eager to enjoy the amenities during their downtime as they rotated on and off duty. According to her dear friend the governor, time-and-a-half, excellent rooms, and a free trip to the beach weren't enough. He'd paid them each double the salary for the job with a bonus.

Max was such a handsome man, and an even handsomer dragon, but what she loved most about her dear friend was the kindness in his soul. Power, fame, and fortune never changed him, and unlike most of his fire-breathing kin, he took great pains to control his raging temper. With his ability to befriend anyone, he would have made an amazing silver dragon.

Ēostre struggled to suppress her anticipation, but once they split to their individual rooms, she found she was brimming with nerves. Nudity had never bothered her. It was natural and normal. Stripping from her clothing to transition to her dragon form was one thing, but wearing a sexy garment to highlight her assets and draw the eye was another. According to Chloe, Ēostre was bound to have the attention of every man on the beach drawn to her.

Looking at herself in the mirror, she was certain Chloe was right. The silver strips covered barely anything at all yet still managed to support her breasts and push them up.

"Last chance to back out," she murmured to herself. The idea was tempting, but the thought of losing the bet spurred her competitive spirit back into gear.

She pulled on a floral cover-up and stepped from the room to find her travel companion waiting awkwardly in the hall. His bare chest was already bronzed from hours spent poolside at his manor, and every inch of him was sculpted to masculine perfection from his chiseled pecs to his trim waistline. Her eyes scanned downward, skimming the carved indent of hip muscle above the band of his shorts.

"That isn't a Speedo."

"If it's good enough for Daniel Craig, it's good enough for me," he retorted. "Besides, I think this is, ah—"

"Much better," Ēostre agreed, sharing his sentiment after another appreciative look. The black shorts — tiny, *tiny* shorts — clung to his hips and defined upper thighs like a second skin. So well, in fact, that she thought he looked better than James Bond.

Ēostre may have been a dragon, but she was also a woman, and she knew a fine human man when she saw one. Between Max and Daniel Craig, there could be no competition, the point proven when a young woman practically salivated over him in passing. The girl, no older than her twenties, stumbled into a wall corner after rubbernecking to keep Maximilian in her view.

Ēostre giggled into one cupped hand. "The young one clearly agrees. Now come. Let's abandon your security team and sneak away."

"I heard that," Vincent said. "For his safety, we prefer to keep Governor Emberthorn within our view at all times."

"If this is what you call 'invisible' you are failing at it terribly," Ēostre fussed at the young man. Technically, none of the security team members who followed Maximilian for his "safety" were young at all, each of them a shapeshifter in his or her forties with a youthful physical appearance.

"We promised to be unobtrusive," the agent said, an irritated edge seeping into his professional tone. "Which is what we've done, Ms. Feuersturm."

Ēostre blew out an exasperated sigh. "There is nothing you can do for him that I cannot do myself. For the love of the Ancestors, I'm accomplished sorceress. There is no bullet in this world capable of causing Maximilian harm." Pride surged into Ēostre's voice, making the words come off in an unintentionally flippant tone. She regretted it at once.

"We've established that, my friend, but they are for looks as much as practicality. Was it not your idea to hire my own private security team until Ian has established his own men in the Secret Service? Discretion is key, Ēostre, more than anything at this point in my career."

"You're right. Forgive me, all of you," she said. Thoroughly chastened by her own conscience and Max's cool, irrefutable logic, she flashed the three-person shifter squad an apologetic smile. "It would appear even I am prone to moments of poor decision and ill temper."

"No harm, no trial," Andrew said, chuckling. "We get it. Our presence is intrusive, and you want to enjoy a holiday without us lurking behind you. We'll endeavor to grant a wider berth for the rest of the weekend."

The wolf's bright, toothy smile eased the heavy weight forming in Ēostre's stomach. She couldn't have forgiven herself if her rare surge of draconic arrogance had alienated his bodyguards.

Thankfully, Hotel Avalon was a brisk stroll from the shoreline, and within a hundred-yard walk, their bare feet were on beach. Ēostre carried her shoes in one hand and enjoyed the sensation of hot, dry sand shifting beneath her toes.

"That feels amazing," Max muttered. "But I'm not sure about this being an entirely selfish venture for you."

If you knew how damned good you look in those shorts, you wouldn't question it, Ēostre thought.

It didn't take long to discover the perfect spot on the beach. A single umbrella shaded two lounge chairs only a few yards from where the water lapped against the sand. The turquoise waters sparkled beneath the late afternoon sunshine.

"I wasn't joking, and I don't believe I made the terms of our wager," Ēostre reminded him.

She pulled off the cover-up and settled down on the cushioned lounger. Once she removed the bottle of sunblock from her beach bag and passed it to Max, she rolled onto her stomach and set her cheek in the crook of one elbow. "Chop chop, my friend. This was your idea."

Max didn't respond, and she didn't dare to look. Instead, she continued to hide her face, long after the first touch of his fingers brushed past her back. He took her hair and guided the long, silver braid to the side of her shoulder to expose the expanse of her back.

After he unfastened her bikini top, Ēostre heard the bottle's contents shaking then squirting over one of his palms. "You'll have to forgive me if I'm heavy-handed. I haven't done this in a while."

"So you've done this before?"

"Once or twice," he answered with a mysterious air to his deep voice.

From the moment his hands touched her skin, Ēostre knew she wouldn't regret her decision. Fingers covered in cool sunblock glided over her back and kneaded the lotion into her flesh. They swept up to her shoulders and down her sides, dangerously close to skimming past the sides of her breasts and breaching the minimal protection offered by her swim attire.

And more than anything, Ēostre wanted to roll onto her back to invite him to finish a more thorough lotioning of her body. To feel his hands easing beneath the bikini triangle to cup skin against skin.

Heavy-handed? No, his hands were as magical as their dragon forms.

Her nipples stiffened, and despite the ambient temperature of the hot and sunny summer day, his touch made her shiver. Ēostre tried to convince herself it was the chilly lotion, then his hands descended again.

It was the closest she'd come to orgasm without sex in a long while.

"Ēostre?"

"Hmm?"

"Are you all right? Your back is stiff as a board," he commented.

She cleared her throat and relaxed beneath his strong hands, letting him work out the kinks and aches acquired over a week of driving, sitting at a desk, and of course, that persistent twinge she'd felt ever since Astrid crashed into her. "The lotion was a little cold is all. I'm fine."

"Well," he said in a husky voice, "I think I'm done with you."

One peek at Max over her shoulder was enough to renew the scintillating tingle gliding over her body. For a split second, she saw fire in the eyes raking over her from head to toe, making her feel like the world's most desirable woman. Once Max tied her bikini top again, she rolled to her back and accepted the bottle of sunblock.

"But you're not finished," Ēostre said playfully. With her knees bent, she raised one leg from the beach chair, wiggled her foot at him, and grinned with unmistakable mischief. "I have legs, my friend, and you are my helpful manservant."

Something dark and turbulent passed over Max's hazel eyes. The change nearly made Ēostre renege on her command and cancel the bet altogether, and then it was gone, prompting her to wonder if it was a figment of her imagination. As he reclaimed the SPF 30, their fingers touched again, and a spark leapt between them.

"Very well then," Max finally murmured. He pulled up the adjacent lounge chair and sat on its edge. Leaning forward flexed the muscles in his abdomen, further defining the dragon's natural athleticism and how it translated to his human body. Behind her shades, Ēostre's eyes flicked to the trail of rust-colored hair below his navel and lingered where it disappeared beneath the waistband of a sinful pair of male swim shorts.

Keeping her hands off of him in public was bound to be more difficult than she expected.

***

"Will I be feeding you grapes and fanning you afterward?" Max joked. Playful comments and remarks helped ease the sense of panic building in his chest. On one hand, he'd never felt a tug toward any female dragoness the way he did toward Ēostre. On the other, she was the widow of his closest friend.

Did she have the capacity to feel again for another dragon and to open her heart to him?

"Maybe I have that planned for later."

Ēostre raised one leg from the lounge chair, bending it at the knee. Once she did, Max's strong hands closed around her calf then began smoothing lotion up and down her shin. His caress traveled to her ankles and skimmed up in a repetitive, circular pass, gliding over sleek flesh until he reached her knee.

A vision played through his head of having Ēostre on a private beach, stripped of her swimsuit, her body arched beneath him in ecstasy. He imagined how it would feel to kiss his way up her shins, to set his bulk between her slim, creamy thighs, and part them before burying his cock in her receptive embrace.

As Ēostre's tension diminished, another kind grew beneath Max's tight-fitting black shorts. Her relaxed body remained at his mercy, and her eyes were closed. Shit. He had to get his mind back in the game and off of the things he wanted to do to her. Childcare legislation, animal rights laws, decrepit female judges, crooked senators. He flooded his mind with thoughts of those things, leaving no room for fantasies about Ēostre screaming his name.

On the subject of crooked senators, he thought. "By the way, I had a call from Duhane this morning thanking us for attending his party yesterday. He said you were, and I quote, 'delightful and radiant.' As usual, you have left an impression."

"Are you surprised?" she asked, her demure tone setting his blood aflame.

"I… no. Far from it. That's why I invited you, after all." His hands paused on her thigh, relishing every second of contact between them.

"I thought you invited me as a buffer between yourself and the eligible women who would haunt your steps from the moment of your arrival."

"That too."

Applying lotion to Ēostre was its own kind of hell, chipping away his willpower with every touch. By the time it was over, he'd fought back the urge to take her like a savage beast on the lounge chair, and she was smiling at him with a sexy half-smirk.

"And what's next on the agenda?" He wiped his hands against his thighs, cleaning off the greasy remnants.

"You tell me," the silver dragoness said. "Saul never tires of reminding me about the things I've missed while sleeping. It feels as if I'll never catch up, and there's always some new surprise beyond the horizon. So tell me, what's a pair of people to do when they're at the beach?"

"Trust me?" Max asked. He offered his friend a hand and pulled her from the lounger. She leaned close, brushing her lips against his cheek in response.

"More than anything."

The rest of the weekend went off without a hitch once Max decided to introduce Ēostre to a century of beachside activities. They did everything from snorkeling off the coast to racing jet skis across the blue waves. Max talked Ēostre into parasailing to experience flight without her own wings keeping her aloft in the ocean-scented wind.

While Max enjoyed every second, he had only a single regret each day after they parted to their individual rooms — that the night didn't end with Ēostre in his arms.

Chapter 9

"Good afternoon, Ēostre."

"Hello Hilary," she greeted Max's secretary. "Is he with anyone at the moment?"

"No, and he's been expecting you. Shall I send in your usual coffee?"

"Yes, please."

She headed down the hallway and gave a nod to Vincent, opening her mouth to greet the wolf when Max's voice exploded from behind the closed door.

"What the hell?"

Ēostre rushed ahead into the office, Vincent hot on her heels, to find Max sitting behind his desk staring at his laptop. A flood of color swept across his cheeks, highlighting his enraged expression.

"What?" she asked. "What are you yelling about? Did we drop rank in the polls? I was sure I checked them this morning."

"No, it's not the polls. We're in the lead as usual, and ahead of Thompson again by a good margin."

"Then why are you bellowing? Has the board tried to rip your company out from beneath you? I thought that was in the past."

"Vincent, please give us a moment. There's nothing here for you to fight."

Vincent swiftly analyzed the office interior for threats before giving a terse nod. The werewolf dropped his hand from the grip of his gun and retreated, reclaiming his former post in the hall.

"Will you please tell me what's going on, Max?" Ēostre asked after the door closed behind the guard.

In answer, Max turned the laptop around. A beach photo dominated the screen, accompanied by an article from a popular celebrity gossip blog. Ēostre and Max were pictured mid-laugh, walking through the surf hand in hand.

IS THERE LOVE IN THE AIR? the headline questioned.

"That's a damned nice photograph," Ēostre commented, impressed. With one palm flat on his desktop, she leaned over for a better look. The photographer had captured the very essence of their holiday weekend away from stressful office days and their fellow judgmental winged predators.

It had been worth every penny she paid to arrange the candid photo. Max would never forgive her if he discovered the truth, but she had a feeling it would be popular among the female voters.

Most of all, she'd wanted a memory of their weekend together for herself.

"There are photos of my chest everywhere," Max grumbled, oblivious to the headline.

And what a fine chest it is, Ēostre decided. "And your back end. Don't forget that," she said cheerfully while scrolling down the page. She checked several sources and found the same photos shared across them.

"Oh, read the comments here. GamerMouse says, 'Are we sure this guy is in his fifties? Looks more like thirty to me.' Ha!" Ēostre laughed. "And AsurKat called my swimwear choice 'bold and provocative.' What did you… think? About the suit," she added slyly.

"It was a brazen choice, I agree, and well worn. You turned every head we passed. I didn't, however, expect it to turn up all over the internet. I'll have Lynette scour the market shelves for any physical copies so we know what we're dealing with."

While he fretted over the possible fallout, Ēostre sat on the edge of his desk.

"We can turn this around to our benefit, Maximilian. Worry less," she said, pressing her thumb against the deep furrow in his brow and smoothing over it. "They are lovely, innocent photos, and now the world knows you have a softer, gentler side."

"They've jumped to conclusions about our relationship," he pointed out in a tense voice. "And violated your privacy. I am less concerned about my own image than I am of—"

"No harm done. It's speculation and I haven't seen any negative remarks in my skim overs. You're a bachelor, so there is no scandal. Only a fun day at the beach for a hardworking man."

She kissed his cheek and waited for the worried wrinkles to smooth from his brow. Once they did, she exhaled a pent-up, relieved breath herself.

After a long pause, he grudgingly admitted, "Perhaps you're right."

"Of course I am," she said in a breezy voice. "Now, enough fuss. What are you doing here when you have a lunch meeting across town in an hour?"

"It's been rescheduled," he grumbled. "I had a few last-minute instructions I thought up last night to leave behind for the company since I'm passing over the reins, more or less."

"And your text asking me to meet you here?"

"We have business to discuss." Some of his usual humor leaked back into his voice. "You've won our bet and it's time for me to pay up. I already informed the team they'll be guarding an empty mansion tonight. I don't want them in my hoard, and they're not comfortable with traveling by your preferred mode of transportation. We decided it wouldn't hurt since you and I technically won't be in public."

She grinned. "That and there is no safer place than in a dragon's den."

"Naturally. I figured we could head from here into the Capitol Building, finish up our next slew of campaign matters, enjoy a nice dinner, then part ways in the public eye."

"Dinner?"

"Yes. I mean to feed you before allowing you to rob me of a precious valuable."

Ēostre crinkled her nose briefly, her mind flitting to an inside joke between her and Chloe. The younger woman had discriminating tastes when it came to romance novels, and they'd once laughed about the common theme among most of them — drop-dead sexy women who do nothing but visit restaurants to eat fancy meals before getting laid by powerful men.

I suppose I don't count, she mused internally. *I'm not his mistress, and we aren't having sex, which is the true crime here.*

"My figure disagrees with our frequent dinners out, but I can't decline a good meal," she said aloud. "You know the best places in Sacramento."

"Nonsense. Your figure is perfect exactly as it is." Maximilian's hands raised to her middle and traced the shape of her body from waist to hips. After gliding both palms over her curves, they retreated from her sleek pantsuit back to the armrests on his chair. "You are as slim as you were three centuries ago. Perhaps even five," he mused.

Lamenting the loss of his touch, Ēostre tucked her chin and studied her own lap. Compliments from Maximilian, while genuine and always true, dredged up memories of her life as a young, unmated dragoness, when suitors hounded her relentlessly with precious jewels. Wanting her favor, no less than a dozen eligible males followed in her shadow.

"Definitely not five," Ēostre said, "I'm afraid I have Saul to blame for that. Anyway, what time shall I retrieve you?"

"Midnight. I'll be waiting for you in the parlor."

The remainder of their day passed with swiftness, despite dull meetings and press calls. Her mind kept wandering to what precious gems and artifacts Max had hoarded over the long years, and how she was going to choose one.

Throughout dinner, Ēostre remained aware of the occasional eye following them from nearby tables, how a few hours in Max's company completed her day, and how he hung on to her every word in a way Fafnir never had.

The internal comparison to her deceased mate took her by surprise, and from that moment on, the restaurant's other occupants vanished. She drove home from their dinner in a partial daze, engrossed by fantasies of confessing her affection to her best friend.

Election night, she decided. *Win or lose, I shall tell him on election night. Until then, I must be practical. I can't divert Bel's attention from what matters now. I must be as patient as the hunter stalking her prey.*

With a clear mind, Ēostre stepped into her apartment at the Adagio and shut the door behind her. Her role as Maximilian's top advisor had required her to stay close, and for appearances, she rented an apartment in the city. Years later, the two-bedroom flat had become her own little slice of urban heaven, a place to retreat after a long day when she craved silence and peace. Usually, she teleported home to the manor and stayed overnight with her family, only to return by morning to conduct business in the city again.

After slipping from her heels, she tossed her purse onto the couch in passing and proceeded down the hall, footfalls muted by plush cream carpet. Portraits of Astrid, Saul, and Chloe lined the walls along with cherished treasures from her hoard. She'd surrounded herself with objects she loved to bring comfort to her home away from home.

By midnight, she couldn't contain her enthusiasm. Promises of a new priceless trinket had Ēostre bouncing on her toes when she crossed via a magical window from her personal home office and into Max's mansion. As agreed, he awaited her in his lavish parlor, the seventy-inch, curved Smart TV playing a favorite show.

"I have lost all respect for him," she commented, eyes on the Viking leader dominating the screen.

"As have I," Max admitted. He grimaced and flicked his gaze back to the fictionalized depiction of Vikings on his television. "If only *all* humans valued their chosen mates as well as we dragons."

"If only. Are you ready, or shall I wait until the end of your episode?" she teased.

"I'll resume once I'm home." He cracked a smile at her and rose from the seat, still clothed in his slacks and button-down shirt. She saw his tie slung over the back of the couch. "Take us to Mount Shasta's satellite cone. It's close to where we must enter the hoard."

Ēostre raised both hands and constructed a perfect portal, shaped from her own will and molded by magic. Its border glimmered brightly, sparkling with the luminescence of a hundred sparkling fireflies with a snowy wonderland framed beyond it.

She stepped into a disused climbing camp near the summit of Shastina. When Max followed, she shut the gateway behind her and surveyed the majestic beauty of the world beneath them. The pristine, snow-covered caps of Mount Shasta remained as lovely as the peaks in her memories. Standing with her face lifted to the frigid wind, she breathed in fresh mountain air and sighed.

"It's been a while since I said this, but you have amazing taste when it comes to homes," Ēostre murmured. "This is glorious."

He chuckled. "We can leave our clothes here before descending the slope." Without another word, he unfastened the line of buttons on his shirt and shrugged out of it. Ēostre watched at first, entranced by how his muscles moved and flexed over his powerful torso, then she snapped out of it and mirrored him.

Max didn't glance at her once. She stole a peek as she set her dress aside to see the ideal and perfect draconian gentleman even had his back to her as he folded and set aside his mortal garments, exposing a backside that could have been carved from marble. He made her knees weak, those hard and chiseled muscles something she'd fantasized about having under her hands since their day on the beach.

Disappointed in his failure to regard her nude state, she took her dragon form and he did the same, giving her an entirely new reason to admire his unmistakable appeal. As a man, Max was certainly attractive, but as a dragon, he was breathtaking.

The ruby plumage of his wings had brightened over the years, and his horns, while only a meter long, gleamed golden. Bold spots of blue color decorated the bend of each wing and reappeared as speckled bits of down near the wing shoulders. He turned to face her, snorting steam from both nostrils.

"Are you ready?"

"Lead on."

With his tail balanced behind him, Max dove forward, resembling a skier on the slopes. Ēostre hung behind a second to giggle before she scrambled behind him down the mountainside. As she followed, moving her claws quickly over the rocky terrain to keep pace, she couldn't help but notice how much he seemed to enjoy their playful race. He knew the mountain best, and she didn't have a hope of beating him to his hidden lair.

Dragons always hid the exterior entrance to their home, but their methods usually varied. While Saul had built a manor above the entrance to Ēostre and Fafnir's former residence, Ēostre preferred to use magic. A bevy of illusions concealed the entrance to the cave system where she'd slept in Switzerland while mourning. As a final failsafe, anyone approaching her lair became acutely, but seriously ill until they were forced to turn back and leave.

She knew they were close when the ice-covered boulders split open, parting to reveal a craggy crevice. Max wiggled inside and led her down a path that widened after a hundred feet of darkness. Eventually, the rough stone walls gave way to smooth, polished rock. Max's scales slid against the walls and created tiny sparks.

The volcanic dragon entered ahead of her and exhaled a single breath of fire, which split into individual spheres of trembling flame. Each one floated in the air until it reached one of the sconces located around the huge room. The result was radiant, exposing beauty she'd never thought possible from one of his kind.

"And you claimed you couldn't use magic," Ēostre teased gently.

Every dragon's hoard was different from the next. Some lived in pigsties overflowing with coin, and some took pride in sculpting their lairs into masterpieces. Max was among the latter, a creature who'd shaped his mountain stronghold into art. Black volcanic glass walls rose from stone floors chiseled by his own claws, decorated with jewels glittering from where he'd embedded them in the walls. They shined in every color of the rainbow, and some had been shaped with tender care.

Obsidian casks and polished wooden chests held every manner of coin and gemstone, while smooth pedestals displayed individual treasures. Vases and sculptures shined at her from every point in the cavern.

"Anything I want?"

"Such was our wager."

She wandered through the neatly laid pathways, pausing to touch and sort through her options. Coins held little value to her and she already had plenty of raw gems in her own horde. The few scrolls Max had collected over the years briefly drew her interest, but she had a copy of almost all of them.

"Where did you find these? The detail is exquisite." Distrusting her claws to handle some of the finer works of art, Ēostre shrank back to her human body. A hot rush of modesty clothed her with magical adornments of silver silk after she considered his earlier avoidance. The sleek garment pooled around her ankles, so thin it was like she still wore nothing at all. Not that she expected Max to notice.

Did he find her unattractive? Or was it something more, the ghost of her dead mate, Max's best friend, haunting their relationship? The thought snaked through her mind, but she suppressed it and glanced over her bare shoulder to find her distracted host lumbering away, oblivious to her inner turmoil.

"I did not find them anywhere," he answered.

"Well, whoever you commissioned has true talent. May I pick from among these?"

"Take your choice," Max said, as if it pained him. He wandered over to an enchanted pit of bubbling magma and flopped down to rest his chin on both claws. He reminded her of a man resting beside a stoked fireplace.

"What if I want to think on it?" she called to needle him.

Max's playful growl sent shivers of desire up her spine. Sensing it, his head raised sharply and a pair of molten red eyes fixed on her face. With his nostrils flared, she had no doubt that he smelled her interest.

But he didn't act on it. Instead, he set his face against his claws again and turned to the pool. He lazily dragged his tail through the magma.

A dozen figurines awaited her inspection, crafted from molded metal and cut crystal. An opal swan rose up in a magnificent pose with wings spread, looking like frozen moonlight. Bronze and gold fused together to depict a majestic eagle with chipped amber for eyes. In fact, most figurines featured a winged creature of some sort, and all were equally stunning.

One, above all the others, captured her attention. A silver dragon with wings carved from diamond poised in flight was set over a large cluster of emeralds. Every exquisite detail had been carefully etched and carved until the metal had the appearance of life. Ēostre practically expected the jeweled art piece to take flight.

"I've made my decision," Ēostre said. "I want this."

Max turned his great head. "You ask for this?"

"Yes. It's magnificent," Ēostre said. She traced her finger over one of the polished wings, fascinated by the uncanny likeness between it and her dragon form. Without a doubt, there could be no argument about it, the figurine was a sculpture of her.

"Did *you* carve these?"

His silence was more telling than any words might have been. Max ducked his head and closed his eyes.

"You have a remarkable talent. Why didn't you ever tell me you were an artist?"

"It has always been a private pleasure for me. Something to pass the time between long slumbers." He turned toward a nearby brazier and blew out a breath, extinguishing it. It set off a chain reaction of dimming lights, smothering their flames one by one until only the orange glow from the magma remained.

Ēostre caressed one of the statuette's opal horns, awestruck by the precision, the detail, and the love that had gone into its craftsmanship. "Must we leave right away? The night is young, after all, and we have no other responsibilities at this hour," she pointed out.

Max's eyes glowed in the dimmed light. He hesitated then with a tender touch of his claw, nudged an untamed lock of silver hair from her face. "I'm certain to return to exaggerated complaints if we are away for long, but..." The corner of his mouth raised and he slipped back down to the polished rock on his side. "For once, I don't care. Shall I relight the lamps?"

"No," Ēostre said demurely. "It sets the atmosphere and adds a certain comfort to the mood, doesn't it?" Once the figurine was safe on an adjacent pedestal, she chose Max's ruby-colored side as a broad cushion to lay against. She crawled over him without invitation and heard his sharp intake of breath. He stilled beneath her, resembling one of his own statues, quiet aside from a subtle purr rumbling from his chest.

It isn't my imagination, Ēostre thought with determination. *The way I feel and his affection for me are real.* Although she didn't dare to act on her desires, for fear he would believe the gift had influenced her intentions, the dragoness stroked her fingers through the dark red mane at the base of his neck. Age had weathered his hide over the centuries, giving it characteristics similar to suede, without the rough, cracking appearance some of the other ancient males acquired. He took care of himself.

"Do you really think this will all work? That the humans will accept us?"

"Kenneth believes a rocky start should be expected, but in the end, going forward and embracing the rest of the world can only benefit all of us."

Ēostre smiled. Max's running mate, Ken Palmer, was the definition of staunch and upright, and had been as supportive as some of her friendlier dragon associates. "Kenneth is a good man. I hope the rest of humanity follows his example."

"As do I. Think of what the humans can learn from magic, from our wisdom, and think of the freedom we could enjoy once we no longer are forced to hide our true selves. Oh to fly again, Ēostre. To fly in the daylight sun and feel its golden kiss against my feathers. I've dreamed of such a day for so long," he confessed.

Ēostre wiggled around until she was nestled firmly against the shoulder of his wing. It made the perfect pillow for her cheek despite airy down feathers tickling her ear. "Mm. That doesn't surprise me, Sun God," she murmured. "I flew once with Astrid during an evening storm, but it wasn't the same. There's nothing sweeter than a summer storm at midday… than the afternoon sun gleaming over the dew on the wilderness below after the rains have ended. I want to show these things to her, Belenos. I want to show my new grandchild these beautiful things the humans take for granted."

"As do I. We have spent so long in the shadows, we no longer remember the blessing of being free. What for? For the pleasure of owning a slave?" He snorted in disgust, wisps of smoke curling from his nostrils.

"I once had a slave," Ēostre admitted. "But I never considered him one. He was a young boy Fafnir brought home, but I believe

I mothered him more than anything. Saul hadn't been born yet, and… I was quite lonely whenever Fafnir left to make war and trouble for knights. And you, my dear friend, hibernated that entire century."

Maximilian looked abashed. "I didn't realize Fafnir left you alone so often. So what of the boy, then? You came to love him?"

"I did. Griban became family, and I loved him very much. I suppose he cared for me as well since he refused to leave my side once granted freedom. He always stayed nearby, and continued to do the few tasks I'd always asked of him."

"And then?"

"He died," she said sadly. "But it was many years later when he was no longer a boy and had children of his own. But his time as my friend seemed too short. Too brief."

"What about his children?" Max asked curiously. "Surely you were able to make friends with many of them. Did you remain in touch?"

"Of course I kept up with his progeny. One of them lives on Saul's property now."

"Leiv?" Surprise filled his voice. "Fafnir chose bear shifters?"

Ēostre nodded. "Fafnir decided he wanted a strong shifter rather than a fleet deer or timid squirrel. Wolves, he said, were too unpredictable. He didn't trust creatures who relied on living in packs, he wanted a loner, like us."

"That sounds like him."

The memory was a bittersweet one and they both lapsed into silence, lost to their own thoughts. Thinking of her lost mate brought pain, but only a shadow of the despair she'd felt a few years ago. Each day since her reawakening had lessened the heartache.

And each day with Max since made her feel more alive.

"We're going to win this, Bel," she murmured as she snuggled in. "And we'll fly sun-filled skies again. You'll see."

"It's a dream to hold onto." His voice rumbled beneath her ear.

Only nights had passed since Ēostre first wished to fall asleep in Maximilian's arms. With her desire made a reality, she turned her face against the softer hide at his throat and dreamed only of him.

Chapter 10

Ēostre and Max overslept. By the time she returned him to the governor's mansion, Lynette had realized he was missing, alerted the wolves, and a grumpy pack of were-creatures awaited them in the parlor. Despite their irritable words and slyly veiled comments, Ēostre smiled because she'd had one precious night alone with Max.

"As far as anyone knows, Maximilian was here the entire night."

"And what would we have done if a government emergency arose requiring his immediate attention?" Andrew demanded.

"You would have called my son, who would have in turn had his genie track me as I've given her permission to do," Ēostre countered calmly while smoothing her fingers down her dress. "You know this, Andrew. We discussed the course of action to take in the past."

Carl shook his head. He was a big, dark-skinned werewolf with chocolate brown eyes. Ēostre had never seen him in his wolf form, unlike Andrew, but she imagined his fur would be dark as pitch and his huge wolf as big as a Buick. "Ian hired us to do more than keep him safe, ma'am, as you are well aware. In the future, we'd appreciate having a direct line to contact Governor Emberthorn."

"Please," Max spoke up, raising his hands. "Let's not turn this into another argument. We've been here before. You're both right, but unfortunately, there's no easy solution to this. I want to enjoy the time I have left before the door slams shut on my freedom. While in public, you are my security. While alone in our natural states, she will hold that honor. Is this understood?"

Carl grunted. The three men weren't happy when they left, but Megan flashed them an apologetic smile and mouthed, "Sorry," to Ēostre in passing. The girl had a more laid-back approach to guarding Maximilian, unlike the male lycan members of the team. Ēostre had to wonder if it was a werewolf trait or if the raven shifters were naturally more relaxed.

Once they were gone, Lynette sighed. "I'm sorry. I shouldn't have told them you weren't home. When I saw you weren't back, I panicked and worried that something had happened while you were both gone."

"Don't trouble yourself over it, Lynette. The wolves will always find a reason to fret. It's what they're paid to do, after all, and I wouldn't have them any other way." Max shot the girl a reassuring grin before adding, "Andrew is the alpha, but I suspect the other two would make fine candidates."

Lynette delicately pursed her lips, uncertainty creasing her brow and squinting her eyes. "Okay, well... Anyway, do you two want something to eat or did you do your Indominus rex thing and run down fluffy creatures in the wilderness?"

Max shot her a look. "I have more grace than that terrible creature, thank you."

"We're starved," Ēostre spoke for both of them. She stepped up, slid her arm around Max's shoulders, and smiled at Lynette. "We would love a breakfast, thank you."

They dined at the kitchen nook on an immense pile of eggs and bacon, chatted about his promise to visit Drakenstone Manor, and her plans to laze with her family for the day.

"Speaking of my family, I had wondered if you would take Astrid under your wing, so to speak."

"For what purpose?"

"Her breath. She's at the age, physically at least, when we'd expect her to use a breath weapon. And like her father, she's..."

Max stared across the table at her with a deep furrow creasing his brow beneath his mussed auburn hair. He looked like a man freshly risen from bed despite wearing unwrinkled clothes from the previous day. "Saul will not teach her?"

"No, no, that isn't it," Ēostre clarified with haste. "Saul loves to instruct her and has taken great joy in teaching Astrid the finer points of using her dragon form. Yet another difference between him and his father." She sighed and stirred her eggs around on the plate, spearing a chunk of thick, diced bacon with the fork. When she glanced up, Maximilian's features were sympathetic.

"I see. It isn't that he has not tried, but that they're both inexperienced. Saul is a rather young father, after all."

"He is," Ēostre agreed. "I'm proud of what he's done with her so far, and I've given what help I can, but… you taught Saul, Max. I was not the one to draw that potential from him. You did it, and I can never tell you how much I appreciate the kindness you showed my child."

"Ēostre," Max began after a heavy pause. He set the fork aside and wiped his mouth with a napkin, his plate glistening with bacon crumbs and a smattering of scrambled egg. "If Saul is agreeable, I will gladly help in whatever way he finds most appropriate."

"Good, because he's agreed already," Ēostre said cheekily. "Chloe and I discussed it first then when I brought the topic to him, he pleaded with me to ask you."

Max became speechless. His stare continued for the length of several heartbeats before the stunned dragon found his words. "He trusts me with Astrid?"

"He does."

"Even after what happened?"

"Even after," she confirmed with a smile. "Saul has never truly stopped adoring you, Maximilian. So please, worry no further about the dark times we've all put behind us, and know that you're a part of our family now."

Ēostre found it amusing that her son was very like Maximilian in some ways and had expressed his doubts personally about the great fire wyrm agreeing. Not that he ever distrusted the other dragon. According to Saul, Max had better things to do than to teach another dragon's cub.

As an inner sense of accomplishment welled within her for a match well made, Ēostre raised her cup of sweet coffee for a sip. The fragrant aroma of vanilla washed over her, and once she finished the sweet latte, she rose from the table and mussed Max's already messy hair.

"Thank you for the meal, Lynette. Max, we'll speak later."

Ēostre returned promptly to her apartment where she spent the next ten minutes seated on the edge of the bed with her new silver figurine balanced on her knee. It wasn't small by any means, at least twelve inches high, but it was a perfect replica of her pre-Saul figure. Before she'd thickened at the waist and she'd grown her second pair of maternal horns. Then, she was a sleek figure with a svelte body, and he'd captured even the subtle nuances that made up her natural poise. The head was slightly canted, the eyes lively, the feathers chiseled from hundreds of diamonds.

Human beings would put a worth on it leading into the millions, but to Ēostre, its price was beyond measure.

As her fingers slid over the smooth silver back, she channeled her magic into three layers of defense to guard it, beginning with a single spell of protection to hide it from mortal eyes. Afterward, she wove a spell of limitation — no human could ever touch it without her express permission, if they could somehow see it, and if such a human were able to circumvent her powerful spell, they wouldn't dare try to steal it. Instead, they would feel an intense, insatiable burning itch in the nether regions regardless of how much they scratched, rubbed, or bathed. And finally, if all other methods of deterrence failed, the thief would be rendered blind. That usually made people throw away their ill-gotten gains and stumble around until she discovered them in the hoard.

She touched the smooth nose of the dragoness sculpture again, smiling at the sight of it. Max cared. He had to, and soon, he'd know she felt the same way.

***

"When did you get here!?"

Astrid's enthusiastic squeal startled Ēostre awake before the child bellyflopped onto her in bed. After breakfast with Max and a few routine errands, she'd snuck into her bedroom at the manor for an impromptu afternoon nap, deciding the rest was needed before she devoted time to family activities. So much for that idea.

Ēostre groggily rubbed her eyes and glanced at the clock. "Thirty minutes ago, give or take."

She was then dragged from bed and treated to cookies and tea with her two favorite girls. Her son lumbered onto the veranda an hour later on the tail end of their chat about taking Astrid shopping for new clothes. He yawned, stole two of Ēostre's cookies, and peered out over the swaying grass while devouring them both in a bite.

"I see where Astrid gets it from," Chloe muttered.

"They never grow out of it," Ēostre agreed. She shook her head.

Saul finally turned back to them. "I plan to take Astrid hunting this evening, Chloe."

"Don't make dinner. Check. Do you plan to bring anything home to me or will I be left here to starve and eat frozen chicken nuggets with Kraft macaroni again?"

A rush of color overtook Saul's cheeks, and Ēostre grinned at her son's embarrassment. "That won't happen again. We were a little carried away that time."

They ended up dragging Ēostre along. The adults trailed behind Astrid in their dragon forms, allowing her to take the lead through the wooded wilderness to the rear of Drakenstone Manor.

The trees grew thick, untamed by Leiv's landscaping, but the deer were plentiful and oblivious the predators stalking them.

Saul's family owned all of the surrounding area near their home, leading up and past the mountains. Everything for miles had been claimed as part of the Drakenstone Estate, and some years ago, he'd even had it declared a forest preserve by the state. With high, twelve-foot privacy fences marking the perimeter, it wasn't worth it for human hunters to poach on the property.

He'd left much of it unchanged since Ēostre's last awakening, claiming he appreciated the untamed wilderness of it all. She smiled as she picked her way across the leaf-littered forest floor, silent but deadly despite her draconic form. Her son surpassed her in size, and the realization of how much her wee cub had grown over the centuries made Ēostre's heart swell.

He is a wonderful dragon and an even better man, she realized. *I raised him well. I truly did. And now he has a child he loves and nurtures with all of his heart. I couldn't ask for more.*

Ahead of them, Astrid balked on the trail. The scent of the herd was all around them, but she hesitated and lingered, uncertain of herself. She hadn't yet developed the sharp sense of smell that would come with age and second-guessed herself frequently while with her father.

At her size, she wasn't yet too large to give the deer a good chase between the trees and abundant growth. Venison was a staple in the diet of most cubs, the next prey creature they learned to hunt after bunnies and foxes.

"Is she truly ready to take on a buck, Saul? What if it hurts her?"

Saul twisted around to stare at his mother. "I wasn't yet half her size when you challenged me to take my first buck."

"I suppose so…" She tried to think back and wondered at her decision. Had it been her idea? Fafnir's? Probably the latter. He'd always urged and pushed Saul to mature before he was ready, too impatient to father him, and equally unwilling to allow him to be a child. "You were almost knocked out." The memory of Saul's injuries surfaced in her mind. The buck had slammed his hooves multiple times into Saul's little body, the frenzied attack pummeling him before he caught the upper hand.

"Almost being the important distinction," her son quipped. "But I remember at the end, I was the one to best him and Father was never prouder."

"I can do it," Astrid spoke up. She turned in a full circle, sniffing the air. After a moment she headed eastward through the trees. Ēostre couldn't help but smile. She had caught the scent of the small group in that direction as well.

"Should—"

"Shh," Saul hushed her before whispering, "Or I will send you home."

Ēostre shot him a dirty look. Falling back, they allowed Astrid to continue alone, relying on their honed, adult senses to monitor her progress through the wood. If they moved any closer, their larger sizes and the noise made by their steps would alarm the herd of their presence. Astrid on the other hand, pressed her body low to the ground and snaked beneath branches, moving with light steps. Suddenly, she stopped.

Much like a cat, the cub crouched low to the ground and tensed. Her backside wriggled right before she leapt forward. The deer didn't know what hit them, and the group scattered as Astrid's strong legs propelled her into their midst like a high-velocity bullet. Her powerful jaws took the creature around the neck, puncturing the blood vessels and spilling hot blood over the grass, onto her golden hide, and down the buck's tawny pelt.

"She needs to—"

Saul shushed her again. As he did, Astrid snapped her head to the side and broke her prey's neck. It was perfect down to the final step.

Usually, she missed the mark, and either Ēostre or Saul had to help her. "A very clean kill, my sweet. The animal suffered little,"

Saul encouraged her. He set one claw between her wings and mussed the downy fluff there affectionately. "Do you know what I think?"

"What?" she asked, wiping her mouth with the side of her forelimb.

"I think you're bound to grow into a fine huntress one day." Saul shot Ēostre a smug look over his shoulder. "And by this time next year, you'll no longer need me to accompany you."

Astrid perked up with pride. As part of her lesson, Saul tasked his daughter to haul her kill back to the manor by her own teeth. He refused to allow Ēostre to help, reminding her she once did the same to him.

"I know you're old, Mother, but your memory seems to fail you the most whenever Astrid is involved," he teased.

She huffed in irritation. "I'm not decrepit and senile, son. I simply seem to have a new perspective on training methods now."

"You're soft on her." Saul wore a wounded expression. "If it were me, you'd have left me there to find my own way back, deer in tow."

"The privilege of being a grandmother. One day you'll understand." Ēostre had to wonder about Astrid's precocious, half-dragon development and whether she'd be setting out on her own in the next decade after all. "It may be sooner than you think."

Saul grimaced. "Don't remind me."

"Mommy, look!" Astrid called at the moment they were within earshot of the back patio. Chloe was sprawled out on a lounge chair with a book in hand, but looked up at their approach.

"Did you catch that all by yourself?"

"I did! Isn't he big?"

"He sure is, sweetie. Looks like six points on his antlers."

"Seven," Saul corrected her. "And she did it all on her own this time from the start to the finish." He plucked the lifeless deer from the grass with his teeth and ambled off to handle the gross parts of meal preparation Chloe hadn't yet grown accustomed to watching. Astrid trailed after him.

Ēostre abandoned her dragon form and slipped into the sundress she'd left behind on the adjacent chair.

"I'm still so jealous of how your boobs look at your age," Chloe said.

"Are they supposed to look different?"

Chloe rolled her eyes. "I forget you dragons pick your looks and never really age like we do. Most women have to get boob jobs to keep a nice, firm rack like yours. Otherwise we start sagging."

"You're not sagging," Ēostre pointed out.

"I guess I have Saul and Astrid to thank for that. Dad says I look exactly the same now as I did seventeen years ago."

"You haven't changed since our first acquaintance. Neither has your friend Marcy. It will be interesting, I admit, to see what the future holds for you both."

Chloe's soft laughter was infused with warmth. "Yeah, me too. I wouldn't change it for the world, though. The supposed immortality is only a sweet perk. The real prize is having all of you guys to spend it with me. Speaking of, looks like they're coming back."

"He certainly makes quick work of the skinning," Ēostre murmured as she watched the two dragons return. "What does he do with them?"

"Leiv uses them for furniture and stuff. He makes a good chunk of change selling some of the stuff he makes." Chloe leaned forward in her seat and waved at her daughter. "Astrid, baby, it's probably time to go clean up."

Still riding the high from her first successful solo hunt, Astrid pounced on her father's tail and bit him playfully. "I got ya!"

Saul roared in pain, tossing his head back prior to flopping dramatically to the grass. "My one weakness. Chloe, save me! She's gotten me!"

"He's a terrible actor," Chloe said, shaking her head. "But she falls for it every time."

"My tail may never move again," Saul lamented, hamming it up.

"Thank the Ancestors that he doesn't star in his own productions," Ēostre agreed.

"Save me, Chloe!" Saul cried out in mock anguish.

"Nope. This tiny human is going to stay over here where she won't get trampled, thank you very much." Chloe grinned at them and bit into another cookie.

Astrid giggled and kept up her playful attacks until her father, feigning his own death, flopped lifelessly to the earth, unmoving and holding his breath.

"Daddy?"

Saul didn't answer.

Astrid scrambled onto her dad's ribs to peer at his face, introducing Saul to her claws. It got him up in a hurry then, her talons sharper than needles, puncturing his tough skin.

Chloe and Ēostre both laughed at him. "How long until dinner is ready?"

"Leiv has the grill warming up as we speak. He's a much better butcher than I am, anyway."

"Why don't you cook it with your breath, Daddy?"

"Because, little one, I haven't completely mastered the fine skill of searing meat, and I'd prefer it not to be charred and leathery. Our fire burns much hotter than the grill."

"I like my meat pink!"

"Then let Leiv cook it." Saul chuckled. "Go on and get changed, now, like your mother suggested unless you plan to eat with your claws."

"Aww. Okay, fine."

Astrid scampered away and transformed when Saul's back was turned. Her naked rear disappeared into the house for a shower as Chloe called out, "Don't forget to wash the blood from under your nails! You forgot last time!"

"I won't!"

"Why'd you fib to her? You do well enough when we camp," Chloe pointed out after the door was shut behind her daughter. Years after their initial meeting in the mountains, the pair continued to take trips away on the weekends, and sometimes Astrid remained behind with Ēostre, granting her parents child-free time alone.

"I know," Saul admitted. "Still, you have to agree that dragon-fired meat isn't as good."

"Nope. Give me your charred camp meals any day."

Ēostre smiled at her son's flabbergasted expression and stepped back to give the couple some room. The love shining in their eyes for one another brought to mind her feelings for Max. Feelings she still hadn't admitted to.

"Mother?"

"I'm going to see to Astrid. I'll meet you both at dinner."

Chapter 11

The one thing voters loved most about Max was his willingness to share his prosperity with them. Sacramento's Convention Center bustled with activity. Long tables yielded a bounty of chips, snacks, and drinks, while backstage Max and his campaign staff stood by, watching screens showing the waiting crowd as well as election results coming in from across the country. Earlier in the evening, he'd given a speech after a catered meal, in which he'd been very candid about his spending and his hope for America's future.

The remainder of October had passed in a flurry of final preparations, interviews, and campaign speeches in a final bid to win the American voters. Ēostre had never been prouder of him, and even if the night ended without a victory, her thoughts on the matter wouldn't change.

There was no denying it any longer. She loved the man so intensely it hurt and tore open the raw wounds left by Fafnir's death.

Was it possible to have two soul mates? Fafnir was dead and there was no bringing him back, but Maximilian was living, breathing, and supportive as ever, hoping to atone for the sin of allowing Brigid to terrorize her son.

Deep down, she'd come to realize he truly did love Saul with all the affection he'd hold for his own son. With all of the affection he'd had for his own cub.

"I'll return soon," Ēostre said abruptly. She stood in a small group with Max, his running mate, and the man's wife, chattering about incoming reports on the large screen.

"Where are you going?" Max asked. "The results should be in soon."

"To make a call." After patting his hand in reassurance, she smiled. "I'll be back before you're on the stage again."

Once Ēostre escaped the noisy auditorium, she strode quickly down a corridor until she found a quiet, semi-private place to whip out her cell phone. Saul picked up on the third ring.

"Mother?"

"Yes."

"What's wrong? Is something the matter?"

"No."

"Shouldn't you be with Maximilian, watching the polls?"

"Yes."

"Please stop answering me with single-syllable responses. What's wrong?"

Ēostre spun on her heels and paced for a second longer. Although she and Max were both of similar age, their gap no more than two centuries, she felt like a child… a cub with her first crush on an older, more powerful dragon. "Do you believe me when I tell you how much I have missed your father over these years?"

"Of course I do, Mother. You slept for decades as you grieved him." His voice softened even more, and in the background, Chloe asked if everything was all right. "I don't know," he replied to his wife. "My mother sounds troubled. Here. Speak with her."

"Saul—"

The phone transferred hands and Chloe picked up. "Ēostre? What's wrong? Do you know something that the news hasn't reported yet? We've been watching the entire thing. Oh my God, this is so exciting."

"This isn't about Maximilian, well it is, but not about the race."

"Saul, I'm starved, baby. Would you get me another one of those tiny cakes Leiv made?"

"Of course."

Seconds later, after her son must have left the room, Chloe's excited outburst made Ēostre wince. "You love him, and you want Saul's approval!"

The weight raised from Ēostre's shoulders, and for the first time in weeks, she felt like crying. "I don't want him to believe I'm replacing his father," she admitted. "As if I have moved on and forgotten everything he meant to us both."

"Ēostre, Saul would never believe that. He knows how you felt about Fafnir and had only the best things to say while you were hibernating. He loves you. Your son loves you so very much that the only concern he has is your happiness."

"I know," Ēostre admitted after a quiet sigh. "You are right. I should make the first step, tell him how I feel. I planned to do it tonight after the elections ended."

"You shou— holy shit, he won! Ēostre, he won! Thompson is giving his concession speech!"

"What?" She spun around and cracked open the door. Wild cheers filled the hallway. "Chloe I need to—"

"Go on! You can call me later."

"Thank you."

Ēostre rushed back to the main room, the cacophonic cheers from the crowd overwhelming the patriotic music blasting from the speakers. Red, white, and blue balloons rained down from the ceiling where they'd been restrained by a net, and party poppers sent confetti fluttering through the air. The energy in the room was incredible, and it washed over her in a powerful wave.

On the stage, Max and his running mate were exchanging hugs and handshakes with their campaign staff. Ēostre had barely caught her breath when Max pulled her out from the side wings and lifted her from her feet, hugging her tight. He spun her in a circle before setting her down on her feet.

"You did it."

"*We* did it," he corrected her. His eyes gleamed bright in his exuberant face.

"Go on. Go say something. Everyone wants to hear from you."

Max moved away from her and stepped to the front of the stage, closer to the joyous crowd. With a handkerchief clutched in her hand, Ēostre watched the group erupt into a fresh round of applause and boisterous cheers.

"Allow me to begin this by saying I've never had a more humbling moment in all of my life. Thank you for coming to celebrate this night with me. Thank you."

The crowd cheered again.

"I want to thank each and every one of you who voted this day. Whether it was for me or the other guy, you chose to make your voice heard. But if you did vote for me," he began, with a proud grin on his face, "I want you to know how much I appreciate your trust. Know that I aim to do my best to live up to the faith you've placed in me this day. It was a fierce battle to reach this point, and I give my respect to Senator Thompson for running an impressive campaign. I respect you, sir, and hope to have understanding between us in the future."

The crowds cheers filled the room.

"Of course, I can't forget to thank the man who stood by me through thick and thin, who worked just as hard as me during this incredible journey. The Vice President-elect of the United States, Kenneth Palmer.

"I'd also be remiss if I didn't thank the mastermind behind our campaign. She's been the rock that has grounded me when I threw out some pretty crazy ideas for the election road — my campaign manager, Ms. Ēostre Feuersturm." Max glanced upstage and caught her gaze, his eyes burning with intensity, before returning his attention to the crowd. "Without her, none of this would have been possible. I am forever thankful for the brilliance and loyalty of my entire campaign team."

Ēostre watched the remaining speech through the haze of triumphant tears. They'd won. In that moment, little else mattered beyond sweet success and the flutters of anticipation in her tummy.

"Thank you, America," Max said to the crowd again as Palmer joined him at the front of the stage. The two men exchanged words and fond embraces before the cameras, and eventually the night wound to its end, and it came time to steal Maximilian away from his supporters and political acquaintances.

He looked so handsome, so sure of himself, exuding an aura of confidence unlike anything she'd ever experienced in his presence before. Before she knew it, she was blinking back tears again and smoothing her palm over his shoulder.

"Maximilian. Come with me," Ēostre urged him. "Excuse us, ladies and gentlemen, but I do believe the President-elect needs his rest," she called out. "It's been a long, very thrilling day."

Blinding camera flashes followed them from the convention center, but the man beside her grinned through every photograph.

Tonight was the night she would share her heart and hope, above all else, he felt the same way.

Frankly, she didn't know who was guiding who to his car, and she didn't care if the crowd continued their speculation about the newly elected president and his campaign manager.

Some journalists were already beginning to put her into the White House as Max's first lady, and while the idea of it all thrilled her, her foremost concern was whether he wanted her at all.

Hoping she hadn't read the signs wrong.

The drive home passed like a blur, and there were reporters camped on the sidewalk outside of the governor's mansion, hoping to glimpse their future president. Max groaned as Andrew, their driver, slowed down to a crawl.

"Should I speak with them on the lawn?" he asked. "I should, shouldn't I?"

"Absolutely not," the security agent said.

"Agreed," said the other agent in the front passenger seat.

Ēostre took their side. "No. You'll do plenty of press conferences in the next few days after you've had time to rest.

"Should they see you entering beside me at this late hour?" The anxiety finally faded, giving way to a crooked grin.

"Actually. You're right about that. I'll see you inside, Max. Goodnight, Andrew. Goodnight, Carl."

Magic surrounded her and she pushed her way through the portal into the formal parlor. As far as any of the reporters would know, Maximilian had returned alone. Even Lynette, his live-in maid, had taken the night off, making the evening ideal for her confession of love.

"Governor Emberthorn, Governor Emberthorn! Can we have a moment of your time!" a woman cried from beyond the waist-high black fence surrounding the immense property.

The security agents hurried him inside and took their posts. After the door was shut behind Max, Ēostre stole a peek through the curtains to see if the crowd was beginning to disperse. It would take some time before the last stragglers were gone.

"I can't believe the night is over. We did it," he mused. "We really did it. Now there are so many things to do and people I must call. Tomorrow will be a busy day."

"I could be wrong, but I believe most newly-elected presidents take a day or two to rest."

"Rest? You must have forgotten who I am. How could I possibly rest when there is so much work to be done? This is only the beginning."

Max loosened his tie and paced the entrance hall before entering the secondary parlor where he often took his drinks and entertained company. He was positively humming with energy and she worried he was at risk of losing his composure *and* his human form.

No, she told herself. *Max is always so firmly in control of himself.*

"Ēostre."

119

"Yes?" Ēostre stepped out of her heels and exhaled a sigh of relief. How did human women do it all day? She'd once thought the Elizabethan corset to be uncomfortable, but by comparison, heels were an exquisite torture device.

"Promise me this was a fair race, and that you didn't orchestrate a preposterous scheme or purchase the vote. Tell me I did this on my own without money or cheating."

Ēostre laughed at her friend's elated expression. "I do so swear on the color of my wing feathers and the silver of my tail. Honestly, Maximilian, this was your hard work. Your talent of persuasion, perseverance, and promises to get things done. You have a silver tongue, my friend, and America loves you."

As he opened the bottle of chilled champagne, she tossed her blazer over the back of a chair. It felt good to sit down and rest, even if the worst wasn't yet finished. After all, supernaturals still had to come out into the open. In the meantime, she relished the chance to have Max all to herself again if only for a few days before he began to appoint his cabinet members.

"Do you suppose they will love me as much once they know the truth?" Max asked. He pushed a glass of champagne into her hands then poured another for himself.

"It's possible they'll love you even more," she said. "After all, humans have believed in magic for a long while. Our existence will confirm the beliefs of many."

"It'll be a new age." He continued his lively pacing, bristling with excitement. His drink went untouched.

Ēostre lowered her glass to the table and abandoned her seat. Crossing to Max in only a few steps, she reached out to take him by the hand and guide him to the couch. "You should sleep tonight," she said. "I know you've been awake for the past week, but even dragons require a nap every so often."

"I'll nap when my presidential term ends. What's another four years but a blink?"

"Eight," she countered. "You won't lose the next race."

"Ha! You may expect them to take this in stride, but we'll see how they feel when the truth comes to light," he said, laughing. "Still, I'm grateful for your unflagging optimism."

"As if the American public would squander the opportunity to instill fear in their opponents across the ocean. The only country with a fire-breathing dragon at the helm."

Maximilian chuckled. "You have a point. Soon the others will be clamoring to take their places in the political arena, no doubt. Especially you silvers."

She waved off his offer to refill her glass but remained lounging on the sofa beside him. She needed the time off her feet, appreciating it after the busy day. "Not this silver. I don't often say this, but that was a grueling, highly exhaustive campaign. I may take a break." She flashed him a smile. "Maybe even retire from American politics until you need me again."

"There won't be an 'until,' Ēostre. I always need you."

His words gripped her heart and squeezed, eliciting a yearning deep in her soul. More than anything, she wanted his words to go beyond their work. Beyond friendship.

"Although this election has been only a fraction of my life, a mere grain of sand in an hourglass, I've never felt more like a winner than I do this evening. I have you to thank for that."

"Unnecessary. We did this together."

Max flashed her a nervous smile, his usually confident demeanor seeming to crumble under the weight of rising uncertainty. She watched everything about him change in that moment and reached out to touch his knee. "I suppose it's time to be open with you."

"Open about what, Max?"

"Ēostre, you are the mate of my best and dearest friend. I swore to him if death ever took him, I would protect you in his absence and look after Saul."

"Max—"

"Let me finish." Maximilian set both strong hands on her shoulders, the touch setting off electric sensations across her skin. His thumbs swept over her collarbones, touching her bare flesh and the straps of her little black dress. "What I did once for obligation, I do now out of love and respect for you."

Ēostre remained silent, sensing he had more to say. In lieu of words, she placed her palm over the back of one of his hands and stroked his knuckles.

"It's taken too long to realize what you mean to me. I care for you in ways I've never loved any mere friend. You have been my faithful companion, my advisor, and most importantly, you have stolen my heart, Ēostre."

All of her carefully laid plans and rehearsed declarations of love fell apart. With three sentences, he reduced her to a state of stunned silence, and she could only stare at him in wonder. A profound sense of relief swept over her.

Before she could even utter a reply, Maximilian dragged her to him by a handful of her silver hair, and he anchored her in place as the heat of his kiss graced her lips. She melted against him, moaning into his open mouth. He tasted like cognac, despite the champagne glasses and the night's dining. Ēostre couldn't determine if it was his natural flavor, or if his favorite liquor had just become a part of him, infused in his very essence.

"Should I… should we go to your hoard?" Ēostre whispered. As he was kissing her, tracing an invisible trail between her ear to the pulse point in her throat, he edged closer and introduced her to the throbbing hardness captive in his pants. Ēostre pressed against it and dropped one hand beneath his belt, stroking upward over the firm length. He responded by nipping her ear and growling low after she leaned away to gaze up at him.

"Why?"

"Our dragons…"

"Mm… No, we will not visit my hoard," he said.

"No?" A dragon's hoard was his most sacred home, and while she had plucked her prize from among his treasures, it didn't grant her the right to mate with him amidst his jewels. Regret dropped a lead weight in her gut, and she wished she hadn't brought it up. She'd asked for too much, too soon.

"For many reasons, none related to my trust in you, Ēostre," Maximilian said, as if sensing her trepidation. "You have it, all of it, but I cannot endure the time to travel home."

"And your other reasons?"

His fingers flowed over her slim waist, continued upward until he squeezed one plump breast in his hand. She shivered in delight. "I will not take you as a beast," he breathed against her jaw, before his lips traced to her mouth and claimed them in another searing kiss. Heat pooled between her thighs and lower belly, and a warm flush spread over her limbs. "But as a man."

Maximilian found her zipper and lowered it until a casual brush of his hands brought the dress down around her waist. Her arms pulled free.

"Beautiful."

He caught her by surprise when they moved from the couch. One moment they were seated side by side, and in the next, he had cradled her in his arms. Quick, decisive steps moved through the opulent mansion, through a lavishly decorated entry hall and to the stairway leading to the upper level. She knew his home from memory. She'd been there a few days to visit when he had the dragon flux a few years ago, lying in his room bedridden and miserable.

Entering his room for a wholly different reason, an entirely different situation, took the breath from her lungs. Unceremoniously, he tossed her onto the spacious king size bed and gripped the hem of her simple sheath dress. He gave in to his urges without wasting time, stripping it from her body. A noisy rumble vibrated through his chest when she was left in only panties, a demi-bra, and thigh-high stockings. The matching silk underwear was trimmed with lace, a scant garment she'd chosen in hopes of revealing it to him.

"You approve?" she asked.

"Very much," Max answered. He bent over her and closed his teeth around the edge of the lace on her hip. A sharp tug yanked the tiny panties down her thighs, then his clean-shaven cheek glided over her skin. She realized then how much she preferred *and* missed the stubble. She loved the scrape to her skin each time she'd kissed his cinnamon whiskers.

When her panties finally hung from one ankle, an anticipative shudder ran through her body. There was no turning back. At least, not for her. It was the moment she'd been waiting for; every plot, every tease, every veiled seduction leading to one moment alone with her best friend. Through the fog of arousal, Ēostre watched him flick his belt through the loops and toss it aside. His shirt buttons came next, parting fine white fabric to reveal a broad expanse of tanned skin.

Ēostre's heart leapt in her chest again. Before she could remove her own bra, Max reached out, quickly seizing her hand. He pinned her wrist to the mattress and tore the offending garment down with his other hand, spilling her left breast from the half cup.

"Only I get to undress you, Ēostre. Just me," he growled low. "I waited too long for anything else." He flicked his thumb over her nipple and circled mercilessly until it was pebble stiff.

"Max, I thought… why didn't you tell me earlier about the way you felt? I could have told you," she groaned as he revealed her right breast and gave it the same treatment. His mouth followed, a balm of warm sensation over the tensed peak. He didn't stop until both ached as much as the dull throb between her thighs, and then he created a scorching trail of kisses from her sternum to her throat, ending with a suckle and nip below her ear.

"Did you think I didn't realize how much you wanted me?" Max asked, his breath a hushed whisper against her cheek. "I *knew* this moment would come between us, Ēostre, and I bided my time until we could be alone without worries or regrets. Did you think it was a coincidence I gave Lynette the night off?"

His index finger traced the moisture down her slick cleft, and up again, bumping against her clit. She writhed against the sheets and raised her hips impatiently for more.

"No... I knew, but... but..." Her words ended on a shuddered sigh, heralding a whispered plea for more, "I need to feel you inside me."

"And you shall."

"Max, I can't... I can't wait another moment." Something about being the only one without clothing made her feel vulnerable, sexualizing nudity when it had always been natural and normal in the past.

"I have waited centuries to have you, my love. Wait five minutes more to have me."

"But you haven't undressed."

She longed to see him, hungry for a body sighted only a handful of times in passing over the years. As a young dragon, he'd been slim, his frame the lithe build of a distance runner. As Max settled into maturity, he'd picked up considerable muscular bulk, broadening his shoulders and adding girth to his biceps. Their entire day at the beach she'd struggled against the urge to touch and explore.

Now she had no such self-limitations.

"You've seen me undressed before."

"Every time is different," Ēostre breathed. "How are you so patient?"

The finger responsible for teasing her sank to the last knuckle, penetrating her body but denying the fulfillment she desired. And then the other hand tightened in her hair again, anchoring her. Testing her desire to kiss him again, his tongue traced the seam of her lips then pressed between them, beckoning her to allow him entry. She gasped as his thumb flicked over her clit then moaned into his open mouth.

In under five minutes, Max had ruined all hope of Ēostre taking charge, and she wouldn't have it any other way. He was raw and sexual, claiming the lead and what he wanted from her body. Her hips moved to the pattern he created with the thrust of his fingers, until he stopped and withdrew completely from the bed.

"Max?"

Her eyes snapped open to find him standing beside the mattress, his slacks falling to the floor to reveal snug-fitting boxer briefs in bold red with a heavy bulge distorting the front. An impatient whine rose from Ēostre's throat until at last, they fell from his thighs, and the hard length of him jutted forward and up. As Max lowered one knee back to the bed, his thick arousal bounced and swayed, the perfect enticement to get a grip of herself — and of him.

"Satisfied?" he asked.

"Not yet."

At first, her fingers traced down the wide shaft until she found the rounded tip. His arousal matched her own, sexual need forming a clear drop of precum at the sensitive crown. The sight of him alone made her breath catch in her throat, but holding his cock was its own sweet reward.

"I don't know if I want to be selfless with you tonight, Ēostre... there's so many things I fantasized about doing with you. To you," he clarified.

The solid length of him throbbed in her hand, the silken skin soft beneath her exploring fingers. She stroked up and down in long, languid strokes, delighted in the way his eyes squeezed shut.

"Be selfish, Maximilian." If she had her way, they'd have many, many more couplings and many centuries to enjoy every carnal delight their imaginations could create. She wrapped her legs around his body and drew him close.

"Will you do the same?" he asked, voice a low, husky growl.

Taking control, Ēostre guided him between her thighs and dragged his sensitive head between her slit, rubbing him against her entrance. Then he slid forward. Her body resisted at first, so long a time passing since her last sexual encounter she'd almost forgotten what it was like to make love. Turbulent emotions became a storm of sensation, physical and emotional, her love for him and the sheer weight of her desire.

The second nudge came with the delicious sensation of being stretched. Her body yielded to his girth, and then Max set his brow against the pillow beside her head. "Now I'm the impatient one," he breathed out.

"No more waiting then." She tightened around his tip, squeezing with silken muscles until he groaned and his eyes blazed with lust.

"Is there a rush?"

"Yes," she cried. "I need you now, fast and hard, Bel. Be selfish. *Take me.*"

Ēostre didn't care. They could go slow the next time. Every time after. But this time she needed him now and she couldn't wait another moment.

The headboard thumped against the wall with the next thrust. He surged deep, seating every inch to join them in the exquisite union Ēostre had craved. He pulled out, almost making her weep, only to ram in anew.

Max created a fast-paced rhythm that resulted in the frenetic slap of skin against skin, of perspiration beading against his brow. Her breasts heaved and the rosy nipples at their tips became victim to his hungry kisses. One tip then the next was claimed between his lips, sending hot jolts of pleasure streaking to her core. She clenched around him and groaned, twisting on the bed sheets.

"More!" she cried. "I want more of you, Bel. I need... I need..."

Without parting their bodies, Max leaned back and drew her legs up. One long limb after the other came to rest against his muscled chest, ankles hooked over his shoulders.

And then he wasn't Max "the man" any longer, but an animal instead, claiming her with a reckless rhythm, his groans and low growls driving her wild.

Her breasts jostled and quaked, her fingers spasmed against his thighs, flexing their grip, and her entire body drew tight. Molten passion burned through her veins and her skin tingled.

On the cusp of orgasm, her head tilted back to the pillow and she keened his name. Her breath was stolen away and her heart raced so fast it was a wonder it didn't burst from her chest.

And then he was gone, gliding backwards from her pussy without a word.

"Max? What are — what are you doing?"

Hands on her hips, he answered by flipping her over on the skewed sheets. She barely had a moment to push up on her knees when he dragged her back and reclaimed her body's tight embrace.

"Will you accept me, Ēostre?"

In all of her many centuries, she'd never heard of a dragon bonding to a second lifemate. And she'd never dreamed she'd find a male wanting the tangled remnants of the soul left in her after Fafnir's death. Max changed everything, and now that his instincts had taken hold, she couldn't deny him.

Her body behaved of its own accord. The slightest brush of his fingertips over her clit returned her to the breaking point, until she was teetering at the edge and waiting to careen into ecstasy.

"Do you accept my claim, Ēostre? Are you mine?"

She responded with a brazen moan as he dipped forward again, his cock plowing so deeply they seemed to become one in every definition of the term. She bowed her spine beneath him and exposed the expanse of shoulder blade perfect for receiving the mating brand.

Her original scar remained, a faded, unrecognizable remnant of a time long past. At first she tensed, waiting for Max to withdraw in disgust or even disdain for the permanent brand Fafnir had left on her.

"Mine." Max lowered his teeth and clamped down hard in response to the unspoken invitation.

A jolt of electricity sizzled through her body, the current flooding every nerve, down to the tips of her toes. It was like liquid fire coursing through her, conducting pleasure instead of burning agony.

As the arm encircling her waist tightened in a possessive hold, Max growled against her skin and came. Her entire body spasmed before her channel clenched around his length in a series of methodic shudders, milking each hot pulse. An elated scream tore from her throat. "Yes! Sweet Ancestors, yes! I'm yours, Bel, I want to be yours!"

The wave of pleasure coursed through Ēostre until the tide swept her further and further away, until she could barely see the pattern of the expensive pillowcase beneath her, until the world bloomed bright white and she was shuddering in the throes of passion. Max leaned over her, drove in deep, and rode her through every second while her features contorted in ecstasy.

Once he was completely spent, she realized only her grip of the headboard and Max's arm around her waist had kept her from collapsing to the mattress. She clung to the former, chips of wood beneath her nails, scraped off the splintered wood frame of what had probably been an antique. She'd broken it. Max glided his palm down her tummy and stroked in calming pets.

He kissed the fresh brand, setting off an explosion of aftershocks in her core. She shuddered and arched again, then his half-hard cock tensed. He felt as good the second time as he did the first. Testing her heat, he pumped a few times.

"Mm... Before... we start again... I need a drink," Ēostre murmured. Her voice had gone hoarse. She cleared her throat to no avail then regretted her own request when Max slipped free.

"Champagne good enough for you?"

"Yes."

Max slipped out the bed as she settled amidst the cool satin sheets. Her body was still humming with pleasure. Giggling a little, she stretched out in his bed, her limbs languid and weak with euphoria but flooded with endorphins.

The glasses clinked against the bedside stand when Max returned a few minutes later. Ēostre opened her eyes to the sight of him pouring fresh glasses, a beautiful Adonis in the golden glow emitted from the nearby lampshade. Playful as a kitten, she wiggled up against his side and claimed the glass from his hand.

"Congratulations, Mr. President."

The champagne soothed her raw throat, but it didn't quench the rising heat between them. He was still hard, after all, and they had a long night ahead of them to celebrate.

There was no going back. Things would forever be changed between them, and Ēostre wouldn't have it any other way.

Chapter 12

Maximilian awoke after a rare, peaceful night of sweet dreams. He didn't have a scrap of the satin sheets on his body, and the cool air raised goose bumps on his skin. It didn't take long to figure out where the covers had gone.

Ēostre lay beside him, a beautiful mattress hog wrapped in a cocoon of sheets. She'd taken all of them, whether by intention or not, and left him with so little space he practically hung from the edge.

Instead of leaving the bed, as he would have if she were only a mortal to warm his sheets for a night, he moved closer and enfolded her in his arms to reclaim the stolen space.

What had he ever done in his life to deserve such fortune? He buried his face in her silver waves, breathed her in, and thought, *I have always wanted you, Ēostre. Since the first day Fafnir brought you to meet me, I coveted you.*

Fighting amongst the other males for a heartless female beast had never appealed to Maximilian, and in his luckiest hour, Mahuika had come to strike a deal. A child in exchange for gold and gems. As payment, the fire dragon had given her half of his worldly treasures on the day she arrived with Brigid, their newly weaned cub. He'd waited thirty long years.

Then Mahuika walked out of their lives. She'd only wanted the money and his jewels after all.

"Mm… I ache everywhere," his lover murmured beside him. "Was I too rough?"

Her gentle laughter sent a chill over his skin. "No, Belenos. You were perfect," she assured him. "My complaints are in the best way possible."

"Good." He dropped a line of kisses down her neck to her shoulder. "Perhaps I can ease your suffering with a lengthy soak. The tub is practically a pool."

"Perhaps I'll let you." Chuckling, Ēostre wiggled away to settle on the edge of the bed with her back to him. The sheets pooled around her hips as she opened the nearby curtains, and light washed over the dimmed bedroom.

The bruised, deep purple outline of his teeth marred the back of her right shoulder, discolored as much from the magical brand as the physical injury it caused.

"Did you plan last night?" Ēostre asked gently when she saw him looking.

"No, but I don't regret it," he said quietly. "Do you?"

Ēostre shook her head. "I wouldn't have chosen last night to accept your pledge," she said as she raised her fingers to the mark on her shoulder. One touch awakened the new bond between them, stiffening his cock in an instant.

Max's nostrils flared. "Then you wish to allow it to lapse. After all, you did not mark me in return to seal our bond." Breathing in the scent of her morning arousal was its own kind of hell. Wanting to touch her, wanting to drive into her and reclaim what was his, but listening to her dismaying words at the same time. Max maintained his neutral expression, but his hope dwindled. "I understand. It was foolish of me."

Ēostre shook her head. "No, Bel. Allow me to finish my thoughts." When she shifted to face him, the sleek satin sheets fell away completely, revealing her body to him anew. Long, lean thighs, full breasts, and a stomach only soft enough to remind him she'd once borne a child. She slipped one thigh over his hip to straddle him.

"I had planned to reveal my heart to you last night, yet you beat me to it. I don't regret our coupling, but I had not expected a bond. As for my claiming you, as you asked me last night, is there a rush?" A mischievous smile touched her lips as she gazed down at him.

"No," he whispered, intoxicated by the very sight of her. The sunlight gleamed over her fair skin and lit her platinum blonde hair aflame in color. If it was lavender in the moonlight, noontime made it spun gold in the presence of the morning sun. The tips of her hair skimmed over his chest, tickling wherever they touched.

"Why not?" Ēostre lowered over his cock, trapping it between the slick, wet folds of her pussy and his pelvis. She moved her hips back and forth. "Am I no longer to your liking?"

"You are. In every way, Ēostre."

"I thought you to be a man who knows what he wants, Belenos." Her hips rolled and teased, but she didn't take him inside the receptive sheath he longed to feel again.

"Don't tease me," he growled up at her.

"I'll tease you as much as I want, my mate."

Max's cock twitched inside her, apparently loving the words as much as his brain did. His physical response brought a bigger smile to her face.

"My mate," she repeated.

"Fuck, what are you doing to me?"

"Exercising my will," she whispered. The playful minx in her emerged as she leaned forward to kiss him, dragging tightly budded nipples over his chest. With a groan, he took a handful of her ass and pressed her down against him.

"Take me. Make me yours as well, Ēostre. Do it."

"Not yet."

His skin felt electrified, the fine hairs standing and his skin tingling. A bond could only be initiated at the height of physical pleasure when two souls were connected by bliss.

"I feel how wet you are for me, love. Let me give you what you need."

Despite her equally pressing desire, Ēostre took her sweet time, raising until the thick inches of his cock glistened between her thighs, only to thrust down and reclaim him again. She did it over and over, taunting him with delicious slowness.

Chiming trills filled the room, breaking the silence.

"Ignore it," Max mumbled against her breast, wishing he'd left her purse downstairs when he'd fetched them snacks just before dawn. "It's probably work."

"And if it isn't?" Ēostre held her hand palm out toward her discarded purse. It unsnapped and the phone flew into her palm. "It's Chloe. She rarely calls…"

"Answer it if you must," Max said, sighing heavily. His cock throbbed within her, aching with the need for his mate to resume the subtle glide up and down his shaft.

"Chloe? Is everything all right?"

Chloe spoke too softly for Max to hear her end of the call, but the overall tone of conversation seemed friendly. No emergency at all. He bumped his hips upward and surged deep inside Ēostre, catching her off guard. Her eyes flew open and her fingers clutched wildly at his chest.

He grinned and slid his hand to the junction of their bodies. One rub of his thumb against her clit made Ēostre's pussy involuntarily clench. Her body was so responsive to him, reacting to the slightest provocation and touch.

"Oh? Well, I'm sure he'll be flattered and pleased. I'll, ahh…" Ēostre closed her eyes and dragged in a ragged breath. "Tell him. I'll tell him. Five? Of course. I will — we will see you then." After ending the call, she tossed the phone aside and leaned down to nip his ear. "Naughty dragon."

"You were taking far too long," he grumbled. "What did she want?"

"They're throwing a celebratory dinner for you tomorrow night." The corner of her mouth quirked. "I think she knows we were having sex."

"You hardly managed to keep your composure so I'm not surprised. Now she'll know better than to call again."

She swatted at his chest but there was no strength behind her silent admonishment. She rolled her hips, seating his shaft deep within. She tightened around him again.

"I want you to know something, Max."

"What's that, my heart?"

"I waited to claim you until I could savor this moment and enjoy every second." She dipped her head down to kiss his cheek.

Having Ēostre above him made Max forget how to breathe. His hands traced out her outline, flowing up and down her silhouette, past her ribs and back down to her hips again. He watched at first, mesmerized by each rise and fall, the tight rhythm created each time her thighs flexed.

Her nipples stood stiff and rosy, ready for the heat of his mouth. He leaned up, his weight on one palm, and claimed one eagerly. His tongue bathed the tight peak, then he suckled it between his lips, provoking another internal squeeze around his dick.

"Take me," he growled. "Faster, Ēostre."

"Can't wait?" she asked, breathless.

Sating her own needs or deciding to heed his request, his lover quickly began to thrust him in and out of her warmth.

"I'm close," he moaned out.

Ēostre's breaths came quick. "I know. Let go, Bel. Let go with me," she cried out. The rest of her plea was lost to her orgasm, and then moments later, Bel was lost within her. He thrust up, groaning as he spilled his seed in a hot rush. One spurt then another. Ēostre pressed her body closely against him, her breasts flattened against his chest.

At first, her lips brushed his collarbone in a kiss, then sharp teeth closed around muscle and skin. His vision went dark, shadowed by a curtain of raw bliss shooting through every nerve fiber. Max's muscles tensed and his entire body went rigid beneath her. The shock of the branding mark lanced from head to toe, and he came until he was dry firing inside her and there was nothing left.

"Belenos?" Ēostre whispered.

"Hm?"

"I think I lost you for a moment." She pushed her hair behind one ear and peered down at him, expression jubilant.

"There are no words to accurately convey what I feel right now," he said quietly. "Amazing, fantastic, incredible — all unacceptable."

"Then don't use words."

Max leaned up to kiss his mate. His beloved. His everything. One kiss wasn't enough, but in one kiss, he channeled years of longing, affection, and all of his devotion.

They napped on and off, ignoring the ringing phone in his office and the buzz from his doorbell. When the wolves knocked again to perform their welfare check, he channeled part of his draconic side and bellowed out a wish for privacy. The pack left them alone afterward.

Finally, Ēostre slipped from the bed, and he mourned the loss of her heat beside him. "I'm going to make tea and figure out how to feed us. I'm starved."

Max chuckled and laced his fingers behind his head. She'd drained him. "Don't walk around my house naked. I might attack you again."

"You aren't attacking anyone in your condition," Ēostre pointed out, calling his bluff.

They ended up in the shower together instead, both too tired to do anything more than soap and hold the other while enjoying the refreshing pelt from the enormous showerhead. Dragons loved the water, whether they were volcanic, tidal, ice, earth, or storm.

He could spend an hour beneath a scalding spray easily. For Ēostre, he had to adjust the temperature to something she could tolerate.

"I don't look forward to leaving," she sighed as Max patted her dry with a fluffy towel.

"I suppose you could live with me," he answered, wrapping his arms around her waist. The towel fell to the floor. "Secretly, of course. Until we're married."

"Is that your idea of a proposal?"

I suppose it is, Max thought. He swore internally, hating that he didn't have a ring, a bracelet, or some trinket of affection for the moment. Humans proposed with dazzling engagement rings and tokens of love. And... all he had to offer was his heart.

Max ran his fingertips through her damp hair, pushing fair strands from her face. "Yes. Nothing would honor me more than to take you as both my mate and my wife." He couldn't breathe, but the thump of his racing heart threatened to drown out anything else he may have said. *Tell me you want the same. Please.*

"Nothing would make me happier," she whispered.

"I know marriage has no meaning to dragons, but I want you to stand beside me in all ways. Come to Washington with me. Let the world fall in love with you as I have. Let them see your charm and your radiance."

"Are you sure we should be seen together so soon?"

His grin stretched across his face. "My darling, Ēostre, they've already seen us together in our swimsuits."

"About that..." She nibbled her lower lip and glanced away.

"You arranged it. I know."

"The press? No, not that at all. You see, my selfish act wasn't me wanting to laze about on the beach. It was about having you to myself for the weekend." She paused, then added in a cheeky voice, "In a Speedo. You failed me on that point, though I *suppose* your substitution was acceptable."

"Now you have me all to yourself." He stepped forward, nudging their bodies closer together. "In nothing." And the wave of exhaustion felt in the wake of her branding mark was quickly fading.

"Yes, I most certainly do."

As Max leaned in and claimed her lips in a searing kiss, he was aware of one thing.

They were going to need another shower soon.

Chapter 13

"Are you prepared for this?" Max asked.

"Hardly. While I may know my son well, I can't predict his reaction to our news." Ēostre wrung her hands together until Maximilian gently took one and interlaced their fingers. She smiled up at him.

"Does his opinion matter?"

"No," she admitted. "But I..." The silver dragon pursed her lips and lapsed into silence, thinking. "I *want* his support."

"You'll have it," Max told her. "You raised a good cub, Ēostre, and he's become an even greater man. You said it yourself." He rang the doorbell and waited. The exterior of Drakenstone Manor smelled of sweet autumn flora. Leiv decorated according to the season, planting robust flower vines alongside pansies in every color of the rainbow. They bordered the walls of the home in a lush carpet of varying hues.

"Their car is here! Saul, sweetie, would you answer the door?"

Chloe's distinctive voice reached them from inside, traveling through an open window. Sensing his mate's worry, Max squeezed Ēostre's hand tighter and nudged her with his thigh.

"All will be fine," he assured her again in a quiet voice.

"I know."

Whether Saul approved or not, Max didn't plan to let her go. He couldn't anyway, since he'd pledged half of his soul during their mating rite, freely giving her part of his very essence.

The anticipation continued to build until he heard Saul's thundering steps approaching the door. The man walked heavy, like he was a giant, though he could be nimble footed when necessary.

"Congratulations, Maximilian, on a job well done," he cheerfully greeted Max. "You as well, Mother. How are both of you? Come in, come…" The big smile on the man's bearded face faded when his golden eyes traveled to their joined hands. He stared.

"Hello, Saul," Max said politely. "Thank you. I'm honored to receive your family's invitation today."

Saul continued to stare, and then his nostrils flared as he breathed in their mingled scents and realized the inevitable. "Mother, why do you and Maximilian…" Saul's voice trailed then his eyes went large with surprise. "You've bonded?"

"Yes." Ēostre raised her chin and studied her only child's reaction. "As of last night."

"I… *Really?*"

Despite Saul's perplexed expression, tension continued to gnaw Max's insides. Confusion was better than outright disdain. Claiming a female dragoness for the first time was difficult enough without submitting himself to the judgment of her adult offspring.

Chloe emerged from the area of the kitchen, drying her hands against her thighs. "Hi, guys!" The discomfort lingered as she reached her husband's side and saw the two older dragons still standing on the porch.

"Hello, Chloe," Max said.

"Uh. Why is there a standoff in my doorway? Saul, move aside and let them in," Chloe chastised him. She bumped him with her hip, then her blue eyes dropped to their joined hands. "So it's official now?" She made a sweeping gesture with her arm, encouraging them to enter. The members of Max's security team remained outside after flashing her polite smiles. Ian had come through and gotten at least a small handful of shifters onto the staff of the United States Secret Service, and in the coming days,

Maximilian would become acquainted with the unique habits of a new security detail.

He already missed Andrew, Vincent, Carl, and Megan, but he was told the latter was in a fine position to apply. Ian had plans of getting her on the Counter Sniper Team, claiming he'd trained her himself.

"Very official," Ēostre said. The uncertain smile on his mate's lips broadened.

"I'm so happy for your both. I knew it was only a matter of time before one of you made the first move."

Saul stared at his wife. "How long have you known this, and why wasn't I told?"

"Since summer… and it wasn't your business," Chloe answered, giving him a cheeky grin. "She's your mother, not your child."

"I know that," Saul grumbled. His eyes softened and a gentle smile came to his face. "I am also happy for you. If I appear upset, I assure you, it is merely shock disguising my pleasure."

"Your mother and I—"

Saul cut Max off with an abrupt bear hug, surrounding the fire dragon in a tight embrace. It caught Max completely by surprise, but it didn't go unwelcomed. He squeezed Saul back in return, overwhelmed by how right it felt to not only become part of the Drakenstone family, but to also receive each of their blessings. He and Brigid had gone about it the wrong way before, but now the Ancestors had granted him a last chance at peace and a happy future.

"I am very pleased for you to become part of our family, Maximilian. Do not doubt that," Saul assured him.

"Does this make you my grandpa, Uncle Max?" Astrid asked. None of the adults had noticed her listening. She peeked through the open archway from the living room, her bright eyes filled with fascination. "Do I have two grandfathers now?"

Ēostre darted her eyes to Max. He didn't need to hear her thoughts to know she was leaving the answer up to him. As Saul stepped back, Astrid came forward shyly. Max lowered to a knee in front of her and smiled.

"I will gladly be your grandfather, Astrid. I have adored you since the moment your mother trusted me to meet you."

"I think I like you more as a grandpa," she told him in earnest. Her big ear-to-ear grin proceeded an exaggerated smooch to Max's cheek. "Carry me!"

"Astrid Drakenstone, you are *way* too old to be carried," Chloe chastised her gently.

"It's all right." Max scooped the girl up as if she were a feather. "Soon enough she'll truly be too big so I may as well enjoy it while I can."

Astrid whooped with glee when Max, showing off his muscle, tossed her up and caught her again.

"I suppose I do not need to warn you to take excellent care of my mother," Saul said.

Max smiled. "I doubt she would allow me to treat her any other way."

Eventually, they gathered for dinner in the infrequently used dining room where formal place settings for eight gleamed against a white tablecloth. Astrid and Chloe had put together one grand feast in Max and Ēostre's honor, originally planned to celebrate his appointment to the White House's top spot. In the end, it became a meal to commemorate their bonding, a reception fit for a pair of dragons.

"Svetlana and I will help you to bring everything inside," Mahasti said.

"No, no. You sit down with the guests. That's what Saul is for. Saul, come bring in these steaks," Chloe called from the doorway.

Saul grunted and left his seat.

"Uncle Leiv taught me how to use his barbecue," Astrid confided in Max as she set down a platter of grilled shrimp. A delectable, chili-lime aroma wafted from the bamboo-skewered morsels. "So I grilled these."

"They look delicious. How did you know I liked spicy shrimp?"

"Because you like spicy everything," the girl explained with a giggle.

"She burned the first ones," Svetlana revealed, peeking from around Astrid's back. "Then Papa had to eat all of them so she wouldn't cry."

"You weren't supposed to tell!"

"But it was funny!"

Max laughed at the expression on Astrid's face. Her cheeks were mottled pink and red, and her lips were pouted out. "It's nothing to be ashamed of, Astrid. There's a reason why I don't do my own cooking," he told her.

"Then it's good you're going to have a chef." She leaned in and lowered her voice. "Grandma doesn't cook either. It always comes out gross."

"I heard that." Ēostre laughed and claimed the first shrimp skewer. "However, you speak the truth, little one. I suppose I will need to take lessons."

For Max, dinner passed with more questions than actual feasting, but he didn't mind a second of it. He couldn't recall the last time he'd spent an evening surrounded by close friends and loved ones, and the more he pondered it, the more apparent the answer became. Never.

"Can I come to your office to watch you work before you leave for Washington?" Astrid asked. "I can help out with whatever you need."

"Yes, you may, and of course once I'm inaugurated in Washington, you'll be able to come visit there as well," Max said. "It should be educational for you at least."

"Sweet!" Her bright blue eyes filled with delight. "Can I see inside the manor? Is part of it still a museum?"

"It is, my sweet. I only reside in a portion of the actual governor's mansion. The rest remains untouched as a part of history," he explained.

Within moments, Max and Astrid had made plans to visit a variety of museums, government offices, and landmarks in the nation's capital.

Chloe shot him an exaggerated dirty look, feigning insult. "You didn't invite me."

"You're not my new grandchild," he teased, "but you and Saul are welcome to accompany Astrid. There's room for all of you, including Leiv, Mahasti, and Svetlana."

Leiv, apparently startled by the invitation, inhaled a bite of steak.

"Excellent. What Leiv wishes to say is that we would be happy to visit," his wife said for him. The bear shifter nodded a couple times and coughed into his fist, red-faced.

"Yes!" Svetlana cheered. "Hey. Do I get to call you Grandpa, too?"

Saul grunted, mock scowling at the two girls. "Neither of you ever ask to come to work with me. Don't you love the movie studio?"

"I still love you and the studio, Daddy. Grandpa Max is just more interesting," Astrid said.

Joining Leiv in a near-death dinner experience by choking on her wine, Chloe set the glass aside and coughed a few times into her hand. Saul's scandalized look made it better. Shifters and children made for dangerous dinner partners.

"Oh, oh! Grandpa Max, I want see your dragon! Mom said you were going to give me lessons for my fire, and you're the only member of the family I've never seen in their true form. Are you really going to give me lessons?"

"I am," he agreed amiably, chuckling at her enthusiasm. "Your grandmother has asked me to teach you as I once taught your father and mentored him. Using one's breath weapon requires great focus and power, but you seem to have acquired a fair amount of your grandmother's magic, too."

"I did?"

"Yes, my sweet. Which is why I plan to let you fight me."

"Max," Chloe began, "I don't know if she's ready to fight an adult dragon."

Maximilian chuckled at the woman's natural protectiveness. "It's only practice. Astrid will have a chance to stretch her claws, so to speak. Years ago during less civilized times, she would have begun to learn to defend herself from the time of her birth. A dragon cub can slaughter a human with ease."

Saul took Chloe's hand and kissed her knuckles. "He's an excellent teacher, my love. I was a bit of a slow learner when it came to my breath, but Maximilian had me up to par in weeks. I trust him with Astrid's well-being."

"Well. All right. It isn't that I distrust him, it's…" Chloe sighed and waved them off with her hand. "Give me a moment for my meal to settle. I'll fetch my camera before you begin rampaging in the fields or whatever."

"I'll meet both of you outside. Come Ēostre, you should join us. Perhaps you and I should do this instead."

Ēostre's startled eyes darted to Max. "Oh, I don't know—"

"C'mon," Max insisted again, nudging her with his arm. As she began to relent, he dropped his voice to a whisper. "We'll put on a show for Astrid, and I'll even let you kick my ass since she's never seen a good battle. What do you say?"

"I say I could kick your ass whether you allowed it or not."

Max raised a brow, intrigued by her mounting display of confidence. He'd always loved that about Ēostre, admiring her spirit. "Is that a bet?"

"Do you remember what happened last time we placed a wager, Belenos?"

He grimaced at the memory. While the moments on the beach with her had been precious to him, he hadn't forgotten the

145

uncomfortable scrap of material tugging its way uncomfortably into the wrong places. "Then prove it," he challenged.

"Gladly."

Max tipped back the rest of his wine and grinned as he stood. "Thank you for this excellent meal, Chloe." *Hopefully I haven't enjoyed too much of it to hold my own against Ēostre,* he thought.

***

They met outdoors in a wide-open space where the ground had been razed and leveled. To reach it, Max walked briskly past the field where Brigid met her end, discovering the wound, even seventeen years later, was much too raw to look upon it.

Max and Saul chatted amicably while he stripped and set his clothes on the fence, but the latter opted to remain in his human form.

"I haven't overstepped my bounds, have I?" Max asked him. He transitioned to his natural state, shedding the human flesh in favor of tough, ember-colored hide. His wings flexed then unfurled, spreading vibrant feathers with ruby plumage toward the sky.

Saul shook his head. "Hardly. I may have taught her to fly, but that seems to be where the line should be drawn. We haven't had any luck, aside from a few sparks."

Maximilian stretched out his claws and raked them over the hard-packed soil, thrilled for the chance to adopt his dragon form. The opportunities didn't come often lately. While they waited, he enjoyed the cool November air against bare skin. No matter the time he spent in human garments, he never quite adjusted to their changing styles of clothing.

Ēostre and Astrid, both as dragons, joined them a few minutes later. As an older girl, Astrid had developed a human's modesty and shyness, so all of the male shifters in her life always respected her privacy by vacating the area for her to shift, if she hadn't already shifted elsewhere. Max's eyes were for his new mate alone, however, roaming over Ēostre's sleek, silver body in appreciation.

My Ēostre is beautiful. I must carve another sculpture of my beloved to capture her radiance as she is now.

"Grandpa Max is bigger than Daddy!" Astrid exclaimed as she bounded up, resembling an energetic pup.

Saul grumbled.

"Indeed, I am, little one. But I am also older and adult dragons do not cease growing until we near our first millennia."

"How old are you and Grandma?"

"Very old," he said.

Astrid sulked, dissatisfied with the vague answer. "You don't look old."

"We both have many years left, Astrid. Be content with that. Now, are you ready?"

"Yes!"

"Now… I wish for you to imagine you are striking a match."

An hour later, Chloe was shivering with a shawl around her shoulders while Saul and Ēostre speculated from the sidelines.

"Perhaps she isn't yet ready," Saul said.

"There is always the possibility Astrid will never acquire the talent for using dragon's breath," Ēostre pointed out, reluctance in her voice. "We shouldn't push her too hard when we don't know how she'll develop."

"Please. If none of you will be quiet, I'll have to ask you to leave," Max said.

Astrid's face scrunched in concentration, giving her a comical expression. She coughed, cleared her throat, and made a few raspy, dry noises in a desperate attempt to produce flames. When nothing happened, her expression fell.

They've made her nervous. It's no wonder Saul has made little progress, Max realized. He would have to forbid them from attending again.

"Forget them," he told her in a low, quiet voice. "Right now it's just you, me, and the target. Focus on the hay bale, little one.

Visualize your inner spark and see it growing. What's your favorite color?"

"Gold," she whispered.

"Then breathe in deeply as I taught you, let the air fill your lungs, and think of only gold. The hottest, purest gold. There can be no fire without air, my sweet." He tapped her side with one of his claws. He demonstrated, taking in a deep breath, letting it expand his ribs, and then slowly releasing it in a steady stream of white smoke and fire. Astrid watched him with awe-filled eyes.

It felt like only yesterday when Saul stood in her place, sniffling and upset. Fafnir lacked both the tolerance for failure and the time to teach his own son. Ēostre, rightfully distraught by the turn of events, had visited Shasta with her cub in tow to ask for help.

All Saul had wanted was to impress his father, so much he couldn't surpass his own anxiety to make it happen.

"Your father will be proud of you no matter what, Astrid, because he loves you and you are the most precious thing in his entire world. He may love your mother with all of his soul, but you are the true reason his heart beats. Remember that," he said in her ear before stepping back. "Exhale."

Astrid's attention darted to Saul. He smiled back at her, warm, welcoming, and with nothing but love in his eyes. Max waited beside her with his own breath held. For her, he maintained his composure, exuding nothing but patience, the direct opposite of the three observers.

All of the air compressed from the cub's lungs at once in a single determined breath. One lightning bolt flashed amidst an explosive jet of gold flames. Chloe squealed and raised her camera.

"Oh my God, she did it!"

The hay bale they'd set up for a target remained intact, but the fence behind it didn't fare so well. Her breath weapon blasted a large hole in the wood and sent flaming splinters flying through the air. Astrid ducked her head and sniffled.

"Don't be discouraged. You did fine."

"I set the fence on fire," she sulked.

"Yes, you did. But you called on your fire — an incredibly large amount of fire, I might add — so that's progress. Next time we'll work on your *aim*."

"You mean, you'll still train me?"

Max ducked his head down and rubbed his cheek against hers in affection. "Of course I will, Astrid. I promised, didn't I? And I always keep my promises."

She peeked upward at him, the sadness leaving her face to be replaced with hope. "Are you still going to show me a fight?"

"Do you still want to see one?" he countered playfully.

"Yes!" she cried, the sparkle returning to her eyes.

"Go join your parents then. Ēostre! We're up."

The corner of Ēostre's tooth-filled mouth raised then she prowled forward, her white talons clicking against pebbles and hard bits of rock in the barren soil. Her wings folded close as she assumed her battle stance and tilted her head to watch him, sizing him up, trying to predict his movements.

"We will be cautious with our dragon's breath," Max said. "I don't want to cause you harm."

"Nor do I want to harm you, my mate. I will pull my punches, so to speak, and tone down my assault. Your hide is too handsome to be covered in scars," she teased.

"No magic," he said.

"Of course. I want to play with you — not harm you. What good are you to me broken?"

Despite their agreement, it was still bound to be one exciting practice round.

Max lunged to her right side and feinted with his right claw. He snapped his teeth at the base of her wing when she writhed to the side to avoid him, only for Ēostre to roll out of the way. She sprang up again before his claws even hit the ground. She struck like a cobra and was on his back, hissing and growling before he flung her off.

Shit! Ēostre was faster than he remembered. He exhaled a line of fire to ward off her ferocity.

It worked. She shrank back from the flames, giving Max the opportunity to steal the upper hand. He dove through them toward Ēostre and hit her with his bulk, winding her. If she'd been anyone else, they would have gone at one another for blood. Instead, they writhed and wrestled across the ground, laughing when Ēostre snuck in a thwack with her tail.

From the edge of his vision, he saw Astrid watching with rapt attention from her father's side. The two elders separated, Ēostre scrambling to place distance between them while Max kept her in his line of sight.

"Use your breath, Grandma!"

Blue-white lightning crackled across the space between them, faster than Max could blink. Lances of electricity seized his body in a state of paralysis, and while neither of them were fighting with the full force of their ability, it still stung his toughened hide. He came out of it in time to bat her away as she lunged forward. She dodged his next slash, darted in beside him, and left a stinging mark down his flank.

"*Ow*," Max said. He twisted around for a look at the scratches in his hide. Ēostre's claws could have cleaved him down to the muscle if she'd wanted. Male dragons might have had the greater size and brawn, but their talons were blunt compared to the terrifying weapons held by their female counterparts.

"Was it too much? Did I hurt you?"

"No, no. Mere scratches," he assured. "Hardly any blood."

"Grandma wins!" Astrid bounced from side to side with her excitement. "Right, Daddy? That means she won, right? Grandpa Max said ouch."

When Ēostre approached to fawn over his flesh wound, Max took the initiative. He tackled her, pinning her to the earth and disturbing a cloud of dust. She squirmed and nipped at him in an effort to regain her freedom, but he didn't budge.

"That's cheating!"

"It's very fair," Max disagreed. "She can't get away without using magic."

Ēostre pushed with her hind claws, but her talons, despite their razor sharp tips, couldn't scratch his belly where his skin was toughest.

"Ugh," she grunted. "You're heavy."

"And you're beautiful." Max touched their snouts together and growled playfully. "But I have won our spar. Do you concede?"

"I suppose I can give you this win," Ēostre replied before nipping his shoulder.

"Get a room!" Saul called.

"Yeah!" Chloe agreed. "Not on my lawn!"

"There are young eyes watching," Astrid said.

Laughing, Max let Ēostre up from beneath him. She shook the dirt from her radiant, white feathers and cheerfully leaned against his side, unfazed by her defeat.

"I see nothing has changed, and you still spar like you've taken lessons from the Patriots, Maximilian." Saul chuckled and set his arm around Astrid's back. "A warning to you, my daughter, he plays dirty, as you have seen. He's crushed me countless times in the past, and my bones still remember it."

"I'm not afraid," Astrid said. "When can we practice again, Grandpa Max?"

"I'll take a look at my schedule and make sure to dedicate a few hours to you as often as I can."

Astrid considered his words before nodding. "Okay. Thank you, bye!" She ran back towards the house, leaving the adults alone.

"Thanks for this, Max. She's never said so, but I know she was down about not being able to use her breath." Chloe smiled up at him. "My little girl is growing up so fast."

Saul rolled his eyes. "That isn't what you said to me a month ago."

"Shut up, you," she grumbled. "So, what's next for you two then? Are you, um, going to take this public soon or wait until after you get sworn in?"

Max chuckled. "It was nothing, I'm happy to teach Astrid. As for coming out to the public. I believe I shall enjoy the pleasure of courting Ēostre in public. We know how the world loves its gossip, and I look forward to giving them something to watch."

Chapter 14

Mahuika entered the premier antiquities store of Boston, Massachusetts with a smile on her face. A scent hung in the air and permeated the open lobby, wafting to her from glossy wooden shelves holding rows of leather-bound books. The place smelled like dust and old things, aged paper, priceless memorabilia, and treasured goods protected by collector after collector.

It smelled like trash and worthless relics to Mahuika, who preferred the gleam of gold and odorless gems. She gave a disdainful sniff as she passed a dress form mannequin clothed in a vintage dress from the 40s.

She had a storehouse full of them, and no desire to revisit the style any time soon. If not for Loki insisting she carry out the task herself, she wouldn't bother to step one foot inside the witch's little storefront shack.

Classical jazz whispered from the shop's speakers, contrasting the junk in the aisles. Mahuika passed old signs and out of print paperbacks lining shelves that were tidy but full.

A bright-eyed young woman in a sophisticated pencil skirt and low-cut white blouse approached Mahuika. "Hello, ma'am. Have you been helped?"

"I would like to speak to the owner."

"She's busy at the moment. Is there anything I may do to help you?"

"Yes, find your employer."

"Can I give her a message?" the associate asked.

The smile slipped from Mahuika's face. When she breathed in, she smelled the saccharine sweet scent of mana clinging to the girl's skin, human magic and sorcery interwoven in a subtle seduction spell. Probably some trick to force men to part more easily with their money.

"Yes. You may pass her a message." She leaned forward and dropped her voice to a terse whisper. "Tell your employer if she values the safety of this dust-infested hut, she will provide her company to Mahuika of Aoteoroa. If you know what I am and understand what I can do to you, you will deliver this message to her without fail, little witch."

The girl's mouth opened, only to snap shut again in wide-eyed terror.

"There's no need to threaten my employees, you old snake," Agnes spoke up from an open doorway. "Let's talk in private. Mira, tend shop for me."

"Yes, ma'am."

As Agnes led the way to the rear of the store, they passed over an enchanted threshold to discourage thievery. The magical charm made Mahuika's skin tingle and nothing more, a mild irritation that couldn't cause her harm even if she did decide to steal. She sniffed disdainfully.

Beyond the initial storefront, they reached a chamber where the decor met Mahuika's initial expectations. Glass cases lined the walls, housing all manner of shiny and expensive baubles, a transformation taking the hag's shop from tacky thrift store to high-end antique dealership.

The witch whirled to face her once they were in private. She'd touched up her appearance with magic, smoothing the worst of her wrinkles and stuffing her old bones into a chic dove gray suit. From ninety to late fifties in a single spell. "What do you want?" She wasted no time with pleasantries.

"I came to enlist your aid in bringing down Maximilian."

The old crone cackled. "And why would I do that when he is doing exactly what I hope? Business will be booming once people realize my spells and fortune telling are legitimate."

"I am telling you, not asking you, Agnes the Black." The dragoness curled her lips back from her teeth.

"You crossed the line by coming into my shop to make demands. Scaring my student that way and threatening my belongings. I don't have to do anything you tell me to do. Now get out of here. I have tricks for dragons like you, and even *you* won't like what happens if I use it."

"Ohhh, yes, your tricks." Mahuika smiled slyly and removed a sleek mobile phone from her purse. "Once I tell the rest of the dragon council about your little trophy, what do you think will happen to you then? Will your little tricks protect you against a flock of us? Perhaps I should call Watatsumi now…"

Agnes silenced. Her features became stony and her eyes narrowed. "Loki told you?"

"Now you understand how much he desires Maximilian's downfall. He and Ēostre must suffer."

"And how should I do that?"

"Release the heartstone."

Agnes paled. "You don't know what you're asking."

"On the contrary, I know exactly what I'm asking — for you to release the one thing on this earth able to ruin their happiness and tear them apart. Now, where do you keep it?"

"What a bossy lizard," Agnes muttered under her breath. "Here." The witch slid an oil painting aside to reveal a digital safe embedded in the wall. Opening it revealed a single treasure, a fist-sized ruby on a soft bed of velvet. It pulsed with a gentle light, rhythmic, slow, and filled with magic.

"How long will it take for the spell to take effect? How long?" Mahuika asked. She licked her lips and followed in the hag's shadow.

"I can't do this kind of work in the blink of an eye," Agnes snapped. "You're a dragon. Have some patience."

"How long will it take?" Mahuika repeated, enunciating each word. Her eyes flashed.

"A year, maybe two. Anything more may be courting danger. It'll risk everything."

Mahuika's nostrils flared. Instinct told her to crush the hag and take the jewel to one of the crone's dark acquaintances, but on the other hand, none of them were likely to understand the spell. "Fine. Keep me updated on your progress. I want Maximilian ruined."

"Why go to such extremes? This won't stop him from going forward to expose us."

"It's not about that anymore. This is revenge."

Chapter 15

Max slid behind the sophisticated desk in the oval office and ran his fingers over the polished wood surface. Despite having more than a year behind him since his inauguration into the White House, every day still felt like a miracle. They were one step closer to accomplishing their dream of uniting shifters, magicians, and humans by coming out to the world.

Although enjoyable, the first year hadn't been all smooth sailing. Between adjusting to the presidency and giving Ēostre the proper courtship she'd deserved, his days were busy and the nights long.

The staff went out of their way to make him happy, and fixtures from his old life in California were brought to add a sense of normalcy to his new but stressful routine. Hiring Lynette onto the housekeeping staff had at least provided a familiar face who knew his personal preferences. It also kept the young woman in a job, since he'd felt awful about laying her off after his departure from the governor's mansion.

For the most part, they kept the truth about his nature a closely guarded secret, and most members of his Secret Service detail remained none the wiser. Key members in the CIA, FBI, and Department of Defense knew, of course — Ian had given them full disclosure. The head honchos had watched Max with greedy eyes during their first meeting together, thrilled with the idea of a leader who could breathe napalm and rain fire from the skies on their enemies.

Max didn't plan to let them use him as a weapon, however. He lacked the volatile nature his fire dragon kin were known for and had visions of peace for the future.

Ēostre entered the office and shut the door behind her. "Aren't you finished working for the day?"

"Not yet. I have a few e-mails to answer, and then we can meet with the planner."

"Mm… well, make it quick then."

The world's most gorgeous distraction settled on the edge of his desk, facing him with her legs crossed. Her navy blue, sleeveless dress would have been knee-length on most women, but her long legs revealed inches of thigh.

"I can't believe it's been over a year already," she murmured. He idly caressed up and down her shin, appreciating the smooth silk under his touch. Sweet Ancestors, he couldn't concentrate on his work with her near, and a year of making love to her in every way imaginable hadn't curbed his urges in the least.

"*I* can't believe we'll be married this upcoming week. Are you excited?"

"It's only a silly human tradition," the dragoness said. Contrary to her words, a warm smile curved her lips and color bloomed over her cheeks, revealing it was more to her than a stupid mortal custom. It had come to mean something to them as yet another manifestation of their love.

Maximilian shutdown the computer and stood. "The rest can wait until tomorrow. I'll answer them before the teleconference with the British Prime Minister."

Arm in arm, they left his work behind and traveled to the covered walkway. Her heels clicked against the ground, a methodic noise amidst the chirping birds.

"Where did you leave Spartacus?" Ēostre suddenly asked.

"In my room. He likes to try and chime in on phone calls, the rascal. I asked Lynette to come fetch him during lunch."

Ēostre laughed. For his birthday, the family had gotten together and discovered an African Grey breeder preparing to retire several specimens from his program. Spartacus was an exceptional creature with a smattering of red plumage amidst the typical gray feathers. They loved him dearly, especially Astrid. He was family to them. "Yes, I can imagine a parrot offering advice to world leaders isn't well accepted."

"Hopefully he hasn't nested in your underthings again. He took personal offense to the last time he was parted from my office, and I think it would hurt his feelings to exclude him from the wedding, too," Max jested. Ēostre had appropriated a few drawers in his bureau for her own personal belongings, dedicating one to French-cut negligee, softening the blow of losing his personal space. As far as he was concerned, she could have the entire dresser and all the closets if she'd fill them with silk panties and corsets.

Max's status as a single man made their occasional nights together scandal-free. No one cared about her sleeping over and warming his bed because it was expected, and most of all, because they'd been labeled adorable by the press. Reporters went out of their way to photograph Ēostre, and they loved her impeccable style.

"He'd better not poop on my dress at the wedding or he'll be a roasted bird," she half-teased, half-threatened.

"Astrid would never forgive you." It hadn't taken long after the parrot became part of the White House for them to discover Astrid had a unique talent with animals that extended beyond zebra keeping. She loved them, and they loved her in turn. Her natural proclivity for animal handling transferred to her dragon form when creatures were given a chance to adjust to her presence.

Max and Teo had never seen anything like it in a cub so young. She was remarkable in every way, and with each new discovery, their full-blooded brethren grew even more intimidated by her, and by proxy, Teo's son Javier, who also was part human.

Their planner waited for them in the Palm Room, a woman in an elegant white and gold pantsuit who greeted them with an amiable smile. She had rosy cheeks and a pleasant face surrounded by a halo of golden curls.

"Are you two having jitters yet?"

"Hardly, Glinda. We were discussing the ring bearer," Ēostre replied, stealing a glance at her future husband.

Glinda's smile widened. "I think it's absolutely adorable to include Spartacus. So long as he minds his manners."

"He and I will have a chat man to man," Max assured her, wearing a big grin on his face.

"Dragon to bird, you mean? Now come along. Let's discuss the final preparations."

They stepped back outside and travelled the few feet to the garden grounds. Tulips in every color bloomed amidst the rose bushes and trees.

"Now, the staff will complete the arrangements on the day. Here is my finalized layout." Glinda opened her binder, revealing digital sketches printed on fine paper. From the garden where the ceremony was set to take place, to the East Room's reception, they reviewed every detail and made minor adjustments as needed.

"This will be more spectacular than Teo and Marcy's wedding, and that's saying something." Glinda winked. "I'll provide a copy of the final plans to your security office, of course."

"He'll hire you to plan a birthday or something to get back on top," Max said. "His ego will demand it."

Both women laughed, but Glinda spoke up first. "More money for me. Now then, I'll keep in touch up until the day but other than that, we'll see each other at your wedding."

"Thank you, Glinda. You really are the best." Ēostre hugged her.

After their planner departed, Max took Ēostre's hand in his and led her back through the gardens. "Last chance to say screw it and elope to Vegas."

"Absolutely not, Bel. We are going to have a lovely wedding."

He brought her hands up to his mouth and brushed a kiss across her knuckles. "We are. One you deserve."

***

Ēostre twisted in front of the mirror to view her reflection from all angles. She was adorned in a masterpiece of champagne silk, flattering her curves where it flared out from the hips and created a majestic train. The lace embroidery reminded her of flowers and matched the chosen theme of their wedding: spring.

At first, Ēostre and Max didn't expect their fellow dragons to show interest in the event, especially those scorned by the recent — at least by dragon standards — decision to end the secrecy, but they proved her wrong when other wyrms and younger dragons arrived in force, even the creatures whom she thought were least likely to respect a mortal-laced affair.

"Tlaloc did not come to attend the ceremony, but he wishes you both well and wants you to have this on your day," Xochiquetzal said for her mate. The black dragoness shook her head and placed the contents of a velvet-lined pouch into Ēostre's hand. Small shards of polished dark blue volcanic glass glittered beneath the lights, connected by strands of silver.

"Xochi, this is beautiful. Did he—?"

"No, Tlaloc did not make this," her friend said, chuckling. "He does not have a single artistic bone in all of his body, but I love him just the same. This was a bauble he commissioned many centuries ago from none other than Maximilian himself, as a gift to me, and now we would both like for you to have it. It is blue obsidian, glass from a special volcano he and Belenos once explored as young drakes. So you see, my mate may not agree with what you plan to do, but he loves you both, and would see you happy no matter the disagreement."

Ēostre blinked her stinging eyes and swallowed through the tension constricting her throat. "Thank you, my friend. Help me put it on?" She adjusted her veil and tugged it aside for Xochi to secure the necklace.

"You're beautiful," Chloe gushed. "This is going to be amazing, you'll be the most gorgeous bride to ever strut her shit through the White House."

"I don't want to strut through shit, I want to look elegant," Ēostre said, scandalized by Chloe's choice of words.

Chloe laughed. "No! It means you'll be on point, fantastic, looking fabulous, and all that."

Astrid twirled in her pale, rose pink gown. She wore a woven flower crown in her hair, the stems artfully twined together. "I feel like a princess."

"So do I." Centuries of experience in preparing princesses for the crown hadn't prepared Ēostre to feel like one herself. "I *feel* beautiful, too."

"You've always been beautiful, Grandmother. Today just means everyone who doesn't already love you gets to know it, too."

She crouched down and pulled the girl in for a hug, careful not to muss her hair. "Thank you, sweetling," she whispered.

Astrid kissed her cheek. "I'm going to go see what Grandpa Max, Daddy, and Uncle Teo are doing. I hope they aren't drunk again. Daddy had so much tequila last night he couldn't walk."

"Astrid!"

"Well, it's true," the girl said, much to her mother's embarrassment.

"They'd better be sober," Chloe muttered darkly.

Ēostre promptly burst into tears the moment the little girl left. "She's so sweet." Once they began, the waterworks wouldn't stop until her chest heaved in spasms and her eyes stung. Chloe and

Xochi, like a bridal rapid response team, descended swiftly with tissues.

"Hey now, no crying. You'll ruin your make-up."

"She is right, Ēostre. This is your day for happiness and peace. Embrace it with joy instead of tears." The Latin dragoness gently pushed a strand of Ēostre's hair back from her face. "For such a silly mortal celebration, I have grown fond of attending these events. Humans are capable of creating the most beautiful and amazing traditions," she mused.

Ēostre sucked in a deep breath. "I don't know why I'm in such a fuss. I know we've already mated, that this doesn't mean anything, but..."

"Because it *does* mean something to you, Ēostre. It's your wedding day, and brides are allowed to get emotional. Still, I'm so glad we opted for the minimalist look," Chloe said while dabbing Ēostre's cheeks. "Because if we'd put a full face of makeup on you, it'd be ruined right now."

The door cracked open again, allowing Chloe's friend Marcy to lean in. "It's time! Come on, chicas... you look amazing and everyone is waiting. We have a full house, all abuzz with dragons, supernaturals, and shade-wearing special agents."

"Daddy's on his way, too." Astrid slid past Marcy into the room.

"Okay. Perfect then. Astrid, you're up first." Chloe turned her daughter toward the doors, but the girl peeked back and blew Ēostre a kiss.

"I love you, Grandma."

"I love you, too."

Astrid led the way down the aisle and sprinkled multicolored rose petals across the grass. Chloe followed behind her daughter in a matching dress, walking on satin slippers in lieu of heels.

"You are the very definition of elegance, Mother." Saul stepped in the doorway and offered his arm. "Are you ready?"

Ēostre looked up at her son. Something told her he was asking about more than the wedding, and she had to wonder if she was ready to officially profess her love to not only their fellow dragons, but to the rest of the world as well. "I am. I really am, Saul." There was no turning back. She'd already given Max her heart.

"Then let's get you to your husband-to-be."

On her son's arm, Ēostre couldn't imagine a day more perfect. As they stepped out into the garden the bridal march began to play, beautiful harp music filling the air with an ethereal quality. Everyone in attendance rose to their feet but she barely saw them. Hey eye, her every focus, was on Max.

"Don't rush," Saul muttered under his breath, giving her hand a squeeze. "While it might be amusing, it's far from dignified."

His humorous observation made her smile and loosened the last bit of nervous tension in her stomach. Each step forward brought her closer and closer to Max. Her mate. Her future.

He filled her vision, a handsome figure in his black tux with a ruby red tie and vest. The smile on his face was brighter than a volcano's heart and his eyes were solely on her.

"I leave you with a good man. One I'll be proud to call my stepfather," Saul murmured in a low voice for the pair of dragons alone. He gave her fingers a last squeeze before he placed her hands in Max's. "Take care of her."

"You have my word," Max promised.

Saul took his place at Max's side as Best Man, the guests retook their seats, and the officiant stepped forward. They had purposely chosen a secular ceremony, preferring to leave religion out of the equation. Dragons, who had been venerated as gods themselves at one time, didn't believe in any particular religious deity.

"Welcome, everyone," the man greeted. "Today is a day of celebration, and even a little bit of history. Before today, the only president to get married here in the White House was President Grover Cleveland, in 1886. But this isn't about history. This is about Maximilian, Ēostre, and their love."

Ēostre listened to the words about love and commitment without ever taking her gaze from her mate's. Despite the show for the human world, she took every word to heart.

"Do you, Maximilian, take Ēostre to be your wife?"

"I do, with everything that I am."

"And do you, Ēostre, take Maximilian to be your husband?"

"Completely."

The officiant smiled at them both. "The bride and groom have asked to exchange their own vows of love and fidelity as they present one another with their wedding bands. Maximilian, if you'd begin, please."

"A moment please, I need my ring bearer."

They reached the moment of truth. Ēostre hadn't actually seen Spartacus successfully perform what Max wanted. Her mate insisted for it to be a surprise.

Movement near the back rows caught her eye, Watatsumi with Spartacus on his arm. Everyone turned then to watch as Max held out his arm. He whistled once and his parrot took to the air.

Please don't fly off. Please don't fly off, she prayed. She had faith in Maximilian, and absolutely none in the naughty bird that had become part of their lives.

The African Grey soared across the garden. For a moment, as he made a circle around the rose trellis that served as their wedding bower, Ēostre was certain the bird would make a break for it with their shiny rings — not that she looked forward to wearing the bands for anything more than symbolism. It was the sentiment behind it that mattered most to her.

He didn't. He landed neatly on Max's upraised wrist and dropped a small pouch into the man's hand. Promptly, without missing a beat, he threw his wings up in the air and cried out, "Special day!" Tilting his head as he remembered the rest of his well-practiced surprise, Spartacus made a kissing noise up to her. "Love Ēostre."

"Good job, my friend. Thank you." Maximilian turned a smug smile back to his mate and spilled the rings from the pouch onto his open palm as Spartacus launched himself off of Max's arm and settled on the top of the trellis. A few attendees clapped or laughed at the display.

"That was lovely." Ēostre took the ring meant for Max and cupped it in her damp palm.

"A wise man once said less is more," Maximilian began as he clutched her hands in both of his. "And when it comes to summing up my feelings, Ēostre, I find no amount of words can adequately communicate my love for you. From the first day we met, I knew my heart could belong to you and no one else."

The simple gold band he slipped on her left hand was adorned with delicate etchings in a floral knotwork pattern. She recognized Max's handiwork in the design.

"I never thought my heart would open again after past heartbreak, yet you snuck in, took me as I am, and brought light to my darkened spirit." Her fingers trembled. Her entire body buzzed with joy and love, so much that she didn't know how she managed to contain it. Her dragon wanted to fly. To break free and soar in an elated aerial dance with her new husband. "You are the sun who brought me clear skies, Max, and each day with you has been brighter than the last."

"Beautiful words from both of you. Here, among your family and friends, and before our entire nation, you have affirmed your love and choice to join your lives. Therefore, it is my honor to pronounce your union as man and wife. You may kiss your—"

Ēostre didn't wait for the officiant to finish. She leaned in first and claimed Max as her own with a searing kiss. His arms came around her and pulled her close while the guests cheered and clapped. There were even a few catcalls.

"Why Mrs. Emberthorn," Max said in a voice pitched low, for her ears only. "Save it for the honeymoon."

"Can we skip the reception and leave now?"

Max's husky chuckle warmed her ear and raised goosebumps across her skin. "Soon, my love. Soon."

Beside them, Saul cleared his throat. "I do believe your audience is waiting to greet the newlyweds."

As one, they turned to face the joyous faces of their gathered audience. With his arm around her, Ēostre had never felt more loved.

"We'd be delighted if you would all join us in the East Room for the reception. There might even be dancing." Max grinned and gave everyone a wave.

Dinner gave way to toasts. Some made Ēostre laugh, while others brought tears to her eyes. Astrid even took a turn at the mic. The young girl won everyone's hearts when she welcomed "Uncle" Max to the family and threw her arms around him.

Chloe was right about my make-up. I'd be a mess by now if we'd gone heavier.

A string quartet and pianist provided the music for dancing across the elaborately decorated room. Ēostre made a special request for their first song, and as Max glided her across the floor in his arms, she came to know true peace and bliss.

At the conclusion of a perfect day, they parted from their friends and family after receiving plentiful hugs, well wishes, and kisses. Their honeymoon had taken months of planning thanks to the measures of their security detail, but Hawaii awaited them along with sun, beaches, and fruity cocktails.

And Speedos.

Chapter 16

Hawaii had always been a favorite place to visit, an exotic delight with plenty of volcanic activity to dazzle Maximilian and abundant flora to charm his new wife. With five activity-filled days already behind them, he was relaxed and in no rush to return home.

As the morning sunlight streamed behind him through the window, he took a moment to study Ēostre's sleeping face. He never tired of looking at her. She slept like a model on a bedroom photoshoot, clothed in only a slinky piece of French negligee she claimed was paying homage to his country of origin. With her hair a wild, silver halo all around her, Ēostre's long lashes lay against her cheek and one fair hand rested just beneath her breast. The lacey trim of the nightie skimmed her naked bottom and barely covered her hips.

They had plans to attend a luau later in the evening, but the rest of the day was theirs to do whatever they wanted. As far as Max was concerned, they could spend it in bed. He was already getting hard, his cock firming until it created a silky tower in the sheets. Fortunately, female dragons matched their mates when it came to libido, and she never exhausted of him.

His cellphone rang, interrupting his building daydream. The device had remained silent for their entire trip and he'd agreed to carry it in case someone needed to contact him for emergencies only. A quick look at the Caller ID made him frown.

"Kenneth, I'm enjoying my vacation. This had better be damned important."

"Turn on the TV now," his vice president said in a terse voice. "I'm afraid your honeymoon must be postponed, Maximilian. We have an urgent problem. Your security detail has been notified of the dilemma and are prepared to escort you to the airfield."

"Kenneth, what the hell is going on?" Max leaned across Ēostre's dozing form and grabbed the remote. "What channel am I looking for?"

"Any of them."

It took only seconds to understand the urgency and tension behind his friend's voice. The imagery on the screen was that of a nightmare.

Mount Rainier Erupts, the news ticker read below a photograph of the majestic mountain.

"Ēostre, wake up." Max put his hand on her hip and gave his slumbering wife a shake. "We need to get back to Washington."

"Max, there's more," Palmer continued over the line. "Initial reports are saying something came out with the eruption. Something large that's still flying around up there."

"What?"

"I'm trying to get more information but that's all we have so far. We can't put birds in the air with so much ash so we're relying on ground cameras. People are uploading videos to Facebook and Youtube."

"Instead of evacuating?"

"There was no warning before the blast. We're getting out everyone we can but… it's not good, Max."

Ēostre groggily sat up for a look at the screen.

"Kenneth, there's no time to wait for our pickup. Ēostre and I will be there shortly."

"What? How—"

"Trust me, we'll be there in less than half an hour." He disconnected the call and turned up the volume on the television. Grabbing the nearest clothes at hand, Max tugged on a pair of khakis and a golf shirt. He tossed Ēostre a sundress.

"Max, look. It… no, it can't be."

He turned his attention to the flat screen on the wall and froze. The news team had zoomed in on the angry mountain and caught the mysterious object soaring above.

"It's Fafnir," he breathed.

"No! This isn't possible. I found his lifeless body with a sword through his heart. I watched you bury his corpse in the heart of Mount Rainier!" Ēostre cried. "He was dead!"

Max set his hands on her shoulders and turned her to the screen again. "It's him, Ēostre. Look at the horns! Look!"

The camera focused on the shape rising in the air. Despite the cloud of ash swirling in the sky, he saw a prominent figure with a crimson hide and black tipped feathers. A wicked pair of spiraling dark horns corkscrewed from the creature's brow. They were enormous, and Max had always envied his friend for his stately appearance.

"Fafnir," she whispered with a palm pressed over her heart.

Adrenaline pounded in Max's veins. They had to get moving, had to return to the White House to begin disaster measures, but at the same time he felt an obligation to the woman he loved more than his own life. Ēostre was breaking right in front of him, and there wasn't anything he could do to help her.

"Ēostre, love, can you feel your bond to him?" he asked.

She shook her head. "I don't... I don't feel him," she whispered on a choked sob. "We were soulbound, but I do not feel him. How could this happen?"

Lacking the answers to her frantic questions made him feel all the more helpless. Silver dragons had an innate talent for arcane spells and made the best sorcerers among their kind. The most magical thing Max had done in all of his life was learn to make volcanos erupt on command for a spoiled little girl and charm a few torches in his lair.

He frowned as he watched the live footage unfold. Ēostre quaked against him with tears streaming down her cheeks, but there was no doubt about the identity of the colossal dragon bathed in the light of an erupting volcano. Maximilian would know him anywhere, and he had personally clawed his way into the soul of the mountain and buried Fafnir as per Ēostre's instructions.

He had cried over that dragon's chilly corpse.

"I'll send you to the White House but I'm going to the volcano."

"Ēostre, you can't go."

"I must! We all must. Until we know what has happened, any dragon in the area should be out there now, helping and *protecting* these people. We don't have time for politics."

"You can't stop an erupting volcano on your own, and there are no dragons in that state. Not a single one!"

"I'll ask Saul to come. Mahasti can send him there in a blink."

"Saul isn't a true volcanic dragon, Ēostre, and he lacks your control over storm currents. We need an earth dragon and potentially a water dragon, otherwise the lahar flood will cause a tidal wave and wipe out everything," Max said as he removed his clothes again. "Send me ahead first, and I'll work my way into the magma chamber to disperse and decrease the pressure. You need to get Xochiquetzal and Tlaloc."

"But Fafnir—"

"Will be seen to," he assured her. "But as you said, the volcano and the people come first."

Ēostre drew herself up and swiped at her damp cheeks. "Yes. Yes, you're right."

"Whatever has happened, Ēostre, we will get to the bottom of it," he told her gently. Max dried her remaining tears and kissed her face, sighing with relief when she let him hold her close. "I love you."

"Where do you want me to place you?"

"Above the volcano."

Even the portal lacked luster and brilliance, appearing as little more than a colorful ring of dimmed light surrounding a window to a world dulled by volcanic debris. Thankfully, none of it came through. Her doorway was exit only.

"Max?" Ēostre whispered.

"Yes?" He paused in front of it, preparing to jump.

"I love you. Be safe."

Holding his mate's words close to his heart, Maximilian stepped through the portal. Seconds later, with his wings pinned close against his body, the fire dragon Belenos was plummeting toward the open volcano.

***

Ash filled the air at an exponential rate, billowing from the top of the de-capped mountain. Its entire peak was missing, but the terrible cloud didn't disguise the mighty silhouette perched on the rim.

Against all logic and common sense, Ēostre wanted to go to the man she'd once loved with all of her soul. But Max was right. Fafnir could wait.

"Where shall I take these ashes?" Thor called from beside her.

Ēostre reached out again with her magic, felt the winds and manipulated them as Thor prepared to take hold of the magical leash she created from their energy. They both hovered a few hundred yards from the volcano's sweltering heat, buoyant on the force of their own storm winds. With a combination of magic and her own innate power over storms, Ēostre had condensed the volcanic matter into a funnel.

As for the volcano, it was stifling even for them, the air so hot she could barely breathe. It issued a never-ending geyser of minerals and pulverized rock. Tiny bits of volcanic glass clung to her hide and silver mane, coloring her body dull gray.

"Scatter them as best you can across unpopulated areas and the sea. I will continue to funnel it toward you!"

When Tlaloc refused to lend aid to the humans, his son volunteered in his stead. Xochiquetzal and Teo wasted no time upon their arrival, and worked as a team. While Teo molded the ground from above, his mother passed through the earth like a ghost. Together, the two created natural but safer paths for the lahar to travel. As Max had predicted, the filthy meltwater spilled down the mountainside, dragging boulders, cars, and wrecked buildings in its wake.

Ēostre couldn't estimate the number of deaths. There were mortals in danger everywhere.

What if this is Fafnir's doing? she wondered. From afar, she saw the motionless ancient watching her in return. He hadn't lifted a claw to help, and Max hadn't emerged from the volcano.

Saul circled low over the ground with Mahasti on his back. The sight of him generated as much terror as the erupting volcano itself, but where they saw fleeing evacuees, they also saved lives. More than one human found themselves instantly teleported from danger to the emergency shelters set up for exactly such a situation. Their wishes for safety made the job easy, and a genie wouldn't act against a human's desires.

Through it all, Fafnir remained perched on the crater's rim overlooking the destruction below. He did nothing to assist but also nothing to hinder. His hulking form remained still as stone.

What is going through your mind, Ēostre wondered.

As Ēostre circled around again, the flare of volcanic debris thinned and began to taper. Half an hour later, little more than a few wisps of steam billowed from within the enormous hole.

Down below, Saul broke away from the other two dragons and approached on swift wings. "Mother!" he called to her. Mahasti floated alongside him in her natural state, a being of pure smoke and fire.

"Mother? Should we go to him?"

She shook her head. "You go home. None of us can predict what will happen next now that the disaster has been curbed. I imagine we'll see news choppers and military aircraft soon."

"But Father—"

"Go home," she repeated. "Let me have words with him."

Saul bowed his head but his reluctance was clear. "I will make things ready for him, should you manage to bring him home."

Mahasti reached up and took Saul by one of his huge claws. "Come, Saul. Let us give thanks to our friends and leave your mother to handle this."

Before Saul could protest, the genie took them away in a puff of smoke.

Time to face the impossible...

"Fafnir?" Ēostre glided down to the crater rim and found a solid perch.

The world beyond the mountain looked dull and lifeless, crushed beneath the rubbish expelled prior to their arrival. Had it been a normal event, seismic activity and other signs may have given the locals a chance to save their possessions and their lives. They weren't so lucky this time.

Fafnir resembled a wild animal. The intelligent light was gone from his eyes. He scrambled along the edge, keeping her within his sight but refusing to approach. His body was poised for the attack, his wings unfurled and ready to take flight.

"Fafnir. It is me. Do you not recognize your..." Mate? Did she dare to call herself his mate now?

He didn't answer. Instead, he continued to stare at her with the same dispassionate eyes. A cool, yellow-eyed glower that traced icy fingers down her spine.

"Fafnir?" she whispered again in their draconic tongue. "Please answer. Tell me what's wrong. Tell me how you're here before me now. We saw your body. You died!" Tears welled at the corners of her eyes and slid down her cheeks. He chuckled, unmoved by her show of emotion.

"What does it matter how I am here?" he finally rumbled. "I am awakened, I am here. Perhaps I never died." He moved closer to approach, reminding her of a predator stalking a rabbit in the field. "I smell the stink of another male on your flesh. What have you done in my absence, Ēostre?"

"I…" Could he possibly blame her for moving on after more than a century of mourning, she wondered? He'd been lifeless at the time, not in a state of torpor, and yet somehow his body seemed exactly as she remembered. "You were dead, Fafnir. It took me years to move on without you."

"And yet you seem to have no difficulty now," he said snidely.

Ēostre recoiled from the stinging words. "I mourned you for over a century after we laid you to your final rest."

The larger dragon snorted.

"And what of our son? He passed my vision once as I regained my wits, but where has he gone? Why is he not here beside me?"

"I sent him away for his safety until I could verify you were indeed… you," she answered. "He has mated and fathered a child of his own."

"My son has a cub? Ah, Brigid must have given him such fine, strong children. And you told me it couldn't be done. That the girl was too willful and disobedient to Maximilian."

She hesitated a heartbeat, then shook her head. "No, Fafnir. Not Brigid. Please, come with me. Come with me far from this mountain to meet the rest of our family. Saul is eager to speak to you."

Ēostre noticed Maximilian climbing the crater at a sedate pace, bits of magma still clinging to his hide. Once or twice, he paused to preen the bits of hardening slag from his feathers then his eyes met hers, and she realized for the first time through the emotions flooding their link, that he was afraid.

Afraid of losing her.

Never, she thought, when he stopped to watch from a safe distance. Fafnir caught his scent and turned his head sharply toward the other red dragon.

"Belenos, why do you smother and calm my volcano?"

"There were many humans nearby who suffered and died during this eruption,"

"Humans," Fafnir spat. He whirled to face his fellow fire dragon with both wings spread and his feathers fanned in a dominant display. "Since when have they ever mattered to you?" His booming voice carried for miles across the skies.

"They've always mattered to me, Fafnir," Max replied uncertainly. He held his ground, choosing neither to approach nor yield. "Perhaps you've forgotten that during your century of sleep."

"A sleep during which you saw fit to steal Ēostre from me."

Maximilian flinched. "I would never have stolen Ēostre from you. After she found your lifeless corpse, I buried you myself with my own two claws. I took you into the heart of this mountain and laid you to rest in the rivers of magma below Rainier."

"If your words are true then how am I here?"

Ēostre and Maximilian exchanged looks.

"That, Fafnir, is exactly what we intend to find out."

***

Max couldn't stop looking at him. He'd spent decades missing his friend, wondering if Fafnir had truly joined the Ancestors who watched over them. Most dragons, especially their earth dragon kin, believed the souls of the departed became butterflies who guided their loved ones in death.

Once, when explaining it to Brigid, she'd asked why dragons could go from being so awe-inspiring and powerful, to something so fragile. It hadn't made sense to her.

"Because they leave their strength to those who loved them, my dear," he'd said to her then. "As we are still alive and need it much more."

Getting Fafnir away from the volcano became easier after promises of bringing him to both his son and hoard. With Mahasti's help, they teleported him to the manor and provided the naked dragon shifter with appropriate clothing to don before meeting his grandcub. Max had to explain the child wasn't accustomed to nudity, much to Fafnir's confusion.

"Why," he asked suspiciously, "is such a trifling matter as nudity a problem for my grandchild?"

"You'll see," Max said. He sighed and prepared himself. With luck, Watatsumi had lingered in the manor to help reacquaint their old friend with the modern world.

Fafnir plucked at his borrowed clothes with a look of disgust on his face. Max sympathized. It had taken him a long time to adjust to the modern era's restrictive clothing styles and synthesized fabrics.

"Tell me, what do you think of the manor itself?" Max asked, quickly changing the subject. They walked from the garage to the front of the home, where Fafnir admired it with him.

"My son has made a palace of my former hoard," he remarked with awe in his voice. He craned his head to gaze up at the extravagant stretch of glass windows and metal framework built into a mountainside — a work of art any dragon could love.

"They're called manors these days, Fafnir," Max said. Fafnir shot him a dirty look, but Max grinned and shrugged back at him.

"But why do we stand about here? I can smell the presence of many others inside this dwelling and yet we are unattended."

"You must understand, Fafnir, your... return has been a surprise to all of us. But yes, you are right. Let's enter." Max opened the door wide and gestured for Fafnir to enter, and within moments, they received an enthusiastic greeting.

"Father! Welcome!" Saul called from the top of the stairs.

Max breathed a sigh of relief as the younger dragon bounded down the flight of stairs. It was shaped like an elegant horseshoe, leading up to a landing and railed corridor that divided the home into an east and west wing. Chloe descended the stairs moments later in one of her best dresses. The cream fabric hugged her curves and flared at the hips into a knee length skirt.

"Welcome to our home," Chloe greeted the two men in strong, fluent Draconic. With nearly eighteen years to learn the ancient language, she spoke it as well as a born dragon. It was a beautiful language, lyrical and harsh like the bastard child of German and Tolkien's Elvish.

"Ah, my son, look at you." Fafnir grasped Saul by the shoulders and studied him in quiet approval. "I see you have done well.

"Hello, Chloe," Max offered quietly.

"Hi, Max."

Undeterred by his father's dismissal of Chloe, Saul grinned broadly and gestured with one hand to a wide archway. "Please, come with me. Let us be seated and comfortable while we catch up. I have much to tell you."

Moving in a brisk pace, Fafnir moved ahead of them and breezed past Chloe without even a glance. "Where's the cub? I would like to meet the fine child produced from our line."

"Mother wanted to talk to her. They'll be down in a moment," Saul said.

"Ah, good. Then send your girl for your finest mead. We must celebrate this joyous reunion."

An awkward hush fell over the assembled dragons before Saul cleared his throat. "Father, Chloe is not my servant. She is my wife, and mother of my child."

Fafnir snapped his gaze toward Chloe then back to his son. He laughed.

"You were always prone to jokes, my son. As if I would believe this concubine to be anything more than a mere pet. Now, enough games. I wish to meet your mate and cub."

Saul's polite smile wavered and finally vanished. "No game, Father. I speak the truth."

"Impossible. A dragon born of a human woman?"

"Quite possible, Father. Chloe nearly died birthing her seventeen years ago. If not for the healing magic Mother taught to me, Astrid and I would be alone. She has dragon's blood in her veins now and appears to be as immortal as we are."

Proud as ever, Saul held Chloe against him with an arm around her waist.

Ēostre and Astrid's appearance at the door stalled any further argument from Fafnir. Max resisted the urge to cross over and take Ēostre in his arms, unwilling to openly flaunt their bond in his friend's face. Things were complicated enough.

"I'll get the drinks," Maximilian offered. Fafnir's arrival had made an outsider of him, no longer necessary, and certainly unwanted. He felt the hatred brimming off of the other dragon every time their eyes met.

He'll never forgive me for taking her away, and how can I blame him? He's right. I took her.

"Thank you, Max," Chloe murmured to him in passing. "Astrid, honey, come say hello."

Fafnir nodded his head in approval. "I see you have named her after one of the Ancestors."

The girl took three shy steps forward before she shook her head and ducked back toward the doorway. Saul caught her around the waist and turned her toward his father.

"No! No!" Astrid screamed, wriggling in his hold. She squirmed her way free from his grip and bolted behind Maximilian. Saul blinked and tilted his head down to appraise his daughter. Of all the people to use as cover, she'd chosen Max. She shook and trembled behind him.

"Astrid? Come meet your grandfather," Ēostre said.

"I don't want to."

"Astrid, please," Saul repeated. "Your grandfather would like to see you."

Astrid buried her clawed fingers into Max's slacks, achieving an unexpected partial transformation most dragons didn't master until they were decades old. He couldn't have parted her from him without losing some skin for his trouble. She hid her face into the small of his back and made a pitiful sobbing noise.

"She will come to see me *now*." Fafnir's voice took on a sharp edge.

Like hell if he planned to just peel her off and hand her over. Max frowned and felt behind him until he found Astrid's shoulder. "Worry not, young one. Why don't you go and play in your room. Your grandfather must be very tired."

"He isn't my grandfather. You're my grandfather."

The room became completely silent. Still. Listening to the thundering sound of his own beating heart, Max watched the other immortals in the room and waited. Chloe spoke first.

"Do as Maximilian says, Astrid. Go play with Svetlana."

Astrid bolted away without needing to be told again.

Fafnir's face contorted into a mask of rage. "What right does this human cockpuppet have to send my grandchild away? Saul, remove your pet from my sight."

"She is my *mate*, Father."

Ēostre also jumped to her daughter-in-law's defense. "I don't blame Chloe for sending her away. And you have no right to insult her in her own home. How dare you!" she cried.

"What is she to me? Where *is* Brigid? How has she tolerated this blasphemy?"

Once again, a hush fell over the remaining adults. Max struggled against the surging of emotion, until Chloe, sensing his pain, stepped forward and raised her chin.

"I killed her. She refused Saul one too many times, and after we mated, Brigid chose to claim him. She challenged me to a fight to the death and I killed her."

Fafnir snarled. "Is this true, Maximilian? How could you bear to defend the human responsible for your cub's death?"

"Brigid made her mistake. She had every opportunity to accept Saul. We knew this, Fafnir. From the moment I told her of our decision, she hated him. We laughed and told each other she'd grow to love him in time, continuing our plans and ignoring your son's discomfort. Chloe cannot be held responsible. As her father, I bear that sin, and I alone."

"You have grown weak in the time since my hibernation. You are not the Belenos of my memories. Be gone from my sight. You are a fraud."

"Father—"

"And you, my son. I never thought the day when come when you humiliated my legacy in such a way. A mortal and a half-breed spawn who has no respect for her elders."

Saul was stunned to speechlessness, and Max couldn't believe his ears as Fafnir continued to rail against Chloe. A quick look at the other adults revealed similar states of disbelief, tears in Ēostre's eyes, and fear on Chloe's face.

"Slay her now and I will consider this behind us and in the past. Kill her."

"Father… I cannot. And even if I were able, I could never harm the mother of my cub. She gave me Astrid." Saul paused, inhaled another shuddered breath, and whispered. "She carries my second child, and I would die before I allowed either of them to come to harm."

Fafnir sneered. "Another abomination. I see what little respect you have taught the first for her elders. I refuse to remain among the disgraced."

He strode from the room without further word, leaving everyone in stunned silence. Ēostre sank against the couch and dropped her face into both hands. Saul, frozen to the spot, merely stared.

"I don't… I don't understand. What's wrong with him, Mother? He's never behaved… the father of my memories wasn't like this."

"I don't know, Saul."

"Is it truly him? Perhaps it's an imposter," Max suggested, clinging to shreds of hope.

"I considered that, Belenos," Ēostre whispered. "But he is aware of things only my Fafnir would know. He knows secrets kept between the two of us."

Her Fafnir.

The words stabbed him with the might of a thousand lances. At the same time, Ēostre recognized her mistake and threw her arms around him tightly. "He was my Fafnir once, Maximilian, but you are mine now. You," she whispered harshly. "I don't know what that thing is, but he isn't the man I once loved."

"He can't be allowed to leave," Watatsumi interjected from the couch. Through it all, he had been a silent spectator to Fafnir's explosion.

Max fell into the seat beside him. "Of course not. Where could he possibly go when he only speaks Old Norse and Middle English?" Max muttered. "He had begun to shy away from mortals long before Saul was born, and if he finds a world populated by them, there's no telling what he'll do."

"He is in the hoard. As long as he is there, I see no harm in him remaining in our home," Saul said. He folded his arms against his chest. "I will keep Chloe and Astrid away from it, and him, for now."

"What are we going to do?" Ēostre asked. "What if he's dangerous? I am not afraid of your father, but what will you do if he snaps or decides... Chloe's presence is intolerable?"

"If he decides such," Saul said dryly, "we have a dragon-slaying sword and a pregnant woman who knows how to use it. I think we'll survive. I don't want to harm my father, but I won't allow him to threaten my mate or my children. We also have—"

"Me," Mahasti said as she materialized. A hazy outline appeared first before the rest of her body followed, trailing smoke. "I will remain vigilant while Fafnir is present. I give my word he will harm no one for as long as I am here. In the meantime, Astrid is safe with Leiv in our home, and the timing is perfect since she and Svetlana asked me about a sleepover only a week ago."

"Perfect timing," Saul agreed.

"What will you do?" Chloe asked Max. "You guys are plastered all over the news. It's panic out there between all of the scientists trying to identify you, the evacuees Saul and Mahasti saved, the government clamming up about it, and the media swearing it's a conspiracy."

"I don't know. Right now, I need to get to the White House. The world knows we exist and want answers. They'll expect me to make a statement about what's happened."

"There's some guy on the television claiming it's aliens, so you better hop to it," Chloe replied.

Ēostre turned to her son and embraced him tightly. "Saul," she whispered. "I am sorry. I am so sorry for this. I will stay to watch also. You should not have to do this alone when he is also my responsibility."

"No, Mother. Maximilian needs you by his side."

"I will stay," Watatsumi informed them. "Perhaps I can make Fafnir see reason in a world gone mad."

Chapter 17

Maximilian and Ēostre discovered a circus awaiting them at Washington, and it worsened when they stepped through her portal into the middle of the panicking vice president's office.

The security agents whirled, one with a hand on his gun, only to freeze before it even cleared the holster.

"Thank you, my love."

Ēostre nodded. "They're in a magical state of sleep, but it won't last long. Speak fast."

Kenneth Palmer stared at her. Once the shock wore away, he turned his glowering face to Max. "Half an hour, you said."

"Relax, Kenneth. I'm here now and perfectly fine."

"Were you one of those dragons on the television?" Palmer hissed at him. "I can't believe you chose this moment to disappear. Your security team panicked, the White House has been in an uproar, and you left me here without any answers."

"Chastise me later, my friend." Maximilian smoothed his fingers over his suit jacket and maintained his poise. "Right now, I need a media team ready for a public address."

"I've had one standing by since this all began. They're set up in the Oval Office. I have reporters from every station clamoring for news."

"They can wait. What are the numbers so far? How many lives lost?"

"The early estimates are about one hundred and thirty-nine. Sixty unaccounted for. Now tell me what is happening and why there were so many of you there. It was something out of a sword and sorcery movie."

"An old friend of mine was buried in Rainier's magma pool once. He was deceased at the time, Kenneth. Slain by a dragon hunter and completely dead, but something seems to have resurrected him." The vice president opened his mouth to speak, but Max beat him to the punch, "I can tell you right now that he didn't cause it, but that volcanic eruption wasn't natural either."

"Shit." Palmer ran his hand through his thinning hair. "Well, we have too many videos on the internet and news to try and cover up this dragon issue. You have to come forward."

"I know. I'd planned on it."

Ēostre turned to address the other room occupants in the room, whispering under her breath. Their blank, slack-jawed faces and motionless poses resembled wax figures, but they awakened within seconds, including the one who had gone for his firearm. One by one, they blinked and shook their heads to clear away the fog.

None of them questioned his unusual appearance among them, and he knew he had Ēostre to thank. A little magic went a long way, but even she lacked the spells to fix the day's events. Sooner or later, he'd have to answer for their abrupt disappearance and the two hours they were missing.

One stepped aside and spoke in a hushed tone through his microphone, no doubt informing other agents Max had arrived.

"Do you want the press admitted?"

"No. They'll get their chance soon. For now I need to speak directly to the American public without interference." They headed down the hall as they talked, where Max noted an increased presence of the Secret Service. One of his own personal protection retinues fell into step behind them. Most remained outside once he stepped into his office, but two men followed inside and took up position by the door.

"Are we ready, everyone?"

"Yes, sir, Mr. President."

"You can do this, Bel." Ēostre hugged him tightly.

"Of course I can." He cracked a half-hearted grin at her. "I'm the president."

Once Ēostre took her place out of the camera's view, Maximilian settled behind the desk. His fingers automatically steepled and the gravity of the recent catastrophe came crashing down on him at once. He'd never felt all of his twenty-seven centuries before. Never. Now he felt every year.

Ēostre mouthed, "I love you" from the edge of the room.

"And we're live in five, four," the cameraman said, counting down the final three in silence.

"This afternoon, the world watched as the United States experienced a horrific natural disaster. In the aftermath of this tragedy, despite the loss of one hundred and thirty-nine lives during the eruption of Mount Rainier, attention has shifted to another development with just cause."

He clasped his hands together, palms clammy, and looked into the camera. He imagined the hundreds of thousands of faces staring at their television screens.

"Tonight, I want to address all your concerns, and to bring you the truth. Supernatural and magical beings of all varieties are real... and I am one of them," Maximilian said from behind his desk, his stoic features concealing the dismay ruling his thoughts.

"Paranormal creatures such as the ones sighted above Mount Rainier are known as dragons. I am still gathering the facts about what has happened so that if wrongdoing has occurred, the responsible parties may be punished. The truth is that we don't know yet why this dragon has appeared. So far, we have no evidence to indicate the creature intentionally executed an act of aggression against the public, and every reason to believe the volcanic activity drew him from a deep slumber."

Max ignored the staring faces in his office and continued.

"My fellow Americans, I have dwelled in this country since its inception, long before its Founding Fathers first signed documents creating our nation. The United States has long been a melting pot of many cultures, and I want you to know nothing has changed since our emergence."

The faces continued to stare. Gaping mouths, wide eyes. One of the Secret Service agents assigned to his protection looked like a fish. He felt their condemnation and judgment piercing him. Their apprehension.

"I will hold a press conference tomorrow evening to address questions from the American public. It is my hope that in the coming days, we are able to pull together as a nation of many cultures, races, and now, other intelligent non-human species. In closing, I want to say here today, in the office you elected me to represent, that no matter your skin color, race, religion, *or species* we are all equal in this country. I ask you to give me a chance to prove that you have nothing to fear from us. Like you, we learn, work, and love. We are people. Thank you."

The light on the camera went dark.

"And we're off the air."

"You're all staring at me," Max said quietly. "If any of you have any questions, speak them now."

The young cameraman opened his mouth to speak, then snapped it shut without voicing his question. Instead he busied himself with breaking down his equipment.

A fresh-faced Secret Service agent assigned to Ēostre spoke up when everyone else failed. "If you're magical, sir, what about the first lady? Does this mean we're no longer needed?"

"I am also magical," she replied gently. "But your presence makes me feel safer just the same."

Max shook his head. "I'm not bulletproof, and you're not out of a job. None of you are out of a job until they've kicked me out of this office. As far as I can tell, you'll be needed even more in the coming days if any dragon-hunters decide it's time for me to make a hasty exit from office. Using the full extent of my abilities to protect myself would only terrify the world at this point."

"Dragon-hunters?" This time the cameraman found his voice. He looked over with wide eyes and pale cheeks. "You're a dragon? Like the thing we saw flying above the mountain on the reports?"

"Indeed," Max replied. He let his gaze turn to every man and woman in the room, meeting their gazes. "I know it sounds fantastical, insane even, but every word is true. We didn't disappear and give our security the slip in Hawaii to avoid our responsibilities," he spoke, addressing the agents currently assigned to him. They'd been giving him funny eyes since his return. "We took action before the volcano could claim more lives. We, along with several other dragons, hurried to Rainier and stopped it."

Ēostre joined him behind the desk and took his hand. Years ago when they first concocted their crazy plan to strive for office, he never imagined she'd stand beside him as his wife. Now he couldn't imagine being without her.

"If any of you choose to step down, I will understand. It will not be held against your service record, and you will be reassigned to a position of equal esteem and salary."

No one moved, though there were a few uncertain glances.

"You did well, Max," Palmer said kindly. "I suspect I'll receive a lot of questions asking if I've known all along about this. I'll tell them I only ran with you because you were a dragon and had to have better economic skills than our last big spenders." The vice president shot him a grin.

Max chuckled weakly. "I should show you my hoard one day, my friend. You guessed right. As for the rest of you, I ask you to keep what was said here off camera between us and key members of the service staff until tomorrow. They deserve to know the truth."

"Of course, sir," the same agent said. "As for requesting a transfer, you'll have to fire me to get me out of here now. My kids are going to lose their minds once they find out their dad is assigned to protect a *dragon*."

***

"What's happening back at Saul's estate? Have you called since we left?" Max asked while unknotting his tie. He fumbled with uncooperative fingers until Ēostre stepped in front of him and deftly removed the knot. "Thanks."

Ēostre smiled and kissed his lips tenderly. "Nothing to worry you just yet. They said Fafnir has spent the entire day coiled around some of his old treasures and counting the additions since he left. Saul removed Astrid to Leiv and Mahasti's cabin, of course, as he mentioned before."

"And Chloe?"

"She won't leave, but the…" She swallowed and struggled to maintain her reassuring smile. "The sword is in her possession. Just in case. As she's currently pregnant, she should be able to use its magic again." She returned to taking her accounting of the belongings in their bedroom as well as those in the rest of the Executive Residence. Somehow, in the span of hours during their wedding, every possession had been unpacked and placed as if she'd done it herself.

Max's figurine, the one he'd crafted and pieced together tenderly with love, had been placed on the stand located on her side of the bed. She liked it there where she could admire his talent.

"I understand," Max said. "It won't come to that, Ēostre. It won't. Fafnir loves his son, and he'd never do anything to make Saul hate him. Despise Chloe, he may, but hurting her and an unborn child is simply beyond his capability."

Ēostre whirled to face him. "The things he said, Bel. He ordered Saul to *kill* her."

Max shook his head. "He had to know Saul couldn't do that. When I look at your son and his wife, I can sense the soul bond surging between them, just as he could sense the bond uniting us. Do you see? It was talk. Foolish words said in the heat of the moment and anger, nothing more."

"Perhaps." Ēostre remained unconvinced. Quietly, she settled on the edge of the bed and gazed out the window. Their new but temporary residence didn't yet have the feeling of home despite the nights she had snuck in to sleep beside him. Making it official hadn't changed things.

"Will you be all right here while I handle this disaster?" Max asked.

"I'll be fine," Ēostre assured him. "This is home for us now, and I know where to find you. Go."

"Are you—"

"Go."

Max nodded his head and stepped from the room, leaving Ēostre to her own activities.

How could this happen? For over a hundred years, I've wanted nothing more than for you to return to my side, and now... our time is over, Fafnir. Ēostre traced tiny circles over the smooth comforter. She tried to estimate the thread count of the cotton blend beneath it, and focusing on the trivial matters helped to blot out the horrors of the day.

"This wallpaper is hideous," she muttered. She stood from the bed and strode over the cream carpet to the window, lush fibers shifting beneath her bare toes. "And I miss my balcony."

The petty complaints brought a smile to her face and grounded her back to the reality of being America's first lady.

With a view of the south lawn and Constitution Avenue ahead of her, Ēostre plucked the mobile phone from her purse and dialed Saul. He picked up promptly, startling her with his speed.

"Is everything all right?" Ēostre asked. "Where's Chloe?"

"In our bedroom resting. Why?"

She exhaled a relieved sigh. "I worried a little, is all."

"Father would have to go through me to harm a single hair on her head. We've been talking." Ēostre heard the hesitation in her son's voice, as he whispered, "I don't think he meant what he said, but I don't intend to trust him with her either. Would you like to speak to Chloe?"

"No, I won't disturb her."

A quiet, peaceful silence fell between mother and son. She stood by the window with the phone cradled between her shoulder and ear, gazing out over the immense stretch of manicured lawn.

"This will all sort itself out, Mother. Have faith in that."

"Saul!" Chloe's voice echoed through the manor, reaching Ēostre's ears through the line.

"Ah, she must be awake."

"Must be," Ēostre replied dryly.

"She's surprised me a time or two. With this pregnancy, she has nightmares. Nothing about it is the same as when she carried Astrid, and once again, we have only her and Marcy's experiences." He paused as Chloe called for him again. "Give me a moment—"

Ēostre chuckled. "No. No, go find out what your wife needs, and call me if anything happens with your father. I love you."

"And I love you. Pass my regards to Maximilian."

Ēostre pressed the little red button to end the call and set the phone on the desk in passing. Not a fingerprint on the polished surface. The writing desk, like all other facets of the master bedroom, appeared entirely brand new from top to bottom without a sign of its previous occupants. If she reached down deeply and felt with her magic, she could find the soul of the room and feel a glimmer of the people once there. Their sorrows, their celebrations, and the events that shaped each presidential era, but even her fine dragon's sense of smell couldn't detect a whiff of their predecessors.

Will it be like this for us? Never really feeling at home? Leaving no imprint of ourselves when we leave?

191

The thought was a lonely one. Before her wistful mood made the full transition to melancholy, Ēostre broke the cycle by snooping through Max's things. She found the bulk of her belongings stored within a walk-in closet behind a hidden panel. There, she continued her accounting of her personal effects, only to come upon a strange chest at the rear of the room.

"That isn't mine." She furrowed her brow and found a note taped to the lid.

Do not open, by order of President Emberthorn.

Ēostre sniffed daintily and popped the ancient lock with magic. The aged wood creaked, smelling of old saline and memories of the sea. She flipped open the lid. Instead of finding pirate booty, she revealed a treasure trove of sweet cakes, protein bars, jerky, packaged tuna, and sardine cans. "What in the name of the Ancestors is this?"

Some dragon had a lot of explaining to do.

"Trash. All trash. Is this what he eats at night?"

Leaving the closet behind, she stepped from the bedroom into the casual west sitting hall. A wide, central hallway connected it to the east sitting hall, stretching from one side of the grand residence to the opposite side where historic bedrooms awaited with priceless relics from another era.

"There you are!" came an enthusiastic cry from Ēostre's rear. She turned to see Max's personal maid, Lynette, emerging from the second floor kitchen to greet her.

"Were you looking for me?"

"Not exactly, but I was hoping to run into you. It feels like forever since we've talked."

"Darling. We see each other almost every day."

"But it isn't every day that you're the first lady of the United States," Lynette said teasingly. Then her bright smile dimmed and concerned touched her brown eyes. "What's happening? Is Max in trouble? Ever since his speech, the staff have been speculating about what's happened and whether it's safe to continue working around all of this. I've been picking up tidbits here and there, I heard one of the housekeepers whispering to another in the linen closet a moment ago about being afraid."

Ēostre's heart thumped in her chest, a miniature explosion of anxiety slamming her ribcage. "All of them?"

"No, only a few," Lynette clarified. "I don't think they're all afraid. The head housekeeper asked me if I knew all along though."

"And what did you tell her?"

"I said hell yeah. I also said he's Tolkien's inspiration for Smaug the Great and Terrible. I don't know if that helped."

"Lynette—"

"I'm joking. The head chef though. He was having a real tizzy, except, I don't think it was an angry one. He's freaking out about how to feed not one but two dragons. He was rambling about raw steers or something when I passed by."

"I haven't eaten a raw steer in… well, not since Leiv asked us to cull his herd of the older animals." Ēostre pressed her lips together and glanced into the wide-open space behind Lynette. Like the rest of the residence, it had been styled to his personal tastes shortly after his inauguration, and the large sitting room window at its end shed abundant sunlight into the furnished corridor. "Wait, how does the chef know?"

"He's an executive chef, Ēostre. That makes him senior staff. Besides," Lynette paused and gave a nervous twist of her hair. "Gossip actually spreads pretty quickly through the staff, but it never goes beyond these walls from what I've seen this past year."

"Should I go speak to him?"

Lynette thoughtfully pursed her lips, then nodded. "I would. We all know you from your visits here as a guest but… you're a fixture now. Let them see you're more than what the stories say. That you're a woman who loves stir-fried rice and sesame chicken as much as the next person.

"I really do," Ēostre admitted. "I could go for a large order now, even if Max claims it's never spicy enough."

The young woman nudged her in the ribs with her elbow. "Then get it done, missy."

They embraced like old friends, much to the surprise of a passing housekeeper tidying a nearby picture frame in the central hall. When they separated, Ēostre drifted to the middle-aged human woman and flashed a friendly smile. "Hello," she offered.

The maid, a portly woman in her fifties with graying wisps of hair at her temples, froze on the spot. She resembled a statue at first, then she quickly regained her wits to speak. "Hello, Mrs. Emberthorn."

"There's no need to fear me. I... understand many of you among the senior staff have reservations about remaining."

"Oh no, not me. I enjoy my job here at the White House," the woman said quickly.

"And my husband enjoys your presence among the staff," Ēostre replied, taking a stab in the dark. "He's had only the most pleasant things to say about each of you regarding dedication to your duties. You're Annalisa, right?"

"I am."

"And I'm Ēostre. Please, I'd like to be on a friendly basis with everyone."

With each person she met along the way to the ground floor, Ēostre lingered for small talk and conversation. While some quickly fabricated excuses to hastily return to their duties, some engaged her eagerly in conversation, fascinated by the answers to their tentative questions.

After an hour, she consulted her phone while standing beside the entrance to the kitchen.

No one's leaked it to the gossip columns and media. Maybe they're as devoted as Lynette says. Maybe they'll keep it to themselves until the big press conference tomorrow.

Her heels clicked over an exquisite, gold-trimmed rug as she navigated the central hall. The White House interior wasn't new to

Ēostre. She'd been a visitor over the year during their public courtship, but marriage gave her new perspective as the woman of the household, as opposed to a visitor who would one day reign over it all.

Nervous, she ran her fingers through her tidy, platinum hair, and stepped into the kitchen. All at once, the scurrying of several employees halted and heads turned her direction.

"Hello," Ēostre said in a gentle voice to them. She waited in the doorway of the massive kitchen as neatly dressed men and women in white jackets hurried to and fro. The man she presumed to be the supervisor of the cooking staff beelined to her as if his pristine jacket was on fire. "You must be Chef Teller. I don't believe we've had the chance for an introduction before."

"Mrs. Emberthorn, what an unexpected pleasure. Is there something you require?"

"No, nothing like that. I only wanted to introduce myself and settle any concerns you might have regarding recent events."

"We are prepared for any eventuality, ma'am. Special diets included."

"Oh that won't be necessary. Continue to feed us both the way you've prepared his meals for the past year, only, ah…" After a brief hesitation, she gently said, "please increase the serving size. Plan each of our private dinners to provide leftovers for three or four people. We're nocturnal and sleep rarely at night. If that isn't possible, sandwiches will suffice. Maximilian enjoys spicy meatball subs — the messier and soggier the better. I fear he's been eating poorly to avoid revealing his night time dining habits."

"That's it?"

She nodded. "No steers are necessary."

The man looked aghast. "That reached you? Mrs. Emberthorn, I'm sorry—"

To ease his mind, she flashed a sunny smile. "There's no need for apologies. We are what we are, after all. My son's caretaker does own many fine creatures of excellent dining quality, and while I do

195

enjoy them from time to time, that will not be necessary here. We would never tax you in such a way."

"If you keep late hours, I can be on hand to prepare—"

Ēostre shook her head. "No. I speak for my husband as well as myself when I say we'd prefer for you to go home at a reasonable hour each night. Do you have a family?"

"Why… yes, a wife and a daughter."

"Then strive to be gone no later than six each evening. Have dinner with your loved ones, Alan. They're precious to us, and even I as a dragon know the value of family. My son and his wife shall be visiting us frequently, I'm sure, and they'll be bringing a little girl with them. We'll always try to give you advance notice."

The chef's smile brightened his otherwise stern visage. "Children are always a welcome addition to the White House halls. Will she have any specific needs?"

Ēostre chuckled. "Astrid is not a picky eater and will enjoy whatever you prepare, I promise."

She and Teller chatted for a while longer before the man gave her a tour of the kitchen and its adjoining rooms. As she discussed their favorite cuisines and let him in on Max's hidden secret — his reluctance to bother the cooks — they shared a laugh about some of the man's stranger antics over the past year.

"Now we understand why an entire roast disappeared over the holidays. No one could account for where it went!"

She left the kitchens feeling lighter and more at home. The acceptance she'd found from a majority of the staff gave her hope.

Would the rest of the human world feel the same way?

Chapter 18

"They look like sharks," Palmer muttered. "I've never seen such a crowd of well-dressed predators."

"You're a former senator, Kenneth. You saw it every time the Senate convened."

He heard a faint, barely audible chuckle from one of the agents nearby. "It's all right to laugh," Max addressed them. "I need laughter right now."

"All right. It's time. Remember the rest of us are behind you one hundred percent," Palmer said to him.

"Easy words from the man who will succeed me once I've been taken out by a dragonslayer's lance," Max said, chuckling at the dark thought.

A concerned Secret Service agent stiffened and glanced their way. Max could only imagine what was going through their minds now that they were abreast of his status as a fire-breathing monster.

With one final prayer to the Ancestors, Max stepped through the door and approached the podium. A solemn weight to the atmosphere crushed the fragment of confidence he'd carried with him.

"Good afternoon," he said. "Looks a little packed today, doesn't it?" He scanned the crowd, meeting eye contact with reporters who either chose to stare him down in return, or abruptly redirect their own gazes. Satisfied, he steeled his nerves and cut to the chase.

"I've decided to answer any question directed at me, so there is nothing too delicate with exception to security-related questions. One at a time. Please."

A woman in a dark blue suit quickly pounced on the chance. "Mr. President, I'm sure I speak for everyone present when I ask you to elaborate on your mysterious comment yesterday. You say you're not human, but if you're not one of us, then what are you?"

A sea of curious faces gazed back at Maximilian, each one person practically on the edge of their seat.

"I am a dragon, and to answer your next question — my wife and I are both dragons."

The room exploded into noise, everyone trying to ask their questions over the others. Max held up his hands in a bid for calm and waited them out.

"Next question please. Let's keep this civil and orderly."

"What else is out there? Americans deserve to know what sort of people are living in our communities."

"Besides dragons like myself, there are shapeshifters, vampires, witches, and other magical creatures throughout the world. We have been here as long as mankind, living among you by concealing our existence as fiction."

"Why hide?" the same reporter asked.

"Why do we hide?" Maximilian managed a quiet smile. "Research the events of the Salem Witch Trials. That is why we hide. Many good, innocent people have died in the crusade against magical creatures."

"Mr. President, has our government been aware of these magical beings and covering them up?"

"The existence of the supernatural is no surprise to the government. It has always known, at its highest tiers of secrecy, that paranormal creatures exist. As of today, the U.S. military currently employs five thousand, three hundred and forty-nine shapeshifters. Many of them have been deployed into war zones as special operatives."

Faces filled with wonder and awe. The conference became a combination of stunned people unable to find their voices, and anxious journalists vying for his attention next.

"I'll take the next question from you," Max said, gesturing to a young lady who patiently waited her turn. Her serenely beautiful face was surrounded by fluffy white curls like ivory down.

Shifter, no doubt. He could smell the scent of bird on her, wafting to him on occasion.

"Do you plan to create legislation to protect the rights of magical citizens?" she asked. Her calm, blue eyes watched him. He had no doubt she was asking for herself as much as any other shapeshifter tuned in.

"Yes. I do," Max said. He cleared his throat and took a sip of water. "My personal belief is that we are all created equal. No dragon, shapeshifter, or human should ever face discrimination."

"Thank you," she replied, retaking her seat.

A blond man, with a smile fitting for a toothpaste ad, rose for the next question. "Sir, if literary sources are to be believed, vampires and werewolves have dangerous reputations and can't be trusted. Will a system similar to our sexual offender registry be use to announce such monsters who move into our neighborhoods?"

"No," Maximilian said tersely after grinding his teeth. He lost his temper for the first time and felt Ēostre's hand on his shoulder. "We are not sexual predators and murderers, nor should we be seen as such. While I invite all paranormals interested in a mortal life to register for the proper identification, nothing will at any time ever publically identify their natures. They deserve, just as you do, the right to dignity and peace."

"What about you, Mr. President?" another reporter asked. "How do you expect the people to continue supporting you when you aren't who you claim to be? Are you even a true citizen?"

"I was not born in the United States as my birth certificate states," Max admitted. "This country was an unknown land at the time of my birth, but I have dwelled here long before this country's inception. I lived here when the first pilgrims arrived, before our Founding Fathers created this great nation."

"So you're admitting your entire identity is a lie," the journalist fired off quickly. "Falsification of identification is an impeachable offense, Mr. President. What do you think this means for your career in the oval office?"

Their questions stung, and no matter how much he'd expected it, nothing could have prepared him for the harsh tide of emotion flooding over the room.

Maximilian retained his composure, dimly aware of Ēostre feeding him bits of her calmer nature through their soul bond. "I hope it marks the beginning of a friendly alliance between all living creatures in this country. At no point did I set out to deceive the American public or this government. Just as your parents create names and the appropriate paperwork for you upon your birth, ancient creatures such as myself have developed identities to live normal lives. I may not have been born to the name Maximilian Emberthorn, but that is who I am today."

"If you are not Maximilian Emberthorn, may we know your true name?"

Max stole a look at his wife, seeking her advice. She tucked her chin in a small nod.

"History knows me as Belenos of Gaul. I was once known as the Fair Shining One. The god of the sun. I saw the rise and fall of the Roman Empire. I watched the birth of nations and saw the centuries claim them."

The reporters quieted. A few of them gazed upon him with reverence, others with disgust or barely disguised fear, but finally Max's mind was clear.

No matter what they thought about him, no matter what they wrote to their papers, he'd been honest. They couldn't find fault in that, and the tremendous weight had finally lifted from his shoulders.

"If you have any more questions, please leave them with my office staff. I will address every concern personally."

He left the podium and noise behind. Cameras flashed and questions were called out, but he didn't have time for any more of them. Or the patience. That was rapidly dwindling and for the safety of the crowd, it was better for him to vacate the area.

"You handled it well," Ēostre assured him.

"Thanks to you. I wanted to snarl at a few of them, but I realized that wouldn't create a favorable opinion of dragons."

Ēostre's soft chuckle ghosted across his skin and warmed him from within. They made it back to his office without further word, where Palmer waited for them. He offered out snifters of brandy.

"Thank you, Kenneth, but none for me," Ēostre deferred.

"You know me so well, friend."

"I knew you'd need this once I gave you the news that's reached me. I have good and bad. Which would you prefer first?" Kenneth asked.

"The good."

"The good news is that the group of you saved an extraordinary amount of lives yesterday. Geologists and scientists have begun recreating the events using some sort of computer software, and they estimated hundreds more in the town local to the volcano would have died. On top of that, you've saved the ecosystem there, thousands of animals, and prevented millions in property damage."

Max forced a smile to his face. It strained his muscles, requiring more effort than usual. "You're right. That is good news. How are the recovery efforts?"

"Good. Red Cross was pleased with the donation you made, and in light of it, I decided to meet your contribution with one of my own. You're a good influence on me."

"What's the bad news?"

"I'm… sorry to tell you this, Max, but Thompson has it in for you. I found out from a friend that he contacted the Chairman of the House Judiciary Committee. He wants Michaels to proceed with impeachment. They're already trying to get you out."

"If Congress feels the same way as those reporters, then I've already been tried and convicted," Max said sadly.

Palmer scowled. "If that happens, you'll still have my friendship, Max. I'll do whatever I can to fight for your people. I'd rather humanity be on the side of the dragons than for this to come to a war. Everyone loses then."

"Thank you. I appreciate that."

Despite kind words and apparent understanding among many members of his cabinet, Max's worries plagued him long after they retired for the evening. Ēostre had recommended rest in face of the coming days ahead, but sleep proved as elusive as ever.

A few centuries ago, he would have passed the time by hunting beneath a starlit sky. Instead, humans brought his food to him on silver trays with napkins and fancy linens.

"Are you still awake?"

"It's far too early to sleep," Max grumbled.

"I know, but…"

"Sorry," he apologized. "It's unsettling being unable to do anything."

"I could use magic to stop them," Ēostre murmured in the dark. "But I know that isn't what you want."

Beside him, his wife resembled every artistic depiction of an angel Max had ever appreciated. Leonardo's finest work didn't compare. Sighing, he reached out to stroke a lock of her silver hair and let it glide around his fingertip. Her hair smelled like lavender with subtle traces of vanilla. The scent teased over his senses to instill a feeling of peace.

"You wouldn't do it if I asked. I know you better than you know yourself, my love, and one thing you have never done is impress your will over a mortal for personal gain."

"You are correct, but if you were hurting deeply enough, there is nothing I wouldn't do to see you happy again. That includes bewitching a few hundred mortals. A thousand if I must. You are my mate, my one love, and nothing will take me away from you." Ēostre rose onto her elbow and looked at him with only devotion in her stormy gray eyes.

"I know," he answered. "But you have your own worries and fears, my love." Maximilian gathered Ēostre into his arms, and she came readily into his embrace, burrowing against the warmth and turning her face into his throat.

"His heart was empty, Maximilian. There was no love there. Nothing of the dragon we knew. I'm afraid."

"Then know that I am here with you through every step, Ēostre. We will discover the reason behind Fafnir's reappearance. Watatsumi claims to have a theory, but he won't share it with me until he can determine the truth."

"He told me the same," she whispered. "If anyone can get to the bottom of it, it has to be Watatsumi."

"Until then, all we can do is keep an eye on Fafnir. Give him his space."

"And your presidency?"

Max kissed the crown of her head. "One day at a time, love. It's in the hands of the bureaucrats now and we'll handle whatever decision they choose."

Chapter 19

Complete exposure wasn't what he'd wanted to happen. Nothing had gone to plan, and as far as Loki was concerned, Mahuika was to blame for the shit storm brewing across the world.

Agnes wouldn't return his phone calls. Any efforts to contact her reached a harried assistant, busy signal, or went directly to her voicemail. Mira, her apprentice, claimed to have no knowledge of her master's whereabouts. On the day of the eruption, she'd vanished into thin air without so much as a note telling the girl what to do in her absence. The old hag had dropped off the face of the earth, and if she knew what was good for her, she'd remain in whatever hole she'd claimed.

Mahuika was a special case. He had no doubt about whether or not she was behind the eruption and possibly the witch's disappearance. Too convenient. Either they were on the run together, or the fire dragoness had snipped a few loose ends by eradicating the evidence of her wrongdoing.

"I should have known better than to trust a petulant child," he muttered. At the time, her instructions had been simple. Release his soul, and together, they'd sit back and enjoy the fruit borne from Fafnir ruining Ēostre and Maximilian's happy new bond.

Could the situation be salvaged? He skimmed over the reports, news articles, and the posts online. Anti-Dragon propaganda had surfaced, blaming Fafnir for the deaths of many within Rainier's range and calling for Max to step down. The worst of them were the petitions asking for all dragons and dangerous supernaturals to be documented and labeled like weapons of war. Some crazy conspiracist had the audacity to suggest supernaturals be put into internment camps.

"Sir? Mahuika is on line three."

Loki snatched the phone from the cradle and raised it to his ear. "Where have you been?" he hissed into the receiver.

"In a safe haven," she replied calmly. "Has our plan caused Maximilian and Ēostre the turmoil we desired?"

"You've caused all of dragonkind turmoil!" his voice boomed. "What were you thinking by engineering an eruption and exposing us all?"

Mahuika's laughter filtered into the phone line, further incensing him. "Don't be so melodramatic, Loki. If we achieved our goal, then no price is too large. We've brought them both pain, after all."

Loki inhaled a deep breath then leaned forward to prop an elbow against the desk surface. When he spoke, his voice was low, measured, but brimming with undisguised fury. "When I find you, I will scatter the pieces of your corpse from here to Hawaii."

"You will do nothing," Mahuika replied at the end of a haughty laugh. "You'll blow smoke from your fancy office and despair, but I did what the rest of us wouldn't. Maximilian would have exposed all of us in time, but I've dealt him a wound Fafnir's mere return could never have caused. Do you want to know why you will do nothing, Loki?" She paused, husky voice filled with amusement. "Because you're as good as dead, too, if the council discovers your treachery. I've done nothing but expedite his awakening, but you... you allowed a witch to violate a fellow wyrm's soul. You stood by as she denied him a final rest in the beyond among our Ancestors, and that, my friend, makes your crimes outweigh mine by far."

As Loki shook with rage, Mahuika ended the call. She'd gotten what she wanted from him, but little did she know, she'd also made a lifelong enemy.

***

"The formal impeachment inquiry failed, Max. Whether it's by the merit of your speech or fear of reprisal, this won't reach trial."

"Was it close?"

"Not even," Kenneth said. "Although I'm certain they would have had you when it came to falsifying records, the House appeared to be reluctant for some reason."

Max slid back in the seat, exhaling a breath of relief. The tension left his chest at last and a weight raised from his shoulders, leaving his body with aches created from days of anxiety. "Gee, I wonder why," he said with a nervous chuckle.

"How long have you been in the office?" Kenneth asked. "Dragon or not, you look like crap right now."

Max raked his fingers through his dark hair and tried to focus on the words floating over the computer screen. Between phone calls to foreign dignitaries, other dragons, council members, and shapeshifter leaders, it was all beginning to blur together as a never-ending stream of making nice.

"Did you even go to bed last night?"

Max grunted. "Nocturnal. I don't like to sleep at night anyway."

"When was the last time you've slept *at all*?"

"I don't know," he admitted with honesty. Three nights ago when he and Ēostre retired to their bed, he'd spent most of those hours watching her peaceful breathing rhythm before inevitably showering, dressing, and returning to work.

"Go catch a nap then. The press conference isn't for," he paused to check his watch and said, "another five hours. Plenty of time for even a dragon to get some shut-eye. You don't want the American people to see you with bloodshot eyes and dark circles, do you?"

"They'll spackle makeup onto me," Max grumbled.

"And that makes for a grumpy dragon." Kenneth's grin widened. "Go. Sleep. Find your first lady and cuddle her. I saw Ēostre moping in the rose garden an hour ago. Spend time with her if you won't rest."

"Moping?"

Kenneth shrugged. "She didn't seem herself, Max, what can I say? We both know Ēostre's usual sunny disposition has been impaired by the recent developments. And considering what you've told me about Fafnir, I can't blame her. I lost my first wife to a drunk driver twenty years ago. I would be a wreck if she were brought back to me now."

"I'll go see her."

After Kenneth stepped into the hallway, Max opened the door leading to the colonnade. It ran the perimeter of the rose garden and he only had to take a few steps to see Ēostre seated on the grass, enjoying a lonely picnic for one.

He should have been out there with her. Feeling like the world's most neglectful mate, he stepped down from the walkway onto the manicured lawn. "Ēostre?"

"Oh, hello dear." She aimed a smile up at him but it didn't make her eyes sparkle as it usually would. "Done for the day?"

"No, but I happened to have a glance out the window to see you here. Where's my invitation?"

She offered out a chocolate-dipped strawberry.

It seemed like years had passed since their wedding day amidst the tulips and fragrant roses. He checked out their surroundings then sat in the grass opposite her to enjoy the sweet confection.

"You'll ruin your suit."

"I have plenty more."

A hint of her usual cheer flitted across her face, only to vanish as quickly. Her sadness inspired a swiftly building idea in his head.

"Join me for dinner, love. Let's go somewhere and leave the White House for a night. Let's see a movie. Let's... enjoy an evening of time alone." He took her hands between both of his and raised them to his lips, kissing her knuckles.

"Can we even do that? Get away, I mean."

"It may take a few days to make the arrangements with the Secret Service, and for that, I apologize—"

"I understand," she said, voice so soft he barely picked up the words. "It isn't necessary, Belenos."

"It is," he insisted. "I'll let someone know we'd like to have a romantic evening out. We'll visit some local restaurant, come back for a movie perhaps." He aimed a sly smile at her, realizing days had passed since he and his wife enjoyed anything but sleep alongside one another. "And move on to other activities."

"I'd like that."

His security team and their supervisors had other thoughts on the matter.

"You can't give us a few days' notice about dining outside of the White House, Mr. Emberthorn. We need time — *weeks* to arrange such an event."

"Well, that's exactly what I'm doing. I *could* simply go on my own and you couldn't stop me if you wanted. I'm trying to give you the courtesy and respect of going through the proper channels."

"Oh hell." The man rubbed his face then leaned back in his office chair. Director Nichols, the head of the Secret Service, was a no-nonsense kind of guy with a gray goatee and serious, deep-set eyes. "All right. I get where you're coming from. You could probably gobble me up if you wanted."

Max grinned. "I gave up humans a long, long time ago."

"Lucky us," the man said, his dry tone brittle as a cracker. "The matter of your security isn't an actual issue here. It's the red tape. Can you give me a week?"

"Gladly if it means my wife can enjoy an evening on the town."

***

It happened in two weeks, not that Max was counting. As the presidential motorcade cruised down the street toward a restaurant of their mutual choosing, he couldn't help but feel a swift surge of pleasure. His mate was smiling again, and every second of it was radiant. He could have basked in it as if she were the sun, and in a way, she'd become exactly that for him.

Riding in the enormous, bomb-proof limousine had become a convenience, but he never appreciated the chauffeured ride until the moments when Ēostre sat beside him. Tonight, she was clothed for their date in a midnight blue, strapless dress, and designer flats that fit her like slippers.

His Ēostre never missed the opportunity to wear heels, and he'd become accustomed to her meeting him at eye level. Being the perfect height for receiving his kisses. On top of the unusual change, she'd let Chloe pamper her with eyeliner, foundation, and the whole nine yards. The woman beside him was transformed.

"Are you trying to go incognito?" he teased, nudging his foot against hers.

"Have you ever tried running in heels? I figured these would be more suitable if we decide to make a break for it."

"Don't let our agents hear you saying that." Max laughed and relaxed back into the seat.

Police officers had blocked the street, and a counter-sniper team watched the approaching vehicle from the roof. They entered the restaurant through a tent and were taken to the upper level where a private table for two awaited them. Nearby, the management had arranged a table for his security detail.

"Hello," Max greeted a few diners in passing. He smiled at an owl-eyed waiter and became the very model of goodwill, with a broad grin on his face for anyone who dared to glance up from their individual meal to look at them.

Max drew a chair out for Ēostre and took the opposite seat. "It's good to see you happy again, love. Perhaps later, you'll speak to me of what bothers you."

A brief flash of guilt flared in her eyes. "No, Max, it isn't like that. I've been worried, is all. The impeachment movement stressed you out so much."

"And it's behind us now," he assured her.

Within moments, they'd tuned out his security team, letting him imagine it was only the two of them out on a normal date. They ordered appetizer plates to share and a bottle of wine, which came with prompt service. By the time their main courses arrived, he had Ēostre laughing like her old self.

"And then, Kenneth came in the office behind me and Spartacus decided it was time to begin singing about all the single ladies. Apparently, Lynette made him into a Beyoncé fan a few months ago." Ēostre giggled into her linen napkin. "She thought if he learned the song, we'd get a move on the wedding sooner, but the stubborn bird didn't decide to actually begin singing it until now."

Max groaned. "I'll have to reeducate him. They warned me having a parrot would be like having a child again, but I didn't listen." He imagined the bird chastising him in its gravelly voice that if he liked it, he should put a ring on it.

"Good practice, then."

Once they were stuffed and unable to have even another bite, Max summoned the check and left a generous tip. It felt nice to pay for his own meal, to spend his own money on something frivolous, and to have a taste of the freedom he'd surrendered when chasing his dream to become president.

One of his usual agents, a lean man with thinning brown hair and a brown eyes leaned close to him. "Sir. We have a slight change of plans. We're going to take you down through the kitchen and exit via the rear of the restaurant. 'The Beast' will meet you and Mrs. Emberthorn there."

"Why?"

Agent Roberts smiled apologetically. "Slight dust up with a restaurant patron out front. Claims we infringed on his rights. Nothing serious."

"All right."

She's so happy again, Max thought, pleased with the night's outcome. He didn't let the security matter concern him again until they were stepping outside of the restaurant into the evening air. The balmy summer weather greeted them, contrasting the air-conditioned restaurant.

"Are we heading back or can we still see a show?"

"Hopefully they'll allow us to enjoy the showing as planned—"

"We need you to get into the vehicle right away, sir," Roberts said. "Security has been compromised."

"Where?"

"Please get into the vehicle," Roberts insisted. "We have no time to waste." Another agent opened the door and gestured for them to enter, but Ēostre lingered beside the door, waiting for him.

When the agent attempted to help Max into the limousine, he found an immobile man unwilling to enter the vehicle. Exercising his inhuman strength required no effort for the stubborn dragon.

"Where?" Max repeated. "What's happened?"

"Possible bomb in a parked car out front. You and your wife are our first priority at the moment. Bomb-sniffing hounds are en route, but we need to remove you from the area."

His eyes darted from the stoic agent to Ēostre's worried features. There was a tainted smell in the air, permeating the alley, and he could tell she smelled it too when her nose crinkled in distaste.

"What is that?" she asked.

"It…"

With an agent flanking them on both sides and many more occupying the narrow alley space, it made an ideal, secure area to usher the president to his vehicle in privacy without subjecting them to cameras and busybodies. But it also made for a cramped space.

The bomb wasn't out front, and if it was, it was only a decoy. The real thing had been tucked into the alley right beside them.

"Move!" Max shouted, dashing toward the trash dumpster mid-shift. He burst from his clothes, sending shreds of a fine dinner suit and linen shirt in every direction. His necktie popped from the dramatic increase in width, and his tail batted aside the young man who was to his left.

The strong odor of oily plastic and tar filled his nostrils. A split second stretched like an hour, allowing Max to see everything happening at once — his screaming mate, the concerned faces of his security detail transitioning to raw fear in the presence of his dragon form, and members of the counter-sniper team above them gazing down with bewildered expressions.

Max went with his gut instinct and tucked the heavy container beneath him, smothering it with his tremendous weight just as the explosive ignited, reducing his world to a curtain of white.

Chapter 20

The narrow alley shuddered, everything happening so fast Ēostre's head spun. She flinched instinctively from the sudden clap of noise, though Max's enormous body had muffled most of it. Seconds after his pounce, he slumped to one side, revealing the detonation had blown a convex hole into the lid of the trash container. Ēostre, as well as the agents, were fortunate they hadn't been showered by shrapnel and exploding debris. He'd taken all of it.

"Bel?" she whispered quietly, clutching one hand against her heart. He crowded the alley with his bulk, a motionless behemoth with a profusely bleeding wound. His tail was still, and then she saw the splinters of metal embedded in his tough hide and protruding from his gut.

"Bel!"

Someone tried to hold her back, but Ēostre's strength was too great. She broke free, slinging one man to the side before rushing forward to her mate. His eyes were tightly squeezed shut, and agony radiated out from him in rolling waves, the intensity warring against Ēostre's attempt to keep her dinner down.

"Bel, please say something," she whispered up to him, touching her palm to his leathery cheek.

Behind her, Secret Service agents who hadn't lost their wits at the sight of Max sprang into action. They relayed harsh demands over wireless communication systems, blockades were ordered to shut down the streets, and one chilling question reached her ears among all of their official babble. They wanted to know how to relocate a dragon for critical care.

She couldn't trust the humans with his life after they failed him so utterly and he'd sacrificed himself in their stead. Ēostre snapped out of her terror to utter a desperate plea under her breath. "Mahasti, I need you. Max and I both need you. I'm afraid he may be dying. I wish to come home right this moment. I wish for you to bring us home."

Mahasti was there with her, the essence of smoke and fire surrounding them. Ēostre heard only the initial words of a startled cry from the suited Secret Service agents before she and Max were swept away on the tide of magic and deposited in Saul's rear yard, the expansive stretch of California beauty behind them. The genie floated to Ēostre's left, jasmine-scented wisps of smoke gradually coalescing to form her brown-skinned body. Bare feet touched down to the ground and concerned eyes turned to Ēostre.

"What happened?"

"Someone was able to get a bomb through the security measures set up by the Secret Service." A thick, viscous river of dark blood seeped from the wound, staining the earth beneath her injured mate. Ēostre's body trembled. "He leapt atop it to save the humans."

"I will bring Saul right away."

Genies didn't have the kind of magic needed to heal wounds. Their powers always leaned toward an ability to grant material desires and wealth. As Mahasti disappeared, Ēostre was struck by how helpless she felt.

Tonight, she'd planned to tell him the greatest secret troubling her heart. She'd wanted to see his face light with joy amidst elated laughter before he swept her within his arms to be loved in the privacy of their bedroom.

It's not too late for him, Ēostre chided herself as the tears fell down her cheeks. *When I found Fafnir, he was long dead. The soul was gone from him, his body cold and unmoving. Max is alive and here with me now. Here to be saved.*

"Mother." Saul had appeared behind her again, clothed in loose-fitting pajama pants. He looked like his father, golden blond in place of black waves with a physical build to match. The realization squeezed unyielding fingers around her throat, then the tears wouldn't stop flowing. She choked on them and ran forward into his arms, caught by him in a strong hug.

"I am so sorry," he whispered.

"They didn't protect him. I... I didn't protect him. I *failed*."

"No, Mother." He took her by the shoulders and gazed down at her. "You did not fail him. What happened was a travesty, but it isn't too late."

Magic flowed with more strength through their natural bodies, leading to both mother and son abandoning their human flesh in favor of sharp teeth and massive talons. Thankfully, Saul's yard was large enough to hold three full-sized dragons, plus some. It had once held the entire council after all, during Chloe's duel with Brigid.

Calling on her magic was as natural as breathing. It bloomed within her, full of warmth and life, love and devotion. Focusing all her attention on Max's wound, she funneled her power into him.

"All right, Saul, pull the chunk out. I'm ready."

Mother and son worked together in tandem to pull each piece of shrapnel from Max's body while slowing the blood flow. They touched him with magic-laced claw tips, channeling the very essence of their ability into his prone body and the gaping wound left behind.

An hour later, he hadn't fully responded to their magic and he hadn't moved. Ēostre swayed, and thankfully, Saul was there to catch her. He set his mother gently to the ground and dropped back onto his haunches, tail flicking in irritation.

"He's injured too badly for only the two of us. We need more dragons. More healers," Saul muttered. "Saving Chloe didn't tax me nearly so bad as this has, and I feel as if we've done nothing at all for him." He rubbed his cheek and gazed thoughtfully at Max's comatose face. "What about Uncle Thor?"

"My brother doesn't heal anyone, Saul. He breaks them."

"True."

Dragons with the capacity for mending flesh were rare, a trait often passed down family lines from mother to son, to grandchild and future progeny. And as she and Thor only shared one parent, he hadn't inherited the gift.

But someone else likely had. The realization occurred to Ēostre the same time Saul realized it. He jerked upright to his feet and rushed for the manor. "I'll get her."

When he returned with the little girl, there were still remnants of a Batgirl nightgown clinging to her slim dragonic neck. Even Saul couldn't keep pace alongside her, proving the speed of smaller feet.

"What happened to Grandpa Max?!" she cried.

"Astrid, listen to me very well, my love. Your father and I have given all we can… and we need you. We need you to discover the magic inside of you. We need your help to save Maximilian."

Astrid nodded. Blue eyes, shimmering with unshed tears, drifted up to Max's face. Even as a dragon, his features were contorted into an agonized mask. Although she was so much smaller than the three adults, she approached the elder dragon and raised onto her haunches, one small claw resting on his ruddy red cheek. She whispered something behind his scaled ear and nuzzled her nose against his skin with her eyes closed.

When she turned her face back to her father, her small face was somber, eyes dry. "Teach me how to heal, Daddy."

Nothing would ever motivate Astrid to learn more than helping to save her grandfather's life.

***

A black SUV pulled into the driveway the following night. Ēostre had expected as much. In fact, she'd been expecting an entire caravan, but with Mahasti's intervention, not even a satellite from space could have discovered Drakenstone Manor.

She should have known Ian would find them.

Ēostre decided to meet him in her human form and went down to open the door as the eagle stepped onto the porch. He was dressed casually, clothed in nice jeans and a flawless polo shirt, the badge on the sleeve promoting his private security firm. He hired shapeshifters when they left the armed forces and sold their services abroad as contracted mercenaries. On U.S. soil, they served another purpose.

"Ian…"

He stepped forward and took both of her hands. "I took the first flight out of Houston. God, I'm sorry, Ēostre. I knew where you guys had him as soon as Mitch called and said Mahasti disappeared with you both, but we've been busy trying to put a lid over this."

"What happened? I mean, *how* did this happen? Aren't they supposed to check everything over thoroughly before they bring him out?"

"One of his agents vanished after you two did. John Kensington."

"I don't… I don't understand. Why would John take off?"

Ian's face grew grim. "We think he planted the bomb. Or at least knew about it."

"What?" She thought back to how the agent in question had tried to escort her toward the limo. Around the side where the dumpster had been.

"We've discovered corruption in the Secret Service," Ian said quietly, rage hidden behind a stoic mask. "It was meant to be a suicide bombing, but Max was the primary target."

"How did this happen, Ian? Who's responsible for it?"

"Slayers have infiltrated the Secret Service. We've apprehended one of them, but according to my guys, there's still two more at large."

A chill flowed through Ēostre's veins, drawing a shiver down her spine. Tears continued to flow down her cheeks as she led Ian to the slumbering dragon in the field. He hadn't awakened yet, and she wondered if he ever would — if the time had come to take him to Mount Shasta. A shudder overtook and a fresh round of tears spilled over her cheeks.

Ian enfolded her in his strong arms and she sobbed until her body ached, crying useless tears long after her lungs were sore from the heaving. "No one's going to get away with this, Ēostre. My boys are on it right now. Russ even came out of retirement to kick some ass in D.C. We're going to find the assholes who did this. They're gonna pay, so don't you worry about any of that. You and Saul get this guy well. He needs you right now. He needs you on your game, understand?"

She nodded through the sniffles, afraid she'd break down again in front of the strong shifter. Eventually, the last of the shakes left, dwindling until exhaustion turned her limbs to lead and only Ian's embrace kept her standing.

"I'm so, so sorry, Ēostre. I feel to blame. I should have insisted on an all-shifter team to protect him."

"No, Ian. You aren't to blame for this. The only person to blame for this is the… the…" Her breath hitched.

They stood together for a while, holding each other up, watching Max's uneven, labored breaths.

Please, Ancestors. You gave me a new chance to love again. Don't take him.

***

"Ēostre? Have you eaten today?" Chloe asked.

She shook her head. Ian had insisted she take a nap after her cry and when she'd awoken, the eagle shifter was gone, sent to Washington D.C. by Mahasti, so Ēostre had returned to her vigil at Max's side.

"Come eat. You can't work your magic if you're too weak. Max knows that and he'd want you to keep your strength up."

"I'll stay with him, Mother," Saul volunteered, sensing the reason behind her reluctance. If he did awaken, she didn't want him to be alone and afraid.

"C'mon."

Ēostre allowed herself to be led away, knowing they were right. She wouldn't be good to anyone, let alone Max, if she was exhausted.

Chloe made herself at home in the kitchen, pulling our pre-prepared trays of sliced meat and cheese. Mahasti kept the fridge stocked with sandwich makings to sate Saul's endless appetite. Crackers, relish, spicy mustard, and apple slices soon joined her prep area.

"He's going to pull through, Ēostre. Max is strong."

"I know he is, but slayers. I suppose we should have counted on them being around."

"Hey, now." Chloe finished making their cracker plate. "You guys survived them in the medieval ages, you'll handle them now, too."

"There's so much to lose... so, so much."

Chloe abandoned their snack and stepped over, pulling Ēostre into her arms. "Talk to me. What else is weighing you down? Because it's more than all this crap going on right now."

"I... may be pregnant," Ēostre whispered to Chloe. "At first, I thought all of the signs were a coincidence due to the stress of adjusting to our public lives together, but then I realized my cycle is behind."

Chloe's eyebrows shot up. "Dragon women have that, too?" she asked at first, flabbergasted.

Ēostre grimaced and nodded as her daughter-in-law grasped the gravity of the situation. Recovering swiftly, Chloe took Ēostre by the arm and guided her to the breakfast bar where they took seats on the high-backed stools.

"You said 'may' which means you aren't sure yet, right? How can we be sure?"

"With Saul, I didn't know I was with child until I felt him kick within me for the first time. That day was magical," she murmured, a wistful tone seeping into her voice.

"And how long did that take?" Chloe, ever restless, left the chair again to fetch glasses and a pitcher of lemonade from the fridge. Ēostre didn't turn it down, nor did she refuse when the woman brought over the snack tray she'd made.

"Close to eight months. Shortly after, other dragons could smell the cub's scent with mine."

Chloe stared at her. "Well, we certainly aren't waiting until then. We have technology on our side and a mountain of unused pregnancy tests in my bathroom drawer. I kinda bought a pack of fifty back when we first tried to get pregnant again."

"I feel terrible in that, all of this, your happy news has been overshadowed."

"Don't feel like that," Chloe said. "We'll get through all of this and then you and I can go buy cute maternity outfits, pig out on ice cream with bacon in it, and drive our men crazy. It'll be a blast."

Chloe's words had the intended effect. Ēostre laughed and the pent up tension she'd been holding onto unraveled. She swiped at her eyes with one hand while picking up her lemonade with the other.

"I'll put myself in your hands then and see what your tests say. How do they work?"

"Oh, you pee on a stick."

Ēostre choked on her drink but Chloe was there to pat her back, a wide grin on her face. "You what?"

"Finish your food and I'll show you. Well, not *show* you, but you know what I mean. It's not as crazy as it sounds. Really."

Contrary to Chloe's claim, it was every bit as crazy as it sounded. She doubted in the accuracy of a human test, but for

Chloe's sake, she tried and emerged from the bathroom with a little plastic cover on the end of the strange device.

"Now what?"

"Give it a few minutes. If two pink lines show up in the window, you're pregnant."

"And if they don't?"

"Then we try again tomorrow morning. Or after a week maybe."

Ēostre looked down at the pink test, doubt in her eyes, "But this is a human test, right? How do we know it will show me anything at all?"

"Well…" Chloe fidgeted before continuing. "When I was pregnant with Astrid, Saul had some scientist friends of his do some tests to make sure there wouldn't be any problems. Completely secret, of course! We found that dragons are a lot more closely related to humans than we would have expected… but I guess that explains how Marcy and I were able to get pregnant, right?"

Ēostre's mouth dropped open, "What about other shifters?"

"A couple of wolves volunteered, and it looks like they're pretty close to human as well. I mean, a hospital would probably still freak about seeing something unexpected in a blood test, but there is definitely a connection back on the family tree. Not that we could tell anyone, though… can you imagine some of the ancients if they thought they might be related to humans?" Chloe made a face, prompting a laugh out of Ēostre.

"Chloe?" Saul called.

Ēostre hid the little stick behind her back when Saul appeared at the top of the stairs.

"Hey, hon, what are you doing up here? I thought you were going to stay with Max."

"Astrid wished to sit with Maximilian for a time, so we've switched places," he explained. "Mahasti is with her."

"That's good for them both. Why don't you go make her a snack then and take a nap yourself?" Chloe urged as she nudged him toward the door.

"Why are you hurrying me away?"

"No reason," Chloe said, the rest of her words flowing in a rush, "but I think I left that pitcher of lemonade out on the counter. Would you put it away before Felix dips his paws into it?"

Skeptical, golden eyes studied Chloe, then flicked back and forth between them before Saul made his way from the hallway and down to the ground level, resigned to whatever mischief they were planning.

"Okay, let's have a look."

Ēostre's heart slammed against her chest as she brought the pregnancy test from behind her back. She didn't know if the results would be accurate, but she trusted Chloe's judgment, and by proxy, had to trust her human methods. Glancing down, she saw two, bold pink lines stretched across the rectangular window.

Her heart skipped, from racing to flutters behind her ribs. Pregnant. Max was going to be a father for the second time. Saul would have a little sibling.

"Ēostre…" Chloe slipped an arm around her. "Congratulations, sweetie. Are you pleased?"

"I'm… I don't know," she answered truthfully. Her fingers shook and fresh tears spilled down her cheeks. "What if he doesn't come back? I practically raised one child alone, Chloe. I can't do this again. Not without Max."

"Shh, no, hon. You won't have to do it without him."

"Mommy! Grandma!" Astrid's voice echoed up the stairs.

"What is it sweetheart?"

"Grandpa Max is waking up!"

Chapter 21

Maximilian's most recent memory was of Ēostre's beautiful face over dinner. Everything afterward was a blur. The evacuation and the bomb had been lost in a hazy white glare.

"Grandma needs you," he heard a young voice whispering beside his ear. "We all do, but Grandma most of all. You promised me you weren't old enough to become one of the Ancestors, and I need you here."

Tiny hands glided over his neck, circling in a soothing stroke pattern that made him quietly sigh. The petting paused and fingers hovered above his skin.

"Grandpa Max?"

How long had he slept, he wondered, opening his mouth to speak, but coughing instead. He cleared his throat a few times and opened his eyes to see Astrid in her human form beside him with huge, owlish blue eyes on his face.

"You're awake! You're finally awake!" She darted off toward the house, screaming at the top of her lungs. "Mommy! Grandma!"

Within moments, adults piled outside of the manor. Max became very aware of a half dozen inquisitive and hopeful eyes watching him, and when he tried to push his weight onto his front claws to greet them, a bloom of pain exploded in his gut, promptly putting him back down. Ēostre hurried forward at once and set one hand to his nose.

"Save your strength, Belenos... please. Don't move."

"Were you injured?" Max asked. His throat, dry and raspy, made the words come out with a harsh cough.

Tears gleamed in her eyes as she shook her head. "No. You saved all of us."

In her human form, Ēostre was tiny by comparison. She hugged the side of his face and sobbed against his cheek. "I thought I'd lost you."

"No. Too stubborn."

"A trait all too common among you reds." Saul grinned at him. "Glad to have you back with us, old man. Mahasti, he must be starved by now, would you—"

"Of course," the genie replied before Saul could finish his request. She snapped her fingers and a banquet fit for a dragon king appeared before them on a gigantic marble slab. A cool vat of water materialized beside it which he drank down to the bottom, sloshing water everywhere in his haste.

While he sated his hunger pangs, Ēostre and Saul approached his midsection to inspect his gut wound. She peeled back the enormous bandage taped over his abdomen then rocked on her heels and stared. Max immediately tried to twist for a better look.

"How bad is it?"

"It's… it's healed," she said, stunned.

"What do you mean, healed? I hurt like hell."

"Exactly what I say, Bel. The physical damage is healed far beyond what it should be."

"There's definite scar tissue left behind, but the injury is closed," Saul commented. His brows drew together in consternation and then he shot his daughter a look. "Did you heal him again, Astrid?"

Ēostre, Saul, and Chloe stared at Astrid while the girl shyly scuffed her toes against the dirt. "I know you told me to rest, Daddy, but I was worried. Am I in trouble?"

"No, no," Saul promptly replied once he recovered his wits. "You're not in trouble." He and Chloe moved up to the child, the former kneeling down to shorten the distance between them. "You did a very brave thing, Astrid, and you may have saved your grandfather's life. I don't know how you found the power to do it, but it was a very good thing."

"Thank you," Ēostre whispered. She hugged Max again and clung to him, motionless, her tears against the ember-hued hide stretched over his broad ribs.

"Yes, Astrid, thank you."

"I love you, Grandpa," Astrid whispered. "I wanted you to get better."

"Thanks to you, little one, I will."

Astrid stepped in and hugged his neck, her parents right behind her in expressing their affections.

Max glanced across the field to see Fafnir's ruby red face staring at him from beside the estate. The other ancient's features were twisted into a mask of unconcealed hatred, his yellow eyes narrowed slits. Without a word, Fafnir turned his back to them and lumbered away to return to the hoard, but Max couldn't shake the feeling that the dragon he'd once revered and loved as a brother, would have rather watched him die.

***

It took the better part of two days for Max to regain enough strength to even attempt to take his human form. When he did, his control wavered, and Ēostre quickly forced him to abandon the attempt.

"At least tell me what I've missed. Bring me a phone," Max groaned as he lay stretched over the ground beside the veranda.

"You nearly died, and you're concerned with having a phone?" Ēostre demanded.

"I need to know what's happened in my absence. Have you kept Kenneth abreast of the recent developments?"

"Of course. He called frequently while you were sleeping, and Ian even visited. His people are turning the Secret Service inside out right now and getting to the bottom of how a dragonslayer got past the vetting process."

Max grunted. "I'm not sure if you realize this, but we don't ask government officials if they have an undying hatred for paranormal creatures during typical interviewing procedures."

"Maybe it should be added to the application," she teased lightly. "I'll get you a phone, or I'll bring Kenneth to you."

After arrangements were made on the phone, Ēostre coordinated a meeting between Max, Kenneth, and a small number of agents cleared to take over Max's protection. They talked White House business while Ēostre hovered protectively at her recovering husband's side and refused to budge. She internally vowed to turn them inside out if they so much harmed a single feather on his wings.

"It's a pleasure to be reassigned to you, President Emberthorn," one of the young men said. He had the smell of a bear on his skin, and the broad-shouldered bulk of a grizzly. One of Ian's, no doubt. "I'm Agent Jim Pellman."

"And I am Agent Charles Price," the second agent said. A normal human nose wouldn't detect anything, but Max smelled wet dog. A hound of some kind with dark brown hair and big, bloodshot eyes. He stood about average male height with broad, muscular shoulders, and had a habit of sniffing occasionally.

One by one the new agents introduced themselves, two humans accompanying the pair of new shapeshifters. Each of them had been selected by Ian himself.

"I'm glad to see you're on the mend, Max, and I won't be the only one. Most media outlets have been hailing you as a hero since it happened. And the ones who aren't… fuck 'em," the vice president said in a rare use of vulgarity.

Max chuckled and pushed up into a sitting position. The sudden movement brought him to a towering height above the group of men. The two human agents fell back a few steps, and their jaws dropped while their eyes focused on his enormous teeth. Knowing he was a dragon and seeing it with their own two eyes changed everything. The slightest movement from him renewed their awe, as well as well-deserved fear.

And he had to respect them for suppressing their flight or fight responses, something many humans failed to control the first time they made contact with a dragon.

"What's the official story as far as I'm concerned?"

Kenneth cleared his throat. "You're at a secure medical facility making a swift recovery. The nation is not without a leader. You should, uh, see the amount of bouquets and other, er, gifts arriving at the White House."

"Gifts?" Ēostre asked.

"Someone sent a longhorn steer all the way from Texas," Agent Price spoke up in amusement. "We found a rancher willing to take him."

"In the meantime, we've asked the public to refrain from further gifts, and to make donations to your preferred charities instead. Military veterans, foster children, and the like."

"Ah. Excellent," Max said. "Anything else?"

"Well… there is one other thing," Kenneth said.

One of the agents snickered briefly.

"What is it?" Max asked, suspicious of the break in Pellman's solemn expression. "If it's funny, I could use the laughter. We all could."

"Did you want us to keep the virgins around? They've been showing up in droves."

Ēostre twisted around to stare at him. "What?"

Kenneth wiped at his eyes, unable to contain his laughter. "We've had women showing up at the gates, asking to be virgin sacrifices. They're out there almost every day now, hoping to heal their president with their, and I quote, 'innocence and purity.'"

Ēostre groaned into her hands but Max's chest rumbled with full-bellied laughter.

"I'm sure a few of them aren't actual virgins, and correct me if I'm wrong, but I thought it was unicorns that had the preference for chastity?" Agent Pellman asked.

"Alas, we haven't seen nor heard from any unicorn in many centuries. As far as I know, they've died out," Ēostre answered. "And really, the whole virgin thing is a man-made myth. They don't taste any different, believe me."

Max's head swiveled around to face his wife. He stared. "You told me you've never eaten a princess before."

She snorted. "As if every virgin must be a princess? Or a girl for that matter? Honestly, my love."

"Right then." Kenneth cleared his throat. "We'll have the virgin matter cleared up soon enough, but I imagine it won't be the last time we see such groupies. Some group held a rally in New York City the other evening to support vampires who have come out into the open."

"Loonies," Pellman muttered under his breath. "How is that going to work, exactly?"

Max and Ēostre exchanged glances before turning back to the expectant faces watching them.

"The vampires," Ēostre began, "have always managed their own affairs with some loose guidelines set by the Dragon Council. Most of their blood comes from blood banks, actually. Or willing feeders."

"It doesn't stop some from killing, though," Max continued. "It's in their nature. However, there are, and will continue to be, severe consequences if they are caught. The same as any other murderer out there."

"Same as with any human out in the world, right, sir?" Agent Newton, one of the two humans, asked with a quizzical expression on his face. "The way I see it, nothing breaks the law as long as it's safe and consensual."

"Correct," Max said. "Which is the stance I shall take over the next few years as I navigate this topic from the oval office."

"Speaking of, when will you be coming back? Not that I'm rushing you, of course." Kenneth flashed him a quick grin. "Everyone has been anxious to see you."

"I should be able to take my human form again in a few days. Ēostre won't allow me to try for now. It's too taxing," he explained to the group of them. "In the meantime, please assure the media of my recovery and health."

"Of course," Kenneth said. "Ēostre, take good care of him for us. We should leave you to your rest. If any other important matters arise, I'll contact you by phone."

Max laid back down while Ēostre saw the men back to the White House, courtesy of magic. Kenneth mumbled something about it being a great way to save on travel costs before he stepped through to his office.

"Can I come sit with you now?"

He turned his head toward the doorway where Astrid peeked out at him. "Of course, my dear. You know I'm always happy to see you."

Astrid moved over and took a seat by his head on the grass. For a while she was quiet, and Max was content with her company alone. Ēostre rejoined them a few minutes later with snacks in hand.

"You look thoughtful, little one," Max told the girl. "What weighs on your mind?"

"It's okay to ask a question?"

"Any time," Ēostre assured her.

"Why do the dragonslayers hate us?" Astrid asked. "What did we ever do to make them want to exterminate all dragons?"

Max inhaled a deep breath. No one had ever asked him the question before, and he wasn't sure if he had the answer she wanted. "Because, my sweet, for every four dragons like your father, Uncle Teo, grandmother, and myself, there is another type of dragon that thrives on chaos. Dragons who live to hurt others

229

by killing humans and causing pain. Dragons like my father and my daughter, who died many years ago, are cruel beasts who live for the glory of battle."

"I don't understand the difference. You and Daddy told me stories about fighting knights and razing villages." Her brows knit, creating a big wrinkle in the center of her forehead. "Dragons brought it on themselves, then?"

"No, it's actually quite different. They would go in search of a dragon, and when a knight brought the battle to me, I ended it swiftly. Of course there were times when it became necessary to rain hell on a kingdom to prove I was not to be trifled with, but for the most part, I desired nothing but peace. This is how many dragons lived, and also how we acquired our hoards. To the winner go the spoils. We occupied a volcano, an island, or even an underwater cave, then we left their kind alone," Max answered her.

"But they hunted you anyway?"

"Yes," Ēostre said.

"Why not move?" the girl asked curiously.

"Do you remember the lovely dollhouse you and I made a few years ago?" Ēostre asked.

"Yes. It's beautiful. It's my favorite toy, and Svetlana's too."

"So it is. Now, imagine you have taken as much time, if not more, to build a real home. You spend weeks, or even months carving your bedrooms. Collecting your jewels. You grow attached to this hoard constructed by your own hands," Ēostre began.

"Okay."

"Now imagine you have stepped outside to collect dinner. A human sees you, and later returns with an army. You are told to leave."

"Hell no," Astrid said, shaking her head.

Somehow Max managed to withhold his laughter at her defiant swear. Instead, he picked up where Ēostre left off.

"They have axes and swords, they have decided to force you to go, or worse, to kill you for reasons which may have nothing to do with actual fear of you. Perhaps they want to pull the skin from your carcass for their mightiest champions, and use your bones for their lances. Would you leave your home to sate their prejudice? It's easy to fly away, little one. Fighting to keep one's home is difficult whether it is against knights in armor or slayers. I have taken many human lives, and while I jest about defeating kingdoms, I don't miss those days of war."

Astrid's lips pursed while she considered everything. "Why haven't dragons killed all of the slayers yet if they're so dangerous?"

"They're not easy to find, Astrid, and only a sorceress like your grandmother can smell the old soul in them."

"Not always," Ēostre added. "I didn't smell the lad who planted the bomb. His blood may have thinned too much from his ancestors."

"Besides, how would that make us any better than them?" Max asked in a gentle tone.

Ēostre nodded her agreement. "Aside from that, do you remember our conversation about witches?"

"Yes. They're immortals like us, but their bodies aren't. They reincarnate, right?"

"Exactly so. Such is also true for dragonslayers. They were born from the blood of a wizard named Merlin," Ēostre explained. "And this is what makes them dangerous, little one. They remember, they hold grudges, they know us. I've encountered the same slayer five times in my life, and he once wounded me so deeply I slept for a year to recover."

"But we don't reincarnate. The reason our soul bonds end upon death is because we disperse into the cosmos."

"Exactly," Ēostre confirmed sadly. "Your... Fafnir is the first dragon to ever return from the dead in the history of our kind."

"I wish he'd go away," Astrid muttered. "He makes everyone unhappy, and he doesn't feel like a person. He doesn't even eat."

Doesn't feel like a person, Max echoed in his mind, as disturbed by her utterance as he was by the realization it was true. Something felt acutely wrong about his old friend. It didn't just feel wrong. It smelled wrong, like the air around him had become contaminated by his presence.

"Is... Is that why you did not want to greet him?" Ēostre hadn't pushed the girl about her revulsion to Fafnir at their first meeting, and in all of the drama that occurred afterward, none of them had thought to ask why.

"Fafnir scares me, Grandma. He isn't like your stories and doesn't feel right." She turned her eyes to Max. "Please make him leave, Grandpa."

"I can't do that, love. This isn't my home," he reminded her in a gentle voice. "Only your father and mother could do that. It's up to them to decide when they've had enough."

In true childlike fashion, Astrid continued to talk and offer up tidbits. Her blue eyes were wide and adoring, focused on Max while she talked. "He and Daddy talk sometimes, and he hurts Daddy's feelings. I don't care what he says about me, but I don't like the things he says about Mom. Or you two." She bit her lower lip and hesitated. "He talks the most about Mom and you, and it's always hateful things," she said to Ēostre.

From the corner of his eye, he saw Ēostre flinch.

Realizing that she'd made a faux pas, Astrid frowned and climbed to her feet. "I should let you rest. Can I come back later?"

Max smiled. "Of course."

"She's right, you know," Ēostre whispered after Astrid went inside. "Fafnir is not right. He..." She sighed and shook her head. "I know our memories tend to shine people in the best light, but his recent displays of malice contradict everything I know."

"Come here." Max wrapped his claws around Ēostre and tugged her against his chest. Maybe he couldn't change the circumstances surrounding her former mate's return, but he could provide the comfort she deserved.

Chapter 22

His return to the White House had been met with genuine warmth and well wishes. Of course, the official medical personnel wanted to ensure his good health and oversee the remainder of his recovery. They even attempted to convince him to see a doctor at Bethesda, but he gently declined, reminding them all he'd survived a couple dozen centuries without anyone's medical expertise.

He couldn't argue with Ēostre, however. She kept him confined to their residence and reprised her role as his personal nurse, little changing between her behavior at Saul's home and the White House.

As much as he appreciated the pampering, long days on the couch and in bed bored him, making Max more than ready to get back to the job.

"Why don't we find a movie on Netflix?" Ēostre suggested from the doorway.

When alone in their residence and away from the eyes of the public, she favored oversized shirts. This one fell off her shoulder, revealing the thin strap of a lace camisole beneath. She wore tight-fitting leggings with it, showing off her lithe silhouette. When she stretched, the shirt raised, revealing the hint of a tummy she'd gained due to her new life in the White House, late nights eating chocolates in bed, and the world-class meals their chef insisted were necessary. Max grinned. He loved every inch of her. "I'll see about when dinner will be ready, and we can... what do they call it?"

"Netflix and Chill, love."

"Yes that. We will chill," she offered cheerfully. A sly smile curved her lips. "I'll let housekeeping know we'll require privacy this evening."

Max perked up and straightened in his seat. Either Ēostre was ignorant to the true meaning of Netflix and Chill, or she'd just discreetly tipped him off that he was officially off bedrest. The lack of intimacy since their abbreviated honeymoon had dampened his spirits as much as the return of Fafnir.

"All right. The news is nearly over," he replied, grinning back at her. "I'll finish that up and find something traumatizing."

She stuck her tongue out at him and flounced into the hall to harass the chef. Everything about her today was a happy contrast to the morose caretaker who had barely laughed since his injury. She was smiling again. Radiant.

And fuck, he really missed the sex, and had secretly feared Fafnir's return had disrupted something between them. Ēostre swore the soul bond between her and the other red dragon had been severed by death, but pain had given Max irrational ideas and thoughts in his head.

Eager to begin their night together, he tuned in to the last news segment. A young blonde woman sat behind the news desk, a bright smile on her airbrushed face. She didn't have a single pore or crease, her makeup applied with absolute precision.

"The exposure of supernatural creatures has brought a variety of people out into the open. While the news has been a dream come true for many people around the world, some are not happy with what's taken place."

The news report cut from the girl to protesters waving signs. A man with a football player's physique stood on the stage, dressed in neatly tailored slacks and a button-down shirt.

Slayer. Without a doubt, it's what the man had to be. The news identified David Mitchell as a retired Navy Seal, forty-three years old with twenty years of service behind him. He had the body of a soldier half his age. Max stilled, able to read the body language, the poise, the shit-eating confidence that David exuded whenever he addressed the crowd. Most of all, Max recognized the face. He'd seen it before. Slayers were eternal.

"Are we going to allow these beasts hold us hostage?" the dragonslayer asked the crowd. "History has proven they cannot be trusted. How can we put our trust in a president who isn't even *human*?"

The gathered crowd cheered the man on and waved their signs in the air. "Down with dragons!" they cried out.

"We need to out these monsters. We need to let them know they have no place among us, or even in this world."

The news segment swapped back to the reporter who gave the camera a solemn stare. "Similar protests have been taking place across the country today and around the globe."

Max punched the power button on the remote, dimming the screen just as the news displayed a poster for the Anti-Dragon Movement. It was only another name — the current name — for the Knights of Merlin, a group known throughout draconic history for persecuting his kind at the behest of a mad scholar. The group to which all dragonslayers belonged.

Their ideas sickened him and caused a general sense of unease in most civilized parts of the world. Instead of banding together, people now accused their neighbors of outlandish acts, from animal sacrifice to cheating their taxes with magic.

Kenneth was right about the media labeling him as a hero, but for every word of praise, he received two more in condemnation.

His mood plummeted.

"Maybe this was all a mistake," he grunted once he smelled Ēostre in the room again. He didn't turn to look at her, only glowered at the remote in his hand. "I should resign."

"Resigning? You want to resign over one news report?" Ēostre whispered. She strode across the room to him and touched his chin, directing her husband's eyes to her face. "Why?"

"They've lost faith in me, Ēostre. How can I possibly lead a country occupied by humans who fear my very existence?" Max shook his head and tossed the remote aside on the cushions. "I was a foolish idealist to believe we could live in peace together."

"A small fraction, Max, and we expected as much." She rubbed her thumb across his cheek. "You are not a quitter, so tell me what's really on your mind."

"No, I'm not a quitter," he replied tersely, "but I understand the grim reality of our future — every dragon's future now that I've exposed us."

"Actually, Fafnir exposed us, so it would have happened at some point anyway. Yes, they've seen some of the worst of us, but they have also seen our best. Your heroic stunt has won people over. What we did at Rainier, saving lives, has shown the people we're not monsters."

"My wife, the voice of reason and my most critical advisor. All right. It was only a brief ponderance. I won't resign," he agreed.

"Good, because *we* need you to remain strong."

"Oh, my love, if not me our kind would find someone else to look to."

"I wasn't referring to our kind, Max. There's more. More I need to say to you..."

"Of course, there's always something more," he half-grumbled, putting a smile on his face.

"I had hoped to speak to you about the possibility on our date, but... well, with everything that's happened there hasn't been a good moment."

His brows raised. "You can always talk to me, no matter the time or issue. You know that."

"I do, but this is different."

"What is it? Are you unhappy here? Are you still thinking about what to do with Fafnir?" Preparing himself for bad news, he rose to his feet and took in a breath. *Calm. Remain calm.*

"No. While the latter does worry me, it isn't what I wanted to talk about."

"Then what? The suspense is killing me, Ēostre."

"I'm pregnant."

Her two words took him by surprise, hitting him like a sledgehammer. For a moment the room spun and his body broke out in cold tingles of mounting excitement.

"Pregnant," he echoed her. "As in have a cub? We're going to have a cub?"

Her lips curved up in a smile. "Pregnant has no other meaning, as far as I know. You're going to be a father."

"Again," Max whispered. He sat down too heavily in the seat, his knees losing control at the last moment. Fortunately, he didn't miss the chair and it caught his weight. "I never thought… You were never in season while we were together. How?"

"Fate, maybe? I could not begin to tell you, though it isn't entirely unheard of to breed outside of our season. Are… are you happy?"

"Happy? Ēostre, I am speechless. Thrilled. I…" He shook his head, unable to find the words, and leaned forward to pull her close. With his arms wrapped around her waist, he set his cheek on her tummy and closed his eyes.

Had the Ancestors smiled upon him somehow, and given him a chance to right his past wrongs? Another chance to be the father he'd always wanted to be?

"I know this was unexpected," she whispered, running her fingers through his hair.

"But gladly welcomed, my love. So very welcomed." *Another chance,* he thought again, only for dark memories of Brigid to shadow his elation. *Another chance to ruin another child.*

As cold waves of dread washed through him, Ēostre stiffened, her fingers stilled, and she leaned back to look down at him. "What's wrong?" All of his doubts flooded through their link, and a rush of shame warmed his face.

"It's nothing."

"It's something," she insisted. "What's wrong?"

His fingers closed over a handful of her shirt. He shivered and produced the worst outcome in his mind, a child just like Brigid, spoiled, selfish, and unconcerned with anyone but herself. "What if… I am a poor excuse for a father again?" he asked quietly.

"Oh Bel…" Her fingers threaded through his hair in a tender gesture. "I am not Mahuika, and you are not Fafnir. I… since his return, I realize now my perception of him was colored by our bond, and with it severed I wonder why I tolerated so many things. I thought the sun rose and set with my mate, but he was the very definition of an absent father. When I needed help, *you* were there for me."

Maximilian digested her words in silence, and when he failed to speak, Ēostre whispered quietly, "Maybe I'm the one who failed you. I should have extended my hand to Brigid."

"Brigid hated you," Max mumbled against the spot between her breasts. "You did try, and she would have nothing to do with you. You tried many times. Brigid was beyond your help and anything you could do."

"Then you understand, my love, that these words also apply to you. There is only so much we may do as parents. Brigid received all of your love, and you taught her right from wrong, but in the end, she chose what to ignore from your lessons."

"I know," he admitted. "I know it in my mind, but I don't yet know it here," he whispered, touching one hand above his heart.

His wife took the same hand from his chest and placed it on her lower tummy. The small bump he'd thought was from her snacking alongside him was something more. Their baby. He wondered how long it would be until their little one would meet them in the world.

"I love you with all of my being, Ēostre. Both of you."

"And I love you, Belenos." A mischievous expression came over her face, brightening her eyes. "Let me show you."

"Show me?"

Her sly smile remained as she seized him by the belt and unfastened it. It pulled free from the loops with a sharp tug, then Ēostre deftly removed his cock and slid her fingers up and down the stiffening length. His body reacted immediately to her, promptly awakening his desire. Growling in response, he playfully nipped her ear. "Should we be doing this now?"

"Why shouldn't we? I sent away all of the housekeeping staff early." She leaned back, a bemused smile on her lips. "Are you afraid you'll harm the baby?"

"I… somewhat," he admitted.

"Mm. No. Trust me, he or she is very safe, and I have… plans."

"Plans?" he echoed dumbly as she stroked from root to head.

"Mmhmm."

With the blood rapidly leaving his brain, Max barely noticed her slipping down to her knees on the floor.

"What are you doing, Ēostre?"

"A surprise." Her fingers glided over him again, practiced and slow, tracing over the veined ridges while he pulsed beneath her touch. "I learned many things recently about humans. They're incredibly imaginative when it comes to sex. More so than dragons."

He shuddered beneath her torturous teases and reached up to loosen his tie. His throat went dry. Kneeling between his legs, his wife looked like a silver goddess. She gave him a coy smile then dipped forward, and the rest was lost to bliss.

Ēostre's soft lips kissed over the head of his cock, then parted to gradually accept him into her mouth. Inch by inch, gentle increments took him deeper, only for the dragoness to withdraw and let her tongue play over the glistening tip. His head fell back as he moaned, clutching a handful of the fabric on the sofa arm.

"Fuck," he swore under his breath.

"Patience, we'll get to that soon enough," she promised as she delivered delicate little nibbles around his ridged crown.

Up and down, she worked him in a slow, leisurely manner that drove him to the brink of madness. With one hand fisted in her hair and the other clutching the sofa cushion, Max moved his hips in time with her set rhythm. She stopped only to catch her breath, and when she did, her fingers took over by curling around his thick girth and pumping until her mouth resumed the tempo, teasing with kittenish licks and tasting the occasional clear drop offered from the tip.

As his pleasure spiraled higher, the tension wound tighter, and heat coursed through his body. Fire burned through his veins and threatened his self-control.

He tried to withdraw to spare her the taste of his seed, but he was too slow, his reflexes delayed by the abrupt wave of rapture sweeping over him. And her hold. She didn't release him, and their eyes met at the moment of his release. "Ēos-Ēostre," he groaned out as he spilled in her welcoming mouth.

Max slumped back against the couch and waited for his eyes to focus. "Wow."

"Feeling better?"

"Immensely, but what about you?" Max asked once he had his wits about him again. He swept a few flyaway strands from her face and tucked them behind her ear. "I did nothing for you." Her lips were plump and swollen from her effort. It turned him on again, knowing his cock had done that to her.

"Please. Having you at my complete mercy was immeasurably nice for me. You dragon men are notorious for wanting control."

"Then I think it's time for the tables to be turned."

"Oh no!" Ēostre called in mock dismay. She hurried to her feet and moved to escape him, but she was too slow. Max scooped her up from the floor and carried her into the adjoining master bedroom, leaving the den behind.

Unlike their first night together, Max didn't abruptly toss her into the bed. He treated her more gently than he handled the fine china in the White House dining room.

"Where did you learn that?" he asked as he peeled down her leggings.

"Secret."

"Uh huh."

"Like I said, I've been learning things."

"Chloe lent you her romance collection, didn't she?"

Damn, she thought. Max would never let her hear the end of it if he knew she'd practiced for a week and was responsible for the shortage of cucumbers in the kitchen.

"No comment."

Max laughed and stripped off his shirt and pants. She drank in the sight of him, sweeping her gaze up his strong legs and over his muscled chest. The scars left from the bomb only accentuated his strength — made him even more impressive in figure. No matter which form he took, he was striking, and made her pulse race and her heart flutter.

The first time they'd mated in their dragon forms, six months earlier, they'd snuck out of the White House in the middle of the night to his hoard where they spent hours alternating from human shape to draconic form until they were exhausted, comparing and contrasting the differences. Giggling like teenagers, they'd decided the humans were definitely on to something.

Most other males preferred their draconic bodies, but Max, her sweet, dear husband, never missed an opportunity to make love to her. She'd never met a dragon like him before.

Struck by a sudden fit of evil, Ēostre spread her legs and glided her fingers over the neatly trimmed strip of silver hair at the apex of her thighs. Max made a rumbly noise in his chest, growling low.

"Tease."

"I haven't teased anyone but myself," she replied, creating a circuit over the slick folds. Her fingers slid up and down, back again, gathering moisture she traced over her clit. She moaned into the quiet bedroom and opened her eyes to find Max watching her with undisguised lust in his eyes.

"Maybe I should take over."

"Have you been in Chloe's romance collection as well?" she teased.

"I'm a man with access to the internet."

Max knelt down on the mattress and grabbed her by her ankles. A single tug dragged her across the silken sheets. His palms glided up her calves, skimmed over her knees, and up her thighs.

A broad stroke of his tongue touched her, warm and wet between her thighs. Every muscle in her body tensed. He licked her again and her thighs trembled, her core clenching in anticipation before his tongue thrust into her receptive embrace.

"Bel," she whispered shakily. She'd seen videos of it, knew what he was doing, but had only briefly entertained the thought of him invading her with his tongue and making her quake in ecstasy.

"Should I stop?"

"No… Stars, no."

He touched her clit with it, teasing or uncertain, and the shock of it jolted through her. Ēostre's fingers flew to his head and took a handful of his hair, nearly pulling it from the scalp.

He paused.

"Don't stop," she pleaded again. He chuckled, warm breath against her damp skin. For the first time since he began, she heard skin against skin, his aroused length in one hand. Ēostre became torn between the desire for him to finish and the need to have him inside her.

He sucked the delicate nerve button again and Ēostre soared, her body cresting on waves of indescribable pleasure. At the moment of her climax, he was above her again, slipping into her in

243

a single thrust. Her legs automatically raised to lock around his hips, and she drew him to a hilted fit.

He thrust in and out, granting her body something to hold onto until long after the timed clenches of orgasm subsided. Then he made love to her again. Face to face, one tender stroke after the next with gentle touches accompanied by whispered words.

When they finally collapsed together in a boneless heap, they were slick with sweat. Ēostre stretched beneath him then sighed, sated and beyond content. "What brought that on? Mm… not that I'm complaining."

"I needed to show you what you did for me goes both ways," he murmured huskily, "and I've wanted to taste you for a long while. I just thought…" He stopped himself and chuckled quietly. "I don't know what I thought."

"That I'd believe you were strange?"

He nodded briefly.

"No, Bel… I…" Her cheeks warmed, a sudden rush of warmth overtaking them. "I think… I want to try everything with you."

"A good thing we have all the time in the world then."

Chapter 23

"What are you doing to her?" Max asked, interrupting the obstetrician for the third time. "She flinched."

"It's only a lubricant. See? You can touch it if you want."

Their doctor came with high recommendations and thirty years' experience. She even gave them an enthusiastic welcome, either naturally fearless or too eager to have the prestigious accomplishment under her belt of delivering a dragon's child. Age had lined her face, and she wore her steel gray hair in a severe chin-length bob. She couldn't be younger than seventy, and despite her unveiled fascination with their dragon halves, she exuded only warmth and a caring, grandmotherly feeling that put Ēostre at ease.

"Max, relax, my love. It's only cold." She chuckled at his fretting. "Chloe told me all about this."

"Oh."

Her husband quieted, but he remained tense as a coiled spring beside her, perched precariously on the edge of his seat and leaning forward to stare at the black screen. Ēostre didn't blame him. Waiting for something besides her name, the date, and the time to appear was killing her, too.

"Now, you're going to see me change the angle and stop to take measurements on occasion," Dr. Shapiro explained. "If you have any questions, feel free to ask." The woman beamed at them, providing the reassurances Ēostre needed. Max was a bundle of nerves, and with their link, it meant all of his anticipation and worries flowed through to her whether he tried to suppress it or not.

The doctor pressed a device into the puddle of clear gel on Ēostre's belly. A spherical shape snapped into focus, and as she rolled the device over Ēostre's mildly rounded tummy, it gained further clarity. "Here's the face. Eyes here, and a nose."

"It's like magic," Max breathed. "How can it see inside of her?"

The doctor chuckled at his enthusiasm and adjusted the angle. "It isn't magic, Mr. Emberthorn. Only science. Now right here is the arm. We'll also listen to the heart rhythm, and I'll be attempt to estimate the due date based on the fetal size. A typical dragon pregnancy is two years, you said?"

"Twenty-five months," Ēostre clarified.

"We'll figure it out." As promised, she saved pictures, measured internal organs, and then a rapid noise whoosh-whooshed into the private examination room, catching Ēostre by surprise.

"What's that?" Ēostre asked, furrowing her brow.

Frozen in place with a bewildered expression on her face, the doctor stared at first. "A heartbeat, but…" The image changed, their fetus becoming smaller, a tiny bean-shaped silhouette beside its mirrored image. "*Two* heartbeats. Twins. It's twins. Are twins typical for dragonkind?"

"No," Ēostre breathed. "Far from it." Beside her in the chair, Max had yet to utter a word. His mouth hung open, amber eyes fixated on the image of their unborn children.

"This is amazing," the doctor told them. "You'll have to forgive me but I—"

"You expected them to look different," Ēostre finished for her without ever losing her smile. "The same magic that allows us to shapeshift also works on the children we carry until they are born. Were we to try this in my natural shape, the babies would take on dragon form as well."

"Can we do that?" Doctor Shapiro's eyes widened and she blushed at her own enthusiastic outburst. Her professional demeanor returned with the utterance of an apologetic, "Sorry."

"No, no need to apologize. Personally, I'd prefer for you to share in our excitement than to judge or fear us. Your idea has merit," Max murmured. Bringing their linked hands to his lips, he kissed Ēostre's knuckles. "I love you."

"I love you too." Twins. The revelation awed her, leaving her and Max speechless through most of the remaining sonogram. They asked few questions, unwilling to interrupt or provide unnecessary distractions. By the time the doctor had wiped Ēostre's tummy clean and lowered her shirt, the shock was finally beginning to fade.

"And these are for you," Dr. Shapiro said, placing a strip of black and white photos into Ēostre's hands. "It's too soon to tell you what you're having as far as gender goes, but we'll do this again in a few months when they've developed further. In fact, if you wouldn't mind, I'd actually like to get an ultrasound each month of your pregnancy for documentation."

Ēostre gazed down at the tiny, twin silhouettes in the photos then turned to her husband and squeezed his hand. "I think that is a marvelous idea. It will be good to have actual medical information if something were ever to happen in a future dragon pregnancy." *Or in ours,* she worried, fretting over the unknown possibilities. While dragons were tough and hardy individuals, she'd known a few females over the centuries who lost their unborn cubs to mysterious reasons.

"Agreed," Max said.

"Excellent. Now, I know I questioned you at length prior to the sonogram, but a few more thoughts have occurred to me since then. You do plan to birth the children in your human body, correct?"

"I believe I will. I like your office, as well as your bedside manner, and would be reluctant to part from that." Ēostre hesitated. "I delivered my older son by myself, and while I was pleased with the outcome, the birth itself was a lonely process.

"Now you said your magic shifts them for now. What about after they're born?"

Ēostre blew out a breath. "It will be a new experience for us all. No dragon has ever birthed in human form before. So the twins will have to learn to shift into their dragon shapes as they grow, rather than the opposite."

"Regardless of the decision you make, we'll adapt our birthing plan to work with you. Please let me know if anything changes."

"Thank you, Dr. Shapiro."

"Michelle. Please call me Michelle," the woman said, voice warm and comforting in the otherwise sterile room.

"Only if you call us Ēostre and Max. I insist. If we're to use your services for our little ones over the next year and a half, at the very least, we must be on a first name basis."

"Deal. Now as I said, I have a few more concerns, and afterward, we'll schedule your next appointment. Join me in my office. It's a little more comfortable than that exam table." She flashed them a reassuring grin, and led the way from the room to a sunny office with two plush visitor chairs. "Water?"

"Yes please."

Michelle's questions never felt like an interrogation — Ēostre and Max answered her candidly, withholding nothing about their species and unique habits.

When it was all done, the expectant dragoness floated on air from the office to the car awaiting them outside. This time, she had no fear of dragonslaying assassins and bombs. Ian worked closely with the head of the Secret Service in providing the best shifters he could find, and their security retinue had tightened without depriving them of further privacy and freedom. He hadn't merely cut through the red tape to make it happen, he'd eviscerated the system and leaned on it until they were happy to accept his "recommendations."

"Are you happy with the news?" she whispered to him once they were safely seated inside "The Beast." "Are you truly happy?"

"Impossibly happy. Thrilled," Max said. He brought Ēostre closer, and she turned her face into his neck, pressing her cheek against the heat her husband naturally exuded. "I can't believe it. Twins."

"It's certainly made you a man of few words," she teased.

"How could I possibly be anything but elated, my love?" His lips skimmed the top of her head. "Today is a day for celebration, we must tell your family—"

"Our family," she corrected him.

"Of course. Our family. Saul, Chloe, and Astrid must be the first to know before we release the information to the media," the dragon mused thoughtfully. "Unless you would prefer for the pregnancy to remain secret. I'll be happy to do whatever you feel is best for you."

Ēostre leaned back to gaze up at him. "Let's tell them. Let's tell the world."

***

Max met a limited number of reporters for a small press release in the rose garden. He loved it there, the serene environment paired with memories of his wedding day to Ēostre. He went without the suit and tie, opting for khakis and a casual button-down shirt, and with the summer breeze rustling his auburn hair he felt invincible, bulletproof, and absolutely in control of his life. Ēostre loved him, the Ancestors had favored them with not one, but two little ones, and the world was gradually coming to accept supernatural existence.

"President Emberthorn, can you tell us when the baby will be due?"

Max's grin widened. "The *babies* will arrive in the fall. A year and a half from now."

He'd expected a stunned reaction. At first, the open yard dropped into silence. Then a flurry of questions broke out. He raised his hands and waited for the noise to die down before he answered.

"Yes, we were incredibly amazed to discover my wife is carrying twins, and we couldn't be happier. As for the time… Dragonkind gestate for two years. Ēostre won't begin to truly show, as you put it, until Thanksgiving later this year."

"Do you know what you're having?"

"Two healthy little ones are what I hope for," Max replied. "Boys or girls, we're happy with whatever blessings we receive. We only ask that the press respect our privacy during this time and in return we promise ample opportunities to get your pictures."

"Do you have names picked out?"

The question resulted in another good-humored laugh. "Not yet, but knowing Ēostre they'll be beautiful and impressive."

"Where is the first lady?" someone asked from the crowd.

"My wife is with her family, delighting in their happy attentions at the news, and I am due to join them. Thank you all for your questions, and I am honored you were able to attend. I have time for one final question."

"Will they hatch from eggs?"

Max, as well as a few of the other journalists, chuckled. "No. My kind are as warm-blooded as your people and quite similar in many ways. She's chosen to birth them in her human form."

After promising to keep them updated on the pregnancy, he was escorted into the building by his security team.

"We'll be at the California estate," he told his security team. "If you're needed for a public outing, Ēostre will send for you. I don't expect for us to be gone past dinner."

"Excellent. Enjoy your time away, Mr. President. We'll remain here, pretending you're still on the premises."

As he took the steps two at a time, Max sent a text message to Ēostre. She told him the portal would be awaiting him in the bedroom, and he found it open, without his wife waiting beside it. The clear window to California displayed the serene interior of Saul's roomy den and enormous sectional sofa.

"Where you going?" Spartacus asked him. He sat on a perch beside the window, eyeballing the portal with uncertainty. Spartacus had seen and traveled through them before for visits to California. Sometimes Ēostre left a pocket portal beside his perch for him to visit Astrid during their busy days. He was never without a friend who loved him dearly.

"We're going to see Ēostre's family. Would you like to come?"

"Yes!"

Once Max held out his arm, the bird flew to his wrist without hesitation. "Astrid will be glad to see you, buddy."

"Spartacus loves Astrid."

"I know you do. I hope you'll love our twins as well, as they will be little ones for quite a while."

Max had missed some of the best parts of Brigid's childhood and looked forward to swaddling them at night and giving Ēostre a rest. He grinned at the thought, excited by the prospect of diaper changing. When Mahuika brought Brigid to him for the first time, she'd been a thirty-year-old cub without a human shape, although that changed once he took her to Ireland to meet her first humans. Within days of their arrival, his beautiful little girl became a fiery-haired toddler.

Why did he still miss her?

Max inhaled a deep breath. Maybe the heartache would never heal, but with two cubs on the way, he couldn't afford to live in the past. He had to move on and be strong for them.

Saul scowled at him when he entered. "You promised to take care of my mother. How is this taking care of her?"

"I made that promise at our wedding, which was technically after I did this to her," Max cheerfully replied. "Where is she? I found a portal in our bedroom, but I don't see Ēostre."

"Looking at magazines in the next room with Chloe and deciding new, extraordinary ways to spend our money. You should know your wife has decided to donate two dollars of your money to charity for every dollar spent while preparing for the twins."

"Excellent."

"You have *no* idea how much Chloe can spend on a nursery. It was cute, initially, until boredom at the end of the lengthy pregnancy led to many unnecessary purchases. Her mind changed multiple times, often after the time granted for the return policies."

Max grinned broadly. "You're not nearly as aggravated as you let on."

Saul grinned. "Of course not. But if I don't pretend to be irritated, my bank accounts hemorrhage dollars by the thousands. It's funny, too. She does it in rare spurts, and will go weeks without purchasing anything elaborate, only to wake up and decide one day the kitchen is outdated, or it's time to engage in a bidding war in another country. When she isn't pregnant, I can't convince her to spend a dime."

"You're here!" Astrid rushed into the room and threw her arms around Max's waist. She hugged him tight, and when he returned it, she giggled and turned her face up to look at him. "Can I take Spartacus outside with the zebras?"

"Certainly."

"Awesome!" She held out her arm for the bird and waited while he stepped from Max's forearm to her shoulder. Spartacus turned his head and immediately began running his beak through Astrid's golden hair, grooming her in an affectionate manner. She giggled.

"You behave now, Spartacus."

"He's always good for me."

"You behave, Max. Be a good boy," Spartacus said to him.

Max frowned. "I'm not the bird. I'm your owner."

"You're his friend," Astrid corrected him before flouncing away.

What the hell just happened there? he wondered.

Saul waited until she was out the door before he released his pent-up laughter. "I wish you could see your own face right now, Max."

"Bloody bird has a mind of his own."

"You'd get bored with him otherwise. If it makes you feel any better, I thought the same about Felix for a time. Now we're old friends, him and I." Hearing his name, the old Savannah cat raised his head and glanced at them both. At the age of twenty-one, he still played frantically with his humans and devoted his days to stalking Saul and Chloe.

They joined their wives in the sitting room, and as was customary, accepted the fragile, tiny cups Chloe poured for them. They wouldn't hear the end of it if they didn't drink her tea, especially since her recent hobby had been to sell tea blends and soaps with her friends Marcy and River online.

"How goes the shopping?" Saul asked.

"I found the cutest bedroom sets," Ēostre gushed. She turned the tablet in her lap so Max could see. "Look. Dragons. This lady hand stitches them and can do almost any color we'd like."

Ēostre had decided early on to make most, if not all, of her purchases through smaller businesses. Max approved the idea and was more than happy to support local vendors. He leaned over for a look and smiled at the pictures on the screen.

"I think those would be perfect for our twins."

"You waste no time, do you, Belenos?" Fafnir's sneering voice came from a shadowed corner of the room. "I never took you for a thief, and yet you have plundered my every possession." He approached them, his yellow eyes bloodshot within an ashen face.

Max grunted, able to suppress the urge to lash out by only a slim margin. He rose to his feet and stood his ground. "Ēostre isn't a possession."

"She whelps incompetent, spineless spawn, and yours will be no different. They will be baying pups forever attached to her teat, unable to thrive on their own."

Saul stiffened in his seat.

"You have an amazing son, Fafnir, and you would realize as much if you gave his chosen mate a chance. If you gave *him* a chance, but no, you wasted your years with Ēostre and spent them running away from your family. You brought this on yourself," Maximilian seethed back at his former friend.

Fafnir hissed and took three charging steps forward until Saul leapt between them with his back to Maximilian. "Don't presume to know my thoughts. I loved my family!"

"Fafnir—"

The furious dragon snapped his eyes to Ēostre. "You have no right to speak to me when you stink of his bastard whelps. I can smell them festering inside you."

"Father, enough."

"And you." He glared at his son. "My Brigid was too good for you. I see that now. A thousand curses upon you for bringing her death."

"How dare you!" Ēostre leapt to her feet, fury making her entire body quake.

"How dare I? How dare you!" Fafnir roared back.

"Saul is your own flesh and blood, and you won't speak to him this way for as long as I draw breath."

"The perhaps it is time your breath ceased and spared us all the shame of your presence. A whore to dragons and humans alike."

A partial transformation overtook Fafnir, his claws elongating and clothing stretched to the seams. He lunged toward Ēostre but

Max was there to block his path, a snarl on his lips as he pushed away the man who had once been his closest friend.

Chloe drew Ascalon and pointed the razor-edged blade at Fafnir. He recoiled from its radiance and stepped back to give them a wide berth.

"To oblivion with all of you."

They quieted as Fafnir stormed from the room, radiating blistering heat with each step. His borrowed clothing went up in flames, thankfully causing no damage to the stone floors or walls, but tiny pieces of burning threads and ash were left in his wake. Ēostre trembled on the couch until Chloe drew her into a tight embrace.

"I'm going to kick him out now. We can't continue to suffer barbs and taunts from him."

"Saul, no." Max frowned, staring out the door Fafnir had disappeared through. "He is too dangerous to loose on the world. We must keep an eye on him until Watatsumi returns."

"What did he mean by 'my Brigid' anyway?" Chloe asked.

"Who knows, love? He's not in his right mind."

"All the more reason to allow him to stay," Chloe murmured, meeting Max's gaze. "You're right, he *isn't* in his right mind, and we'll never forgive ourselves if we send him into the world. He's gotta stay here where we can keep an eye on him."

"Are you certain, Chloe?" Ēostre asked in a tremulous voice.

"Positive."

Saul sighed heavily. "In that case, I believe Leiv and Mahasti deserve a long overdue vacation. We can send them and the girls to Teo's island, or wherever they like for that matter."

"Thor would be glad to host them at his home and I know he's spoken many times with Leiv about a hunting trip," Ēostre suggested. "They'll have a good time and it'll get everyone away from the stress of babysitting Fafnir."

"To be honest, I would feel better if you both went with them." Saul looked from his wife to his mother.

"Nope, I live here."

Saul released a long sigh. "I figured as much, but I had to suggest it."

"And I love you for it, but your mother and I won't leave you guys here to handle this alone."

"Correct," Ēostre said. She swallowed and raised her eyes to Max.

Max and Saul exchanged glances, but they both knew it was useless to argue with the women they loved.

Chapter 24

Watatsumi opened another book and breathed in the smell of ancient paper and old leather. He'd known from the start that the books wouldn't have the answer to their problem with Fafnir, but he'd hoped something in their rich history would jog his memory.

Could a dragon come back from the dead? Was it possible Belenos and Ēostre were wrong? In their grief, they could have mistaken a grievously injured dragon for dead.

No, he thought. If such was the case, why wasn't the soul bond between Fafnir and his mate intact? Why had it taken him more than a century to recover?

Most importantly of all, why did he feel the most sinister, dark intentions from the dragon who was once one of his closest friends? Watatsumi shivered, unable to forget the animosity sweltering from Fafnir whenever their mutual friend was near Bel. A century ago, he would have been hard pressed to name two dragons closer than Fafnir and Belenos, and while he'd like to blame Ēostre's new bonding for the change, he knew the hatred ran deeper. It festered in Fafnir, a disease of the soul, and Watatsumi's sensitive talent for empathetic magic made it difficult to bear. He couldn't talk to his old friend for longer than five minutes without nausea rising in his stomach.

A tiny rap at the door brought Watatsumi's attention to one of the servants.

"May I enter?"

"You need not ask permission, Nagisa. We have discussed this."

"Perhaps, but it's polite to ask," the doe shifter replied. She stood in the doorway watching him with kind brown eyes. She, like all of his servants, preferred tradition over modern ways, and wore an exquisite blue kimono with silver thread woven into a water print. "This arrived for you, but it bears no name."

"No name?" He abandoned his seat and crossed the room to meet her halfway. Bowing deeply, she presented the dragon with a neatly wrapped package addressed from the United States.

"No. Only that. It's a store in America."

Watatsumi glanced at her.

"I may have Googled it briefly before bringing it up to you," the girl said with an impish smile.

Nestled inside of the packaging and bubble wrap, he found a beautifully painted volcanic dragon with curving horns and enormous black claws. His brows raised at the resemblance to a certain, recently awakened wyrm.

"Why would an antique store mail you a ceramic dragon? I don't understand."

"Neither do I, but it requires investigation." Watatsumi glanced at the package again, then his brows knit together. "I know this address."

"You do?"

"Yes. Strange that it isn't postmarked."

"It wasn't delivered by the mail service, actually. A villager brought it to us. He said a strange man in a hooded cloak delivered it to him at dawn."

"I see." He turned the dragon over in his hands again, inspected it for latent spells or charms, and upon finding nothing, returned it to Nagisa. "You may keep this."

The girl chuckled and clutched the gift against the plush, pale silver obi encircling her torso. "It's lovely, but you know I prefer blue," Nagisa said with a wink. She kissed his cheek and slipped from the room, only to squeal in the doorway when the paint bled away to navy and cerulean colors. "Thank you!"

"You're welcome."

Watatsumi stepped through the air, leaving the office behind to appear on an open sidewalk. Fortunately, the abrupt change in time zone took him from a sunlit morning to a Boston night. Except rather than darkness, he discovered a blazing inferno and a busy street occupied by emergency service workers.

"This will not do," he said to himself. "This will not do at all."

The uncontrolled fire raged, fierce flames climbing toward the night sky. He slipped through the gathered spectators and beyond the police line.

"Sir, please, we need you to stand back," an officer called over.

"Allow me to help," Watatsumi said politely.

Before the firefighters could protest, he made a sweeping gesture with his left arm to cast them all aside. With the humans clear of the danger, Watatsumi transformed — his kimono vanishing in the instant his human body expanded to monstrous proportions. Azure feathers dappled with green and white elongated from his powerful wings as he stretched them out. His tail curled into the busy street, thankfully causing no one harm.

Several screams sounded from the rubberneckers and a few of the officers pulled their guns. Phones flashed as people caught him on their cameras.

A single shot rang out and plinked into his hide. Watatsumi sighed, twisted around to face them, and rumbled, "Not now, children." With a single spell, their guns vanished and they were left empty-handed. It was only a temporary displacement spell, and the firearms would appear where they belonged within minutes.

"Holy shit!"

"Did you see that? He used magic."

"The bullet didn't even phase him!"

Ignoring the crowd, the dragon turned back to the burning building. Three fire engines tried to douse the flames enveloping the antique store, but they were making little progress. The stench of magic permeated the air and tinged the fire a crimson red.

Watatsumi recognized dragon fire, and while he was puzzled by its appearance here, it remained a mystery to determine later. First he needed to put it out. He drew in a deep breath and then he released a swirling jet of tidal water. The waves washed over the building and through the blasted windows, dousing the flames in an instant.

"Well I'll be damned." The fire chief stepped forward and stared. "You extinguished everything."

"And I am pleased to do so," Watatsumi replied. He retook his human shape, kimono perfectly in place, and stepped toward the ruined storefront.

"Wait a minute. You can't go in there, it isn't safe," the chief said. He argued weakly, a half-hearted attempt to uphold the duties of his job despite witnessing the impossible feat of a water dragon putting out a fire.

"An acquaintance of mine owns this building, and I would like to know if she survived. I assure you, there is no effort you may take to stop me, so play nice and wait your turn."

"If this is a crime scene we can't have you going in there, er, sir." The chief made a last-ditch effort, and Watatsumi admired him for it.

"I promise I will not disturb anything. Unless I must. This is a witch's den and there may be magical hazards in place your men are not trained to tolerate."

The fire had consumed all of the wards and protections, obliterating any defenses the witch may have left over her haven. Watatsumi stepped through the steaming wreckage.

"This must be where the fire began," Watatsumi murmured. The front room was unsalvageable. Nothing had been spared the fire's wrath and the metal framework of the building had been affected, ruining the support beams. The entire building would have come down if the fire had burned hotter or longer.

It started in the center of the space, leaving a blackened scorch mark on the floor. Deeper grooves of blistered, charred wood radiated out where the fire had initially tried to spread but had been contained. Whatever Agnes used to protect her building had put up a daring fight, but lost in the end.

The stench of dragon fire filled the air, masking the scent of the perpetrator himself. As Watatsumi moved beyond the storefront into the rear offices, he found jeweler displays with melted glass and ruined contents. He followed his senses into a ransacked office, its desk tipped over, precious contents strewn over the soggy rug. Waterlogged books awaited him on shelves and a hidden safe door hung open.

Witches are known for hiding secrets in plain sight, he thought. All of the books, save one, had been damaged when he quenched the flames. He pulled the single dry book from the shelf and ran his fingers over the spine. It hummed with hidden magic, powerful for a human but child's play for a dragon sorcerer.

As if tuned to the book, other items in the room buzzed in harmony. The first was a silver wolf figurine with emerald eyes. It pulsed in his hand, as if it had a heartbeat of its own. Beneath the safe, buried in piles of mushy, disintegrating money, he discovered two gemstones — a sapphire and a black diamond — with the same rhythmic beat. A palm-sized crystal ball and an amethyst geode made up the final two objects bound to the spellbook.

He gathered the strange collection up and gave the store a last glance-over. The humans outside were starting to come in, but he had what he wanted. There was no sign of Agnes or her apprentices, not even a pile of ashes.

Work done, he opened a portal to his home and stepped through.

Chapter 25

Despite the warm presence of Max's hand on her tummy, Ēostre slept like crap the morning after Fafnir's confrontation. She couldn't put her finger on it, but something about his behavior, his mannerisms, and the outright hostility toward Saul unsettled her more than his actual return. Fafnir had never loathed their child. He'd never hurt Saul's feelings and had only shown him love whenever he was in their lives.

My Brigid, she thought again, letting the words echo through her mind. The solution was on the tip of her tongue… but behind a wall her stressed mind couldn't crack.

Dragons never returned from the dead. But he had. Fafnir had loved his family, especially his son. Now he loathed them.

It was unusual for Maximilian to remain in bed past noon, but White House employees had gradually begun to acclimate to what they called "Dragon Hours" by beginning the office day hours later than usual. Max and Ēostre discovered most of the staff appreciated the opportunity to sleep in, and their silent support touched him deeply. On top of the approval from his employees, a few top advisors claimed the president's unusual schedule improved the response time for communications with foreign leaders, especially with those in Asia and the eastern parts of Europe.

So he slept in beside her, Ēostre tucked against his chest with her head beneath his chin. Sometimes she pretended to remain asleep long past the hour she awakened, basking in the warmth of her husband's body.

"I know you're awake," Max whispered. His arm squeezed her tighter, then his fingers skimmed down her ribs until his palm cupped her lower tummy. "What's on your mind?"

"You," she teased. Ēostre traced a fingertip of the back of his knuckles and listened to his even, deep breaths behind her. Technically, it wasn't a lie. He and their babies ruled her thoughts, but she couldn't get Saul off of her mind.

How could Fafnir hurt him so deeply?

"Was it this part of me?" Max asked playfully, nudging with his hips. He was hard as stone behind her, the thick girth of him cradled perfectly between her thighs.

"The entire package, but especially that part of you."

"We still have some time before work calls us for the day."

As if jinxing his words, the phone rang. Ēostre frowned at the cellular on her nightstand, but she dragged her toes over Max's shin again, encouraging him. "One second." Ēostre placed the device to her ear after pressing the button. Her husband stilled behind her with limited patience. "Hello?"

"Ēostre, it's me," Chloe greeted her. "We need you guys here as soon as you get a chance."

"What's wrong? Has something happened?"

"No, nothing has happened yet, but Watatsumi arrived a moment ago with news he'd like to share with all of us."

"We'll be there," Ēostre promised. "Thank you."

"No problem. See you soon."

Ēostre clicked the phone off and set it aside. She twisted around to look at her husband, who'd already withdrawn from their bedroom play, sensing that the call was important. "That was Chloe. Watatsumi returned to the manor and has news. He'd like us to meet with him there if we're able."

"I suppose we should get up then and see to it. I'll make sure any meetings I have are rescheduled."

Ēostre took her time brushing her teeth and washing her face, but as she dressed, her nerves tore at her. Tension kept her gut

263

coiled tight and knotted her shoulders until Max stepped in behind her and circled her waist with his arms. She dreaded the news.

"No matter the news he's brought for us, I'm behind you. I'm with you every step of the way."

"I know. It's only that I'm…"

"You're worried about Fafnir. So am I. It is my deepest hope, Ēostre, that we can help him. He… didn't seem well. Physically well," he said with emphasis.

Ēostre whirled to face him. "You noticed, too?"

"How could I not? I had to jump between both of you."

While she dressed, Max handled calls and consulted the security agents assigned to them. In less than thirty minutes, they were prepared to step through the portal to Drakenstone Manor to handle a "personal family emergency" in which the agents, shifter or not, were not permitted to accompany them.

The quaint, open floor plan of the living room greeted them, but her son and his wife were nowhere to be seen. They tracked them down to the sunny solar where there were no shadows for anyone to hide within. Fafnir's magical talents, especially the ability to hide in darkness, had survived his death unharmed.

Saul embraced her tightly and guided her to a chair. It didn't take long to determine Watatsumi had already shared his findings with them. Their grim faces told Ēostre everything.

"Ēostre, Belenos, my apologies for calling you at this hour."

"No, no need to apologize. Please, just tell me what happened, Watatsumi."

"As you wish. An anonymous delivery was made to me from the antiques store owned by the hag, Agnes. No note, no letter, only a ceramic red dragon. I, of course, went to the store afterward to see what I might discover."

"And…?"

"Agnes is missing and her Boston store was burned to the ground. By a dragon."

"I know. News of it reached me last night because an enormous blue dragon—" Max straightened in his seat. "That was *you*? I spent hours dealing with your shit. But how does her store have anything to do with Fafnir? Are you suggesting he snuck away and did it himself?"

"No, I am not suggesting he stole away in the night and did it himself," Watatsumi said politely. "What I am saying is that I know why Fafnir has not been himself. Listen to me, both of you. Listen to me clearly."

"What is it?"

"That thing is not the mate you knew and our beloved friend. It's a corpse. Fafnir never returned to life when the volcano exploded."

Ēostre sharply inhaled. "That isn't possible. We both saw him walking. We both talked to him. If Fafnir never returned to life from hibernation, why is he beneath my son's home living in the hoard we built with our own claws?"

"He is the undead, Ēostre, neither deceased nor truly alive. I have researched many books in the time since I left Drakenstone Manor, hoping to find an answer to this miracle."

"And this is the only one you've found?"

"The only one," Watatsumi said. "We both saw Astrid's reaction to him. We both know she is a special child with an unknown, unique gift. I have a theory. I've spent many centuries of my life researching our kind and the unique traits which set us apart from other magical creatures. We alone are excluded from the wheel of life. Once a dragon is dead, we do not return to flesh and blood. We aren't reborn as the witches, dragonslayers, and many other souls who complete the cycle do."

"We become energy," Max said. "We've discussed this before."

"Correct, my friend, but we have company who does not understand," Watatsumi said with a gesture to Chloe. "We become part of a greater force, dispersed throughout this world to protect every soul, every person, every tree. We are each comprised of two

265

parts, a bestial nature and a calmer aspect. Just as Ēostre brings gentle rains to nourish the earth, she is also the fierce storm."

"What does this have to do with Fafnir?" Ēostre asked.

Watatsumi pulled out a book and several items from his pack. "I discovered these in Agnes' shop. This tome, this vile book of shadows, details how to capture souls. And these?" He gestured to the wolf figurine and various gemstones laid out on the table. "Each one holds a soul. Or at least a piece of one."

"No… that's cruel," Ēostre breathed. Max clenched his jaw.

"Tell her the rest, Watatsumi," Saul said gently with sorrow in his eyes.

"I believe Agnes attempted to capture Fafnir's soul in a phylactery. But a dragon's spirit is far too large for such tricks. It would be comparable to holding a lake in a bathtub," he explained. "Only a portion could be contained. Fafnir's body should have turned to stone after he was interred, becoming one with his surroundings, but instead, it entered a sort of magical stasis, likely due to the magical connection to the vessel. In short, the magic tethering his soul to the stone has confused his body, and it no longer knows whether it's dead or alive. It is in the in-between."

"Like hibernation?" Chloe asked.

"Yes. Most of us choose to hibernate once we have grown exhausted with the world or feel the need for prolonged rest. But this was not a hibernation. I believe someone possesses the phylactery, and has loosed his soul to serve their own agenda."

I won't cry, Ēostre thought stubbornly. *I've shed a century of tears for Fafnir and I won't cry now.* Instead, she dragged in a shuddering breath and raised her chin. "What can we do?"

"He must be put back to rest and his soul released. The longer it is imprisoned, the darker it will become," Watatsumi warned. His silken robes rustled with each step toward the open window. "And it may take several of us to do it. As Fafnir is already deceased, we will have to destroy this undead body so the remnants of his soul have nothing to adhere to. Unless we can find the phylactery."

"Why can't we find the phylactery?" Saul asked.

"I believe Agnes may be dead. Death is the only reason I can suspect for why the witch's favorite lair was left unattended. When I consulted with several of her sisters in the coven, they confirmed their belief that she's no longer among the living."

"Can they call her in a séance?" Max asked.

Watatsumi shook his head. "No, it's too late."

"Did you find out who sent you the figurine?"

"No. Her apprentice claims no knowledge of the piece. Someone else wished me to find her dark secrets without revealing themselves. Someone who either assisted her, or at least had the knowledge and never reported her.

"But why burn her store after warning us?" Chloe asked. She leaned forward, blue eyes shining. "I don't need to be a dragon to smell something about this situation is foul. No. There's two people involved. Unless the sender was hiding evidence of their own wrongdoing, there has to be a second party who was aware."

"It's possible," Max said thoughtfully.

Ēostre slumped back weakly in her seat, feeling dazed and nauseous by the revelations.

"Let's call them Person A and Person B. Person A and B knew about what Agnes did, but maybe they argued about the morality. Person A wants to keep this powerful dragon soul, and Person B wants out of it."

"Person A, a dragon, burned down the store, but the second party sent a warning to Watatsumi," Max said. "But why would one dragon want another dragon's soul? That is… it's an abomination."

"It's a death sentence," Watatsumi said. "Such magic is prohibited. Regardless of the guilty party's identity, the rest of the Council and I would execute the perpetrator immediately."

Ēostre swallowed the dry tension in her throat. "Where is he now?"

"He's still down in the hoard," Saul replied. "He doesn't eat and doesn't appear to sleep either."

"Well, at least down there he can't fly away from us," Chloe said. Saul leaned back in his seat and flashed her a look, his brows raised questioningly. "You guys," she corrected.

"He's still a volcanic dragon and this is a mountain," Max warned.

"Even in his maddened state I don't think he would risk destroying his hoard," Ēostre said in a tentative voice. "It may be the best place to confront him."

"Saul and I will do it," Max offered, breaking the silence. "You're pregnant, Ēostre. We can't risk you in such an endeavor, even for Fafnir."

"I will not be left behind like a hand-wringing damsel," she argued. The dragoness rose from her seat, the abrupt movement sending it backwards to the floor. "I won't run and hide while you grant him peace."

A roar outside brought their planning to an abrupt halt. Saul swore and ran for the veranda doors leading out to the side yard, the others right behind him. Motionless, red-smeared white and gray shapes littered the expansive green pasture beyond the livestock fence. Saul leapt over it nimbly at a full sprint, and they followed. Ēostre moved past her son only to come to a horrified halt when she reached the closest corpse.

"Oh no…"

A slain goat from Leiv's herd bloodied the ground, and a second lay several yards ahead with claw marks down its side.

Max came up short and stared. "You said he doesn't eat," he said.

Ēostre staggered forward to the next body, surveying the pasture of carnage left in Fafnir's wake. There wasn't a bite of flesh stripped from the delicate bones, and each goat had been left to rot in the morning sun.

"He didn't eat them," Saul said dryly. "This was a massacre for fun."

"Thank the Ancients you sent the girls away with Mahasti and Leiv," Watatsumi remarked as he followed the path of death. They moved with him, in awe of the brutality.

"He's never done anything like this before. Even when we raided villages, we never killed unless necessary," Max muttered. "Never wasted our kills when we did."

"He's not the same dragon," Watatsumi reminded him gently. "There!" He pointed as Fafnir zipped across the pasture, in hot pursuit of three terrified zebras. The third one, lame and smaller than its two herdmates, fell behind.

"Fafnir, stop!" Ēostre didn't know what came over her, but she knew the pain Astrid would suffer if she returned to find her beloved animals dead, slain by her own bloodkin. Swift as an arrow, and without thinking of her own safety, she transformed to hurl herself forward, a spear of silver. She knocked her former mate off course seconds before his claws could close around the smallest creature. Fafnir turned, snarling at her and snapping his fanged jaws. Max was beside her in a moment, between them, their collision like thunder.

"Enough, Father!" Saul roared. "Stop this now and let us help you. We know what brought you back. We can put things right again."

He didn't answer. Fafnir and Max's talons snarled together, like two stags locking antlers over a doe. They rolled across the pasture, growling and hissing streams of fire from their open mouths.

Ēostre no longer recognized the dragon she had once loved. He resembled a rabid animal, pink-tinged froth flying from his mouth each time he twisted and flipped over Max, biting him and tearing with his claws. Red feathers flew in the air, and she could no longer tell which dragon had lost them, who had spilt blood. She stood frozen on the spot as Saul leapt into the fray, a fraction of their size and outclassed by their enormous strength.

"Saul!" Chloe screamed from the edge of the pasture.

"Stay back!" Saul growled.

Ascalon in hand, Chloe remained at the edge of the pasture. Worry etched furrows into her brow and her hands twisted on the hilt. Despite his own great size, Saul resembled a cub darting in between two adult dragons. He couldn't lay a scratch on either of them, but the same wasn't true for Max and Fafnir — streams of blood ran down multiple wounds to Max's chest, and then he was pinned beneath the other fire dragon's bulky body.

Saul clung to his father's back in a desperate effort to pull him away. "Father, please!" he pleaded again.

Feral noises bubbled from Fafnir's throat in the place of words. His bloodshot eyes were glassy, vacant, and filled with mindless rage as he thrust his head toward Max's throat and went in for the kill. As he did, Max kicked up with both hind legs, tearing his claws into Fafnir's toughened gut. It barely dislodged him in time.

"Help them!" Ēostre screamed at Watatsumi. "Don't stand beside me, help them!"

"I am," he replied tersely, voice raising higher than his normal placid volume. "By remaining here to tell you the rest of my plan. Do you see them, Ēostre? Fafnir no longer feels pain as we do, if he feels it at all. There's only one way to help them. You must seek out your bond with Fafnir and find the phylactery," Watatsumi said.

"It's gone," she cried, curling her claws into the thick grass in despair.

"No, it is not. A portion of your soul became his when you bonded. Try and find that connection now, however tenuous it may be. Focus! Use what you now know to find the magic animating this body."

"And trace it back to the phylactery," she whispered.

"Yes, and to whoever holds it."

It was difficult to focus when her son and husband were in a fight for their lives. Fafnir's unrestrained tactics could kill either of them at any moment. In a blink, she'd be without her son or her mate.

No!

Ēostre redoubled her efforts. She stretched beyond the comfortable boundaries of her magic until an infinitesimal force flit at the edges of her perception. "I feel it," she said in a quiet voice. "Far away from here."

"Can you pinpoint it?"

"Yes, I can take us there directly."

It became a tiny melody only she could hear. A weak tugging on her soul acted as a beacon, and Ēostre allowed it to guide her, her consciousness soaring across vast, open ocean and serene waters until she opened a portal. Green hills and thick forest waited on the other side as the foreground to smoky-topped mountains in the great distance.

The soul-deep tug drew her onward into a craggy gully damp from a recent rain. She and Watatsumi were halfway down the narrow track when a third dragon came out to meet them.

"You're trespassing," the dragoness hissed. Beneath the cloudy sky her feathers were a dull brick red. Her hide, the color of burnt sienna, had the dry texture of scales — a byproduct of spending too much time in the fire.

Brigid had been prettier, and it was no surprise, considering who had fathered her. As a dragon, Mahuika was as plain on the outside as her soul was ugly within.

"Mahuika. I should have known." In hindsight, the way Fafnir had called Brigid "his" made a sick sort of sense.

"What do you want?" She snapped her head toward Watatsumi. "What business do you have here in my home?"

"You have something that belongs to me." Ēostre gave her no warning. She rushed the slender red dragoness and lunged to the right, dipping her body low to the ground to protect her belly.

In the case of fighting another dragon, the only defense was a good offense. Ending a fight sooner than later saved lives. Ēostre stole first blood when she sank her jaws into her opponent's flank and ripped out a mouthful in passing, too swift for Mahuika to do anything more than swat her tail.

"I'll find the jewel!" Watatsumi shouted as he scurried past. "Keep her here!" His sinuous shape slithered into the mountainside as Mahuika whirled and exhaled a jet of flame. It singed his side, and the water dragon's hide blistered beneath the force. Then he was gone and Mahuika scrambled to catch him.

"You have no business in my home!" Mahuika shrieked. She exhaled another jet of flame down the tunnel in a controlled stream that raced along the curves and disappeared from sight. The water dragon's pained roar echoed from the cavern.

"Mahuika, no!"

The skies split open and a lightning bolt fell from the heavens, the precursor of the assault soon to come. Seconds later, the true light show began. One lightning strike after the next fell with the flash storm, and black clouds rolled in from the horizon.

Mahuika countered with a firestorm. The lightning charred and split her hide but it didn't deter her from belching a twisting ball of white-blue flame at her opponent. A quick dodge brought Ēostre out of harm's way but the heat was searing enough to raise blisters on her shoulder and neck.

Back and forth they went, Mahuika's flames against Ēostre's thunderstorms and pelting rain.

"I'll rip those bastards from your cooling corpse," Mahuika hissed. "It should have been me. I should have been the one ruling beside him. *Me!*"

"You will never hurt my babies, Mahuika. Belenos turned you down because of your spiteful nature. Your selfishness. What you did to Fafnir only confirms the ugliness in your heart."

The red dragoness shrieked in rage and took to the air. Her fury made her reckless and savage. Careless. Ēostre dodged her first attack and leapt up into the skies. They circled one another in an aggressive aerial display, slashing with their claws and biting at each other.

"I will have everything that is yours," Mahuika screamed. "It's mine! It should all be mine!"

Claws sharp as obsidian raked down Ēostre's flank, bloodying her silver plumage. She cried out and summoned the wind to pound the enraged dragon back to the ground. Mahuika tried to resist but the gale force winds were too much. She hit the ground hard and Ēostre followed, landing atop her.

Seizing the volcanic dragoness by the throat, Ēostre snapped her jaws shut with all of her might. She held on, balancing with her wings, tumbling with Mahuika to the hard earth and refusing to relinquish her hold. For the sake of everyone counting on them at Drakenstone Manor, she couldn't let go.

Mahuika's desperation grew as her air supply depleted. Ēostre tasted blood, smelled her fear, and buried her claws deeper. She was like a cowboy on a rodeo stallion, pleading to the Ancestors to hold her grip for one more second. Ēostre held for more than that — refusing to let go even after Mahuika's tail gave one last shuddering thump against the ground before everything stilled.

Watatsumi found them in the same position five minutes later when he emerged from the cavern scorched and limping, his beautiful blue skin bubbled from mid spine to left flank. He nudged her with his nose, still panting with exertion from his own trials inside the deceased fire wyrm's lair.

"Ēostre. She's dead. You can release her now."

***

A wild animal. Max was reminded of a wild animal. There was no recognition in Fafnir's yellow eyes, only a terrifying sort of hatred that burned hotter than any fire. He and Saul panted as they

273

distanced themselves from the great beast, red rivulets streaming down their ribs.

He growled and circled around him again, resembling gunslingers in the old west meeting for a showdown. With Saul and Max on one side, Fafnir on the other, it became easy to see the great wyrm wasn't even remotely wearied from the battle. His body was dead, and Max had to wonder if Fafnir had known all along, if he'd hidden in the hoard to conceal it.

If only they'd looked closer.

"Fafnir, some part of you must still be there. Speak with us."

A flash of intelligence returned to Fafnir's eyes, accompanied by a dry chuckle. "Don't waste your words. When I finish ripping you both to shreds, I'll turn my ire to the rest of this world. No one will escape my vengeance, and all will suffer for what was taken from me."

"Father, you can't blame the humans for this."

"What do I care for humans? They are little more than rodents scurrying through their own filth, I will clean this world of them and usher in a new dawn of power for the dragon race." Fafnir sneered, revealing every tooth.

"Fafnir… you once loved them as we do. You made deals with them. You helped them achieve glory," Max said. "Do you remember Sigurd and what you did for him?"

"Those days are gone! I am ashamed of my own people, who let the humans rule them and hide behind the shifters like scared little lambs. We are dragons! They should be cowering beneath us!" He charged forward at Max only to turn at the last moment and crash into Saul instead. The younger dragon braced as best he could for the impact but his father was larger and stronger. Saul toppled to the ground.

It all seemed to happen in slow motion. Max twisted to face Fafnir while Chloe screamed and raced for her husband. Saul struggled to get to his feet as he fended off Fafnir's slashing attacks.

Then, in an instant, the crazed animosity in Fafnir's face vanished, replaced by horrified agitation. The large dragon leapt backward away from his son, and stared at his own bloodied claws.

"What have I done?"

"Fafnir...?" Max edged closer, putting himself between his old friend and his new family.

Fafnir's eyes darted from his blood-smeared talons to Max's face, his features brimming over with anguish. "Belenos, while I am still myself — while I can speak these words to you — put me back to rest. Kill me."

Max raised his claws, but like Saul, he couldn't bring himself to use them. When it came to the moment of truth, he'd failed. "I can't. Fafnir, I can't," he whispered.

"You must."

"You're my friend!" Max cried in anguish. He blinked his stinging eyes rapidly.

"Then I'll do it! One of us has to put him to rest, Max!" Chloe called. "He's suffered enough!"

"She is right," Fafnir rumbled. "What little remains of the dragon Fafnir will soon be gone. What stands before you is a twisted shadow of the creature you both loved. Mahuika no longer holds the stone binding my spirit, but soon she will possess it again with her vile influence. You must release me." His eyes darted to Saul, filled with sorrow. "Your cub is beautiful, my son. You put me to shame."

"Father... I thought... we could do this, but we can't. Forgive us."

"I can't kill you, my friend," Max agreed mournfully.

"No one will have to do it," Watatsumi announced from their rear.

They turned to see Ēostre and Watatsumi emerging from an open portal, singed, limping, and bloodied. Watatsumi grimaced with every step, but he held his head high, a gleaming, vibrant ruby in his clenched claw. The light shone from it in slow and rhythmic, radiant pulses. Beside the water dragon, Ēostre's determined stride occasionally hitched. Max hurried to her.

"You're hurt."

"No more than you are," she assured him.

"Chloe, we will need your sword," Watatsumi called over. "Mahuika no longer draws breath, but time is short. If you have goodbyes, I would say them now."

Fafnir hung back and refused to move. "No. No goodbyes. Do it now, I beg you."

A deep sadness rose in Max's heart. "I wish there were another way, my friend."

"My time is long past. I have brought you nothing but pain and sorrow, and for that I can never apologize."

Ēostre touched her cheek against her former mate's face. "Part of me will always love you, Fafnir."

"But our bond has ended and death has separated us." He turned his eyes to Maximilian, cool, dead eyes that held a minute bit of warmth, a flicker of what belonged. "Thank you for keeping your oath to me. Protect her. Always."

"Always," Max agreed, choking on the word. "Always, my friend."

Fafnir stepped back from them, folded his molting wings against his body, and proudly raised his chin. "I am ready, brave girl."

Chloe drove the tip of Ascalon into the gem. It shattered, a hundred fragments skittering in every direction into the grass amidst particles of ruby dust. At the same time, the light dimmed from Fafnir's eyes and his body slumped to the earth, motionless, gray, and hardening into stone.

"Father?" Saul whispered.

A warm breeze stirred through the pasture, several multicolored butterflies dancing on the swirling eddies. The delicate creatures took perch on Fafnir's body for the span of a heartbeat until he crumbled away beneath their feather-light touch.

Only a pile of ashes remained.

Epilogue

They left the pasture defeated, numbed, and heartbroken.

"What about his ashes?" Chloe had gently asked.

Ēostre couldn't answer. Max had taken over a week away from Washington to be at her side, and together they got through it with days of mutual tears and hugs. At first, she blamed herself for failing to observe something was amiss when she discovered his body, back when Fafnir had first died. Or maybe if they had acted sooner when he first came back, if they had suspected that someone else was controlling him, maybe they could have saved him from unnecessary suffering. Eventually, her regrets culminated to a deeper hatred for Mahuika, and she wished she could have killed the dragoness again.

Although Mahuika was certainly mixed up in the current events, she wasn't at fault for such a treacherous act. It was Agnes. Agnes, who had already died. Agnes who, as far as Ēostre was concerned, would always be her enemy.

But how does one punish a witch who follows the eternal cycle of rebirth? Watatsumi and the rest of the Council had promised to locate the witch in her next adult form, swearing to make her pay, but confining her for a mere lifetime wouldn't satisfy Ēostre. In fact, she nearly allowed her bitterness to consume her, until one night, she found Max alone in his private office and remembered he had been grieving, too. He needed her as much as she needed him. Their family needed them.

A month was a trifling time for a dragon to mourn, but she'd reached the end of the tears she was willing to shed for Fafnir. The true Fafnir, the real dragon with an uncorrupted soul, wouldn't have wanted her to suffer for another century. Days after she emerged from her depression, Chloe surprised them with a lovely memorial. She'd secretly called Mahasti to return and gather the ashes, and the djinn had placed an immense but elegant urn in the hoard. The pair of them had waited until the right moment to present it.

Crafted from semi-opaque blown glass swirled through with reds and golds, the vase's glossy surface shone from within as though it held a flame in its heart. An engraved obsidian plaque displayed an ancient Norse poem Saul had always said his father favored. It wasn't his volcano, but Fafnir had loved his hoard as much, if not more than Rainier.

As the months passed, Ēostre watched her son's wife swell with child, and when Chloe birthed their little boy, she joined them to welcome him into the world and assist with the expected complications. Astrid was overjoyed to have a baby brother and promised to be the best big sister any dragon could ever have.

Losing Fafnir for the second time had dealt a blow to the family, but as the year waned into cooler months, life resumed its natural rhythm. He was held in their hearts but not forgotten.

***

The late October sun warmed the air, creating a pleasant autumn afternoon for a picnic. It was perfect for entertaining family. Ēostre turned her face to the breeze and inhaled the fragrant flowers perfuming the rose garden before smiling at her company. While she missed Leiv's landscaping, the skilled White House gardeners made it easy to appreciate their talents.

"You're going to regret sitting on the ground when it's time for us to get up," Chloe teased her. "I know your baby marathon is only halfway over, but man are they big."

"There are hot guys in suits I can call to put me back on my feet," Ēostre reminded her.

Chloe stared.

"What?"

"I've been a terrible influence on you. I hope Max can find it in his heart to forgive me."

"Forgive you for what, Chloe?" Max's strong voice carried across the lawn.

"Whoops! Busted." Both women giggled.

"Are you two creating trouble?"

"Who, us?" Ēostre gave him her most innocent smile and smoothed her hand down the skirt of her navy blue sundress. The light, airy fabric flattered her blossoming shape. "Do I look like a troublemaker to you?"

"No, you look radiant as always." Max leaned down and kissed her cheek. "Chloe, little Brandt also looks well. How is he enjoying his first trip to DC?"

The infant bundled in Chloe's lap yawned and blinked his eyes open, as if he knew he was the subject of discussion. The newborn gray was gone, and in its place, the bold golden amber of his father's eyes peeked up at her from beneath sleepy lids.

"I thought some fresh, east coast air would be good for him. I was afraid to bring him out so early until Ēostre called with a few pleasant reminders."

Dragon cubs typically wandered out of the hoard with their mothers from birth. It helped them to grow strong, and likewise, Brandt seemed to appreciate the time away from home. He could already lift his tiny head and support his own neck, unheard of for a human child that young. In some ways, her half-dragon children developed slowly, and in others, they excelled.

"He looks like Saul, right down to his ginger hair." Max grinned after making the observation.

"He never told me he was a carrot-top as a baby. It's kind of hysterical. When the doctor passed him to me, I was confused for an hour until Ēostre explained."

They all shared a laugh, which fully awakened the baby. He smiled up at them and waved his tiny fists. Chloe hugged him against her and closed her eyes. Brandt was the miracle baby she and Saul didn't expect to ever have after long years of trying to recreate the magic that gave them Astrid. Once again, she had a close brush with death, and she'd decided two little ones were enough. Human bodies weren't made to deliver dragon-blooded infants.

Max kicked off his fine leather loafers and took a seat on the blanket with them. "So, am I interrupting work or pleasure?"

"Both," Chloe replied, chuckling. "Ēostre invited me to lunch to discuss her plans for the charity."

"I also wanted her thoughts on a few matters. Saul told me Chloe's mother was…" As Ēostre's voice trailed, her eyes cut to Chloe and studied the woman's reaction. Her daughter-in-law smiled at her, unfazed.

"My mother was awful, and I ended up in the system once because of her."

"I'm sorry to hear that, Chloe," Max said after an awkward pause.

"Don't be. It's over, she's gone, and I've spent all of Astrid's life trying to be the mother I should have had. I don't mind talking about it, especially if it helps Ēostre figure out what direction to take her program. A lot of people fall through the cracks out there."

"I think grants to help with adoptions and changes to improve our foster system are noble goals. If anyone can do it, Ēostre can."

Chloe's grin brightened her face. "Damn straight she can. I'm proud of you guys. You've done so much for everyone already since getting here, Max."

Something fluttered in her belly. Ēostre tuned out her two companions, held her breath, and waited to see if it was her food settling or something more. Another quivering wriggle confirmed her hunch, and with an excited squeak, she seized Max's fingers and moved them to her belly. Two swift kicks bumped up against their palms, followed by a flurry of activity.

"Is that…?"

"Our babies," she whispered.

"They recognize Max's voice," Chloe said. "It happened to me whenever Saul was around, both pregnancies."

"They're so active." Marveling over the movement, Max leaned down and said, "Hello, my little ones," directly to her belly.

"It's like they're dancing in here." Ēostre laughed in delight and rubbed her enormous curve. Tracing slow circles always seemed to calm her babies down. Her fascinated husband assisted, and within seconds, all became peaceful in her tummy.

"I don't envy you two at once," Chloe said. "Astrid was a handful on her own."

"Speaking of my favorite granddaughter, where *is* Astrid?" Max asked. "I'm surprised she's stepped away from her brother for even an instant."

"Visiting with Marcy. Last I heard, she was spending her time with the hippocampi herd."

"Not with Javier?" Ēostre snagged a strawberry from the basket and nibbled on it. She'd been on a red food kick for over a week now. Strawberries, apples, bell pepper, ahi tuna, and every red meat available under the sun had been on her cravings list. The chefs called her obsession cute and strove to provide everything their pregnant first lady required.

Chloe shook her head and shrugged. "Nope. I don't think there's much love there. Saul and Teo are incredibly disappointed that the kids aren't getting along the way they wanted. I had to remind them Astrid has the maturity of a woman, or at the very least, an older teen now. She's nineteen and can speak her own mind."

"We spoke at length about their plans for Javier and Astrid," Max admitted. "I didn't want them to make my mistakes, so they've decided not to press the matter or encourage it further."

"Good. If it happens, let it happen naturally," Ēostre said.

"Especially after she punched Javier in the nose yesterday and left him laying out on the sand," Chloe commented cheerfully. "You wouldn't know anything about that, would you, Ēostre?"

Ēostre choked on her strawberry and Max patted her back. "Absolutely not," she wheezed before making a great effort to put on a neutral facial expression. "I might have told her to make her feelings clear, always, but I'm certain I made no mention of hitting. I think."

"I believe," a new voice chimed in, "that she is merely following the example that a dragon woman is a strong woman who doesn't let anyone bully her."

"Ian!" Ēostre waved at the man as he crossed the grass toward them. "I hadn't expected to see you today."

"I had some positive news I thought you'd like to hear. Unless you'd rather it wait for an official meeting, of course."

"Nonsense," Max told him. "Grab a bit of blanket or grass and tell us what's happening."

"Thanks. First, though, how are you two lovely ladies doing?" Ian asked, taking a seat.

"You know me, busy, busy, busy," Chloe replied. "I'm hoping all this fresh air makes Brandt take a good long nap so I can have one as well."

Ian laughed and reached over to smooth his fingers over the baby's reddish hair. "I remember those days. And you, Ēostre? Are you looking forward to your upcoming sonogram?"

"How did you know about that? The Secret Service has been going through hoops getting it arranged. It's top secret, down to the location, and apparently even my doctor isn't allowed to know until a day before the exam."

Ian's good-humored grin made him appear ten years younger. "I've been working closely with Director Nichols, remember? I refuse to let anything or anyone slip through your security details again. Which brings me to the good news I came to share."

"Well, don't keep us in suspense, old man," Max said. "You have us on the edge of our figurative seats."

"I have it on good authority that the slayers are twisting in circles. Some of them want to end the hunting," Ian announced.

"Some?"

"They're divided on it. Word on the street is there's a faction of new blood opposing their traditions. They were born to the old guard and don't want to murder dragons on their parents' word that you're evil."

"Imagine that," Max mused. "Kids having minds of their own."

"It's a changing world. I don't expect that'll be the end of it," the eagle shifter drawled, "but we'll remain vigilant and on the defensive."

"Yes. The slayers may be silent, but we don't want to take any risk with Ēostre's safety." Max's warm hand returned to her tummy, inciting a new series of flutters inside her womb. Ēostre raised her eyes to his face and drank in his elated features.

"I told you everything would work out," she whispered up to him. "No more hiding in the darkness and obscurity. If we can win over the slayers, show them there's no need for more bloodshed, imagine the life we can have. The life our children will have."

Max took the hand she'd lifted to his cheek and drew her fingers to his lips, brushing a tender kiss across her knuckles. "I'm as smitten with you now as I was the first day we met, and I could never have done this without you.

And if all went to plan, he would never have to.

About the Author

Vivienne Savage is a resident of a small town in rural Texas. While she isn't concocting sexy ways for shapeshifters and humans to find their match, she raises two children and works as a nurse in a rural nursing home.

www.ingramcontent.com/pod-product-compliance
Lightning Source LLC
Chambersburg PA
CBHW021220250626
47155CB00008B/2885